KAIROS

NAOMI KELLY

Cover Design: Juan Padron
Interior Formatting: Saltwater Book Design
Map Designs & Closing Image: Naomi Kelly

Also by Naomi Kelly:
Trial by Obsidian
Meraki: A Syren Story

This one if for you. Yes, *you*.

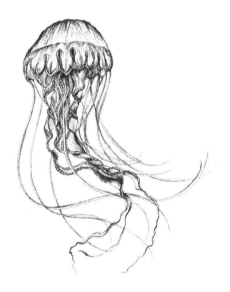

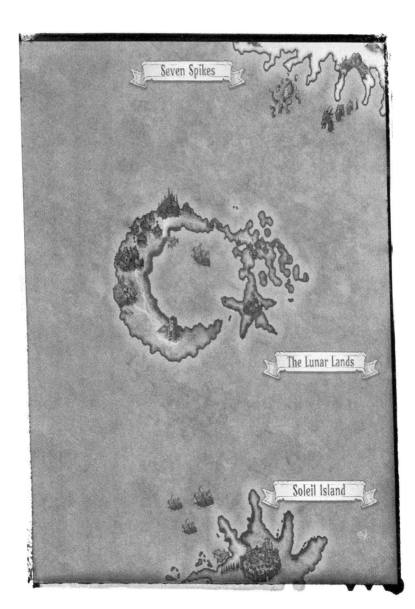

Seven Spikes

The Lunar Lands

Soleil Island

Eight Years Ago

"What you think?" Iseult asked breathlessly, as she finally put down the paintbrush. "This one definitely looks more like a rabbit, right?"

Lachlan gazed upon the vaguely bunny-shaped blob of the side of the hollowed egg and drowned his laughter with the end of his rum. "Have you ever seen a rabbit, love?"

"Ugh!" she protested, crossing her paint-covered arms, and stomping her foot. It took all of Lachlan's minimal self-restraint to tell her the way she thumped the ground resembled a rabbit more than any of her egg-decorating attempts.

"I remember you saying that you'd stop drinking once the new baby came," Iseult chastised, taking the empty glass from his hands.

Although she was not a Descendant of Ares

herself, she had a temper to match her husbands. A temper which was only heightened in her condition.

"I remember saying I would *try*, and I will. But he isn't here yet, is he?" he says, running his opened palm across Iseult's heaving belly.

"Well, it wouldn't hurt you to start practising," she said pointedly, before softening slightly as she lightly thumbed his splayed hand over her bump, "You know I worry about you. Your heart palpitations-"

"Have not returned in weeks!" He cut her off and rose to his feet to stand behind her.

Tugging her in close, he lightly kissed her neck. "Don't be fretting yourself and the babe. Rum won't break my heart, only you could do that."

He said the comment with his usual flair, but Iseult didn't respond with her normal eye-roll nor laughter. Instead, she turned within his hold and held his gaze. They both knew his words hadn't been truthful, for Lachlan's heart had been fractured five years ago when their infant son, Rhys, had been born without breath.

This fracture deepened further when he found their one-month-old son, Rhett, had never awoken from his nap. He had sworn to wife and to the gods, that they would never have more children. They would just have Kellan and Callum, and be content with their *Lazy Twins*, but little did they know Iseult was already pregnant when he spoke those words.

"If anything happens..." Lachlan said under his breath, removing his hand from her bump and curling into a fist as if to threaten the gods, to challenge destiny.

"Nothing will happen," Iseult soothed and lightly kissed his knuckles, "This baby feels strong and feisty, and this pregnancy feels different. Perhaps a daughter for a change?"

To this Lachlan laughed. "You thought Kellan would be a girl too. And the same with Callum, but I've told you a *dozen* times the only girls in my family tree are the women we married in."

"Don't you mean kidnapped?" Iseult smirked, before moving out of his hold to nestle her decorated egg within the Ostara garland which hung across their mantlepiece. Bright daffodils, pale snowdrops, and dense greenery were draped through every inch of the Lunar Lands castle, and their own chambers were no different.

"Ah, that's simply the Lunar family way," he countered with a beaming grin, "But I still married you, didn't I?"

For the rest of the evening, Lachlan traipsed around the gardens with outstretched arms to carry whatever flowers and greenery she plucked. He may be the King, but he was not above doing chores for his wife. Besides, he enjoyed the way she waddled and struggled to right herself after bending over to pick bluebells.

Hours later, the boys sprinted their way through the lawns after their lessons, eager to share all their news, and for a moment Lachlan took in the scene before him. His golden-haired wife smiling broadly at their two boys, their two princes who would one day rule these lands, and suddenly the weight of the hipflask he always kept tucked within his waistband weighed too much.

If it would make Iseult happy, if the health benefits she spoke of were true, then he would give it up. He would leave the rum behind, along with the darker days of his life. His son's deaths, the waring over islands and the need for alcohol to numb his mind enough to sleep- he could abandon these darker days.

He vowed to the gods if the winter of his life had passed, he would never drink again. With a new season about to bloom, he began to feel hope for the first time in a long time.

"The last one to the castle is a rotten egg!" Lachlan declares as the sun lowered toward the horizon.

A lanky Kellan sprinted past him instantly, almost knocking Lachlan off his feet. Callum chased him, yelling cries of protest about his brother got a head start.

"I cannot run, and I've had enough bloody hassle with eggs for one day." Iseult sighs, not even attempting to jog.

Lachlan juggled with his armful of flora, so he could place a guiding arm across her lower back. He slowly accompanied her home, making sure he always stayed one step behind her.

The King had a competitive nature, but he would rather lose every game and gamble known to man to keep her happy.

ONE

had previously thought to myself the castle lawns of the Lunar Lands would be beautiful in full bloom, and it turns out for once in my life I am right. Tulips and daffodils grow in neat rows, whereas snowdrops and bluebells sprout up haphazardly across the luscious grass. From my hilltop view, I see lanterns spark to life across the town square as twilight descends. The little dots of light bursting into existence resemble emerging stars, and they bring a sense of warmth to this crisp evening.

Yet neither the fresh blossoms of spring-time cheer, nor the candlelight which banishes darkness can alleviates the sense of dread in my core.

Dread which only intensifies as my gaze lands upon the bay. Sailors hustle and bustle their way up and down the dock in preparation for this evening's arrival, and as much as I've successfully avoided any involvement all day, that luxury is about to come to an end.

With a weary sigh, I pluck a lone bluebell, tucking it into my hair for good luck and continue my reluctant trudge to the bay. Thankfully, the crunching of the gravel underfoot masks the sound of my teeth grinding so perhaps something would work out in my favour today after all.

Once I've successfully weaved my way through the growing crowds, ducked under the painted egg-shell garlands hanging from house-to-house and skirted my way past the heaving tables of sticky buns, fresh fruits and roast meats, I have reached the pier. Which like most of the Crescent Cove has recently been rebuilt following the battle with my mother, Kestrel.

Finding a slightly less hectic area at the end of the pier, I plop myself down. I'm fully aware the new timbers are probably lodging splinters into my thighs, but I don't trust myself to stand with shaky legs.

Instead, I slip off my canvas plimsolls, letting my bare feet dangle into the cool waters below. Ignoring the organised chaos of a dozen sailors around me, I focus on the ebb and flow of the currents against my legs. It reminds me of my immortal life underwater, but also the mortal act of breathing.

In and out.

In and out.

In and-

"Oi!" Callum's bellow from behind causes me to leap, "All these boats have to be moved to the other side of the bay too."

He gives a wide sweeping gesture to all the ships and rowboats currently in the harbour. Sailors scramble to get to work, replying in a chorus of *"Right away, your Majesty,"* and *"Consider it done, sir."*

Spotting me, Callum strides down the long pier but halts half a dozen yards away.

"Gods above, I can scarcely look at you," he says with mild disgust as he stares at my submerged feet. He tugs his jacket collar up around his neck, so I purposely splashed my feet to watch him shudder.

"I'm trying to enjoy the *warmer* waters before heading up north. I'm convinced the seas surrounding Seven Spikes are enchanted to never freeze fully, yet they're somehow colder than ice," I say with a light laugh, but it brings no smile to Callum's face. I don't blame him. He must be dreading this evening as much as me.

Callum swallows hard, maintaining his hard and apprehensive gaze across the bay, as he mutters, "You don't have to be here."

Feeling wounded, I withdraw my feet from the water and tuck my knees close to my chest.

"No, I...I just mean unlike some of us, you don't *have* to be here," he amends, reaching out his hand to help me up, "You wanting to be here is a valiant gesture Wren, but I wouldn't blame you for hiding away for the evening. Gods know I would if I could, but *he* insisted I be here. Yet he's not even here himself yet."

He being King Kellan, and I knew first-hand how insistent he could be. When Kellan suggested a citizen exchange scheme between the Lunar Lands and Soleil Islands, he finally won back some approval from his disgruntled councillors who were still pissed-off he seized the neighbour isle in the first place.

The councillors went about arranging the exchange. A small fleet of Lunar Lands visitors departed last week, tasked with teaching the Soleil people new skills and trades to help them diversify. The southern isle always had a poor reputation for employment with poverty rates higher than any other. An issue which drastically increased following the destruction of their naval fleet, and the fact castle guards have been made somewhat obsolete since the death of Alistair. With the throne of power now belonging to Kellan in Crescent Cove, the castle of Soleil needs a new purpose. Fletcher recommended it be transformed into a library, whereas Aveen wants a theatre. When asked for his opinion, Callum gave none, and simply asked that the prison cells be demolished.

"Kellan was on his way, but he was summoned to the castle. I'm sure he'll be here shortly," I reassure, accepting Callum's outstretched hand to haul myself upright.

"Surely nothing is more important than for him to greet our *wonderful* guests?" he mutters, only loud enough for me to hear as he wiggles out a hipflask from his pocket.

I bite my tongue to avoid saying "*Isn't it a bit early?*" and instead busy myself with fitting my shoes back on. I also resist the urge to tell him Kellan was called to settle Aveen who would not stop screaming about the "*boatful of bad men coming to rob her.*" I doubt knowing his young sister shares his fears would help improve his mood.

Instead, I reluctantly offer him my third thought, "Well, at least the guests of honour might feel some guilt for what they did for you. Me on the other hand? They're going to absolutely loathe me."

I am the one who sunk their fleets with a few words. I am the one who lured the guards to fling themselves over the towering cliffs. It was my slaughtering which torn apart so many of their families.

Granted, I'm no gambler like Kellan, nor a mathematical genius like Fletcher, but with the number of lives I ended that day I would bet good gold every Soleil citizen had to attend at least one funeral because of me. I told Kellan I would *try* to be here today, although I distinctively did not promise.

"It was Kellan who ordered the attack," he says firmly, "You were simply the weapon he used."

Weapon.

I wince as the word cuts through me as if it were a dagger itself. My heart shrinks a fraction as my whole chest tightens.

A familiar urge to swim away itches within my legs. If I leap off the dock now and started swimming, I would be across the bay and weaving my way through the rocks of Meteoroid Spit in no time. Sure, I might split my arm open against the rough shale again, but it seemed like a less painful experience than greeting the exchange citizens who were due to arrive at any-

A shrill bell chimes through my thoughts.

"Ah shit," Callum grumbles, his eyes locked across the harbour.

On the other side of the bay, standing proud on the rope bridge between the sea stacks is young Ludwig. He tosses his entire arm up and down, ringing his bell as loud as possible.

The young boy had taken Kellan's flippant comment about being 'Herald of the King' incredibly seriously, making it his duty to announce the arrival of each and every boat, much to Fletcher's annoyance. Unfortunately, this isn't another trawler Ludwig eagerly welcomes.

Two long wooden vessels slowly lower their billowing sails as they edge their way into the bay. Even with the billowing sails slackening, the crest is clearly visible.

Gone is the old crest of Soleil Island, and instead the boats don the new emblem. The gold and bronze crescent moon and lone star sigil of the Lunar Lands has been altered to include a golden sun alongside it. Fletcher was quick to point out the geographical inaccuracy of the crest for Soleil Island was nowhere near that close to the Lunar Lands, but Kellan insisted it was vital to have them represented side-by-side.

A symbol of unity and equality. He wanted his newest citizens to know they were part of his Kingdom, not simply an isle he raided.

Townspeople begin to pour out of narrow alleys, eager to catch a glimpse of the new arrivals. Fletcher makes his way through the growing crowd and gives a wave in our direction.

With both Callum and I keeping our arms firmly crossed, his wave is not returned but at least I manage to muster up a smile. It would be easy to miss him amongst the sea of sailors, for they all wear the same crisp, creamy linens and deeply tanned skin, but only Fletcher dons the golden anchor pin which signifies him as Master of the Sails. And only Fletcher is brave enough to approach a moody Callum with a nonchalant smile.

"Oh, come on now, Prince's do not pout," he says gently, tugging his husband's arms out of their tense hold and lightly squeezes his hands, "Like I said this morning, there is no need to be nervous."

"I'm not nervous," Callum lies unsuccessfully before adding, "I'm just annoyed that this is the one-time pain-in-the-ass levels of punctual Kellan decides to be late. Yet if I'm ten seconds late to a council meeting, he-"

His rant is interrupted by the sudden movement in the crowd. A collective rustle from the movement of fabric and feet echoes across the water as hundreds of people bow silently.

Walking through the centre of the genuflecting crowd is Kellan.

"Speak of the devil," Callum mumbles, causing Fletcher to smirk but I do not react.

I cannot. The sight of him captivates me wholly.

Donning his full ceremonial attire, and bronze crown atop his golden hair every inch of his tall frame looks nothing but regal.

On his left arm he wields the Shield of Ares, a not so subtle reminder that is he is protected and favoured by the gods. He extends his right forearm to the more elderly member of society and aids them to right themselves from their bowing stance. I have no idea how one man can appear utterly intimidating yet approachable at the same time.

I know Callum calls him the devil as a turn of phrase, but if the creatures of the Underworld were to rise and choose Kellan to be their King as well? Then I would accept my role as the Mistress of Hel as there is nothing I wouldn't do to remain by his side. Come to think of it, I'd already done some unthinkable things under his rule...

Naturally, my gaze drifts away from Kellan towards those whose lives had already felt the brunt of my destruction. As the visitors gather their bags from cabins, a bridging plank is extended from the dock to the side of the vessel.

Kellan continues to make his way towards the ship, towards us with the wave of bowing preceding him. With Fletcher now lowering himself onto a bended knee, only Callum and I are left standing.

A Soleil woman scoops her young son of five or six years old onto her hip as she carefully disembarks the boat. The excited boy wiggles within her hold, twisting to take in all the new sights and sounds.

A combination of the distance between us, the spring breeze and the boys soft-spoken voice means I do not clearly hear what he cries to his mother, but perhaps it's a blessing from the gods because the way he points at me with a terrified expression says enough.

"Maybe the kid's never seen such a handsome man like me?" Callum shrugs, noticing the child's gesture locked in our direction.

It might only be a chubby finger, but the way my guts twist at the sight of it, it might as well be a knife tip pointed at me.

I try to roll my eyes at Callum's response, but the action threatens to free tears that are building up.

I don't know who will reach me first, Kellan or the Soleil men, but I suddenly know I don't want to stay and find out...

"I can't do this..." My mere whisper drifts away with the evening breeze, but thankfully he catches it.

Without breaking his gaze from the disembarking visitors before us, Callum asks, "What's wrong?"

Everything!

"I...I think there's something wrong with my lungs or my gills, I cannot seem to catch my breath," I explain, with a staggered sigh, "It's as if I'm drowning on land."

"Ah." Callum snorts without humour. "That's just a panic attack. You get used to them."

When I don't respond, he casts me a side-eyed glance. I must look terrible, because without sarcasm he adds, "There's a narrow alley tucked behind the weeping willow tree. Take it, turn left at the end and it'll lead you towards the cottage. There's normally a key under the mat."

"Thank you," I say breathlessly as relief floods through me, "Tell Kellan I'm sorry...I just, I can't.."

"Run whilst you can Wren," Callum offers with a forced smile towards the Soleil citizens beginning to line up on the pier awaiting Kellan's warm welcome, although his face twists into more of a grimace, "At least one of us should have a tolerable evening."

Swallowing hard, I nod and step away, fully aware that Kellan is now close enough to see me.

As I reach the draping, wispy branches of the willow, I pause momentarily but I do not turn around. I do not wish to see the disappointment in his eyes as my habit of running away creeps up once more.

TWO

hankfully, Callum is right about there being a key under the mat. I let myself in, noticing some subtle changes through the cottage.

The original stained-glass window which imploded has been replaced with new panes of clear glass. The fading daylight outside only allows a slim, silvery rectangle of light to slant across the cobbled floor, which barely illuminates the table before me. But even in the dimness, my well-adapted and seafaring eyes spot the subtle difference between the table legs. One of them has been repaired with a lighter shade of pine. The wooden leg I had shattered into oblivion was now a distant memory.

As I spark up the oil burner, I notice that although any evidence of my destruction had been removed, everything else remained untouched.

An empty bottle of rum and a handful of golden coins lay strewn across the table as if Kellan and I had finished our game of 'Face or Fin' just moments ago, instead of almost three months ago. By the bathroom door waits my half basket of candles and soap. And although so much has changed from the first time I stepped a foot in here, it offers an undeniable sense of familiarity.

I click the door shut behind me but opt to leave the latch unlocked. The only thing more predictable than my habit of running away is Kellan's need to find me. It might be in five minutes or five hours, but as long as there are stars in the sky and syrens in the sea, you could bet on him coming for me.

I untie my capelet, carefully draping it over the edge of the table. Shelli, the Lunar Land seamstress, had been kind enough to alter all of my clothes to accommodate my wings. When I commissioned this particular piece, she gave me a sincere look of pity and hesitance, but she crafted it nonetheless.

Granted, I still get some strange glances for wearing a velvet cloak on these warmer days, but those looks are not half as intense as the stares my wings receive. Even though every citizen on Lunar Lands knows I have them, keeping my lengthy, dark wings concealed beneath my custom-made capelet at least allows them to focus on my face when talking to me.

Finally free from the weight of the velvet, I roll my shoulders and stretch out my wings to their full span. As useful as the garment is, the constant constriction of the past four days has left me stiff. I intended to only wear it for short durations like when walking around the town, or shopping at the agora, but with Kellan being exceptionally busy, that's pretty much all I have done since arriving.

As if the deep bathtub is a hippocampus, it calls to me, and suddenly I can think of no better place to be than in water.

"*Gah*, I'm such a syren," I sigh to myself, scooping up my basket of soap and candles and making my way towards the bathroom.

I've been submerging my stiff wings in the deep waters for almost an hour when I hear the cottage door creak open.

"Wren?" Kellan hollers from the doorway. The sound of my name on his lips making my toes curl.

"I'll be out in a minute!" I call, trying to reach for

my towel, but the words have no sooner left my mouth then the sound of Kellan's gait fills my ears.

He swings open the bathroom door, but upon seeing me doesn't move an inch past the threshold.

"Gods above," he says breathlessly. He swallows hard, and lightly grips the doorframe.

My cheeks blush lilac under his unrelenting gaze. I try to cover my body with my wings, but it doesn't really work, and I don't really mind.

I've waited weeks for him to see me...for me to show myself to him, and I know he wants it too. The mountain of letters he sent me whilst we were apart proving it. Each one detailing how badly he craved the sight of me, how he yearned to feel my body against his. I'd folded and unfolded each letter a hundred times as I read and reread his promises to me by candlelight in bed each night. I memorised every tantalising word so when I finally steadied my racing heart and fluttering stomach enough to sleep, his utterings became the script of my dreams. Not the nightmares that once plagued my existence, but dreams. Real dreams.

I extend my hand and beckon him forward, "Come here."

"Why? Are you going to haul me into the bathtub and have your way with me?" he asks with a wicked grin, taking my hand as he crouches beside the tub.

"Well," I start, trying my best to muster up confidence, "I'd prefer if you hauled me out of the bathtub and had your way with me, but I'll take what I can get."

His smirk slides from his face, and his gaze turns heavy-lidded as he realises I am not kidding. He brings my hand to his lips, kissing each finger, then my wrist and then trailing his mouth along my arm.

"The water's gone cold," he rasps as a water droplet trickles down from my shoulder to saturate his lips. He licks away the rogue drop and lightly swallows as if the bathwater dripping from my body is the finest rum he has ever tasted.

"I can't feel it," I say absentmindedly, struggling to think about anything other than his mouth all over me.

"Oh, can't you?" he whispers playfully into my ear, sending shivers down my spine.

He knows damn well I mean the coolness of the water, but Kellan being Kellan he takes the opportunity to taunt me instead. His kisses shift to the softest part of my neck.

His hand slides into my hair, tilting my head away to give him greater access. "Well, can you feel this?"

He nips at my skin, locking his warm lips against me. I know his sucking and biting will leave a bruise, but I do not stop him. I cannot stop him.

I can't do anything except arch my back and lean further into his hold. His hot open palm inches its way down from my hair. His fingers glide past my sensitive feathers, dipping beneath the waterline to graze my breast.

A moan slips from my mouth. Instantly, the water around me responds to my sound. The accidentally lured water surges up the sides of the tub, slapping Kellan in the face.

He gasps, lurching upright. His entire top half now drenched.

"Shit!" I gasp, sending the wall of water sloshing back down.

The descent creates a secondary wave, which crashes out every side of the bath.

Tucking my knees to my chest, I bury my flushed face into my hands. "Ugh. Is there anything I won't ruin today?"

Kellan shakes the excess water from his head as if he were Cerberus. He rakes his fingers through his sodden hair, but a lone limp strand hangs free and frames his face.

"The night is young yet," he starts, peeling off his jacket, and laying it across the puddles between the cobblestones. "It would be bold of you to assume your bad luck has peaked already."

I momentarily unveil my embarrassed face, just long enough for him to see my death-stare.

"I'm only joking," he sighs, scooping me out of the bath despite my protests. "You have not ruined anything, *lígo pouláki*."

Little bird.

He sets my bare feet on top on his jacket but keeps me in his hold.

"I'm sorry," I mumble into his chest with a weary sigh. "Sorry for soaking you. Sorry for leaving the greeting assembly. Sorry-"

"Wren," he says firmly, "Do you know the main reason I'm here right now?"

When I don't answer, he lightly peels me off him, holding me at arm's length. "I came to fetch you for the Ostara feast because dozens of people keep asking me about you. Shelli, Arthur and many others came up to me asking where my beautiful consort is. I decided to stop answering on your behalf and simply bring you straight to them."

"Con-sort?" I ask, stumbling over the foreign word, "Isn't that a bit...formal? Stiff?"

He kisses my forehead before leaving the bathroom, gesturing for me to follow, "Until you and me decide on official terms that's probably the most suitable title for them to refer to you."

Huh.

Consort. I guess I've been called a Hel of a lot worse.

"Now try not to moan." Kellan winks playfully as he strips in front of the tall mahogany wardrobe, digging out something dry to wear.

Over his shoulder, he hands me a folded dress. I shake it out to find it's the same figure-hugging, gold gown with bronze beading across the bodice that I had not worn the last time I was here. Knowing it would delight Shelli to see me finally wear it and realizing Kellan would drag me to this party whether I want to go or not, I sigh and shimmy the dress onto my body.

"Is that something we'll have to do? Decide official terms?" I ask, running my fingers through my navy tresses. Most merfolk and syrens go their entire lives without even trimming their hair, but they don't have to deal with wind or frizz. I've half a mind to march to the sailor barracks and get a crop-cut like most of the men.

"Eventually, yes, we will, I'm afraid. Along with a ton of other paperwork I'm sure the councillors are eager to shove in our faces," he says, fixing the buttons of his shirt, "But there's no rush with any of that, and I don't mind your people continuing to call me consort either."

I nod, and suddenly busying myself with slipping on my capelet and fumbling with the ribbon.

"That is what they refer to me as, right?" Kellan asks, slapping my hand away and undoing my capelet before I even tie it. As much as he appreciates Shelli's craftmanship, he hates the garb, deeming it an insult to the gods to hide my wings.

Without answering him and knowing I won't win the fight over my capelet, I turn on my heel and head for the door.

"Well?" he presses, following me. "Are you going to tell me? Or am I better off not knowing what Aengus calls me behind my back?"

"It's nothing bad. I just doubt your prim and proper councillors would approve," I shrug, stepping out of the cottage into the crisp night air. A loud hum of laughter and music drifts feely from the town square.

"They disapprove of everything," he exhales with knitted brows, rolling up his sleeve to offer me his forearm as we descend the stone steps. "But you've piqued my interest now, so I *must* know."

Even without glancing, I'm reminded of the scars marring his skin for I feel them beneath my fingertips.

The lengthy, risen slit where he slashed his own flesh to perform the Chant of Life and save me had healed...ruggedly, to put it kindly. The wound might have stood half a chance had a harpy not sunk its talon into it less than three days later.

And who knows, maybe he could have even recovered from that if he'd had sufficient ichor in his veins at the time, but he did not for he had given it to me.

By invoking the rite of Meraki, he had given part of himself to me and although we no longer bound by an oath or ritual, we are most definitely entwined somehow. For I can no longer picture my life without him.

My captor, my saviour, my-

"Mate," I finally say in a hushed tone, as we reach the entrance to the feasting hall. "They call you my mate."

As the golden glow of candlelight floods out the doorway to illuminates us both, the crowd pause their wining and dining to bow their heads. Yet Kellan doesn't even spare a glance in their direction. He's far too busy beaming at me with a wolfish grin, and a glint in his eyes as primal as the ancient term.

"Mate?" he repeats with a hint of awe, making no attempt to whisper, "You're right. The councillors would loathe it, which means I absolutely love it."

With a guiding hand across my lower back, he escorts me into the hall, always staying one step behind me.

THREE

lthough I usually despise being the centre of attention, for once I'm grateful to be seated at the top table. At least I'm kept well away from the wary Soleil citizens who have congregated into one corner of the hall.

A steady line of Lunar Lands welcomer's queue to introduce themselves to the newcomers. To my utter dismay, the Soleil people scoot over on their benches to make room for the greeters. Without prompt, they begin filling their flutes with wine and passing around the basket of bread from the centre of the table.

It should be wonderfully reassuring to see these people getting along, to learn the Soleil's are more gracious and kinder than my mind would wish to believe. But it does not feel wonderful, nor reassuring.

It feels like a rock sinking to the pit of my stomach

as if I'm Cronus.

"I thought you were fetching Wren, not having a bath and an outfit change," Fletcher jests, jerking his chin towards his King's dampened hair, and shuffling along the bench to make room for us. Callum doesn't even glance up from his glass to greet us.

Before Kellan can retort with his usual flair, a different male voice interjects, "Well, a King must always look his best, mustn't he?"

An older man, sitting between Fletcher and the Master of the Coin, lifts his glass towards Kellan. He dons a shiny, golden pin similar to Fletchers. Except his is not an anchor- it's a sword.

"Luckily for me, I always look my best," Kellan jokes, selecting a glass from the table, filling it with rum and raising it towards the man. "Yarrow, it's my immense honour to introduce you to Queen Wren of the Water World and Seven Spikes."

The man I don't recognise keeps his glass high but lowers his head in a bow like fashion. "The honour is all mine."

He keeps his head lowered for many beats, which I take as either a sign of deep respect or blatant fear. Unable to catch his gaze to signal his rising, I clear my throat and offer, "Yarrow, was it?"

He finally rights himself, nodding, "Yes, your

Majesty."

"Let us continue our drinking," Callum says flatly, "I'm sure Yarrow is weary after his long journey and in need of refreshments."

As everyone lowers themselves into their seats, I cast a glance at Callum, who only subtly nods to confirm my fears before taking another long, deep sip from his glass.

Apparently, I wouldn't be able to avoid all Soleil citizens after all. *Great.*

"So, you're from Soleil then?" I ask, not knowing what else to say.

"Bred and born," he beams proudly, "This is actually the first time I've ever been away from home. I'd never stepped a foot off the isle before."

"Are you not homesick?" I ask, my tone sounding more bitter than I intend.

"Wren had not strayed far from home until her visit to the Lunar Lands either," Kellan says, stabbing a forkful of honey-glazed meat off the nearest tray, "Ye have that in common."

I almost retort how kidnapping someone *isn't exactly* a holiday, but I figure it would be rude table manners, so I fill my mouth with bread to stop me saying something stupid.

"I'm not homesick...*yet*," he admits with a small

smile, "I've spent the last forty-three years on Soleil. It's about time I get more acquainted with travelling."

Forty-three years.

This man has lived through the reign of Alistair and his father, and now Kellan with the possibility of Aveen in the future if Kellan gets his wish.

"I'm glad to hear the Lunar Lands have made a good impression enough to warrant another visit in the future," I say, picking up a soft cheese phyllo and handful of grapes. Fletcher and I tend to prefer a plateful of nibbles, whereas Kellan opts for hearty dinner that barely fits on his plate. And Callum...well, Callum's plate is too empty, and his glass is too full for my liking.

Yarrow looks at me with slight bewilderment, before glancing around the table. I've obviously missed something...

"Yarrow has been selected to become a fellow Master," Fletcher offers, tossing a warm, reassuring smile in the newcomer's direction, "So he'll be splitting his time between the two isles."

I glance towards Kellan, only to find him already watching me. We know the struggles of splitting time between two isles. The travelling back and forth. The constant quick hello's, chased by catch up meetings, followed by goodbyes again a few days or weeks later.

If Yarrow's circumstances pan out to be anything like mine, he will find himself spending more time on one isle than the other- The Lunar Lands. Perhaps we'll have something else in common after all.

"He was only appointed an hour ago," Kellan mutters into my ear in an attempt to make me feel less out of the loop, "He hasn't even been announced yet."

"By rights he shouldn't be wearing the official breastpin until the paperwork is signed," Master of the Coin pips up, just to serve as a reminder for how dreadfully boring and pernickety a man he is.

"Oh, let him have it," Callum mutters.

I twist to look at the Prince, struggling to believe the words of support came out of *his* mouth.

Callum shrugs and continues, "I tried and failed to best the Soleil guards a dozen times whilst they held me captive. But they were fierce. Impenetrable. Merciless even. I once insisted Aveen and I be placed in the same cell. Hour after hour, day after day, I demanded and later pleaded, that we should not be separated. On the ninth day, they finally gave in and I won. Or at least I thought I had won."

Callum laughs at himself without humour. He clutches his tumbler tightly, his tense grip heating with glass and drink within. He throws back the last dregs before continuing.

"Finally, I was dragged across the narrow corridors of the prison and thrown headfirst into Aveen's cell. Whatever relief I felt swiftly disappeared later that evening when they came with our rations. The ever-generous Alistair ensured we were fed once a day. I suppose he couldn't bargain with our lives if we were dead." Callum chuckles drily.

Yarrow and Kellan become taut with tension. Fletcher subtly runs a palm down his husband's back, but it does nothing to soothe Callum. I fear he's too far gone for that.

"You see the guards pointed out that I had demanded for myself to be moved...but not my cot, nor my food. When the meagre rations arrived, they set my tray by the original cell door, and handed Aveen her tray with only a twisted smile for me. This continued for days. A mound of decaying bread heels and porridge grew just outside of my reach. As the weeks grew on, mushrooms began to sprout from the rot. When Aveen fell asleep, I would sit on the cobbled floor and stare at them for hours. Their white hoods glowed in the moonlight. They were nothing more than fungus, a common garden mushroom, but in my mind, they would have tasted like the realm's finest truffles. I almost dislocated my shoulder trying to reach for one. Silently straining in night as I inched my bony fingers towards the muck pile. At this stage, I'd lost a quarter of my weight. I survived solely off of whatever scraps Aveen didn't eat. The rations sizes were barely enough to keep her going, let alone feed me as well. Knowing she needed it more, I lied to her, telling her they used to feed me when she was asleep. But gods above there were days I hated her. I think that was the bastards' plan. To starve me until I snap at my own sister."

The table descends into stiff silence and stillness.

"But hey, at least we're rewarding their creativity and tenacity with shiny new medals, right?" Callum spits, pointing a finger at Yarrow's pin.

"Callum."

Kellan snarls the threat, his rising tension radiating to everyone at the table...except maybe his brother, who doesn't seem to give a Hel.

Ignoring the growl, and shaking off Fletcher's touch, Callum clumsily rises to his feet. He clatters his knife off his glass with enough force I'm surprised the stem doesn't shatter.

The ringing crystal summons the attention of everyone in the hall. He waits a beat for the shuffling to cease, before clearing his throat.

"Ladies, and gentleman, it gives me *great* joy to introduce you to Yarrow, our newest council member and our first ever Master of the Sword."

As applause implodes through the crowd, everyone at our table remembers how to breathe, although poor Yarrow's mouth still gapes open and closed like a coy.

Master of the Sword.

My leg begins a nervous bounce under the table. Kellan glides his hand up my thigh, giving me a reassuring squeeze but his steely gaze doesn't leave his brother.

"Isn't there an old saying? If you can't beat the tough bastards that held you hostage, employee the man that trained them?" Callum slurs slightly as he sits down and raises his empty glass towards a paling Yarrow.

"I think some of your friends would like to congratulate you," Kellan says to Yarrow, jerking his chin towards the Soleil corner where applause is the loudest, "You are free to join them."

Yarrow visibly relaxes, understanding Kellan's offer is an escape route or a dismissal, "Thank you, your Majesty."

Kellan nods stiffly, and then turns his attention to the rest of the top table, "Why don't you all dance before dessert comes, hmm? It might help make some room for the spring-fruit pies."

Taking his not-so-subtle hint, everyone vacates the

table. But before I even think of escaping, Kellan's grip tightens on my thigh.

"Dancing sounds delightful," Callum announces, wobbling his way to his feet once more.

"Sit. Down," Kellan says flatly, somehow making it more menacing than if he roared.

Callum mutters a curse, rolls his eyes, and flops back into his seat awaiting his chastising. Fletcher and I remain awkwardly perched on either side, acting as bookends to keep the tension from leaking to the rest of the hall.

I've seen Kellan angry before, many times, but this is the type of anger he does exceptionally well. His silent fury. Crossing his arms, he leans back and watches his brother with a heavy gaze.

"What?" Callum snaps with an Aveen-style pout when Kellan continues to just stare at him.

"I will never understand what you went through on that island," Kellan starts, sobering Callum instantly.

"I know they shackled you, starved you, and tortured you, but I'll never truly understand the utter despair you must have felt. I can't imagine falling asleep upon the cold ground, wondering if you'd ever see your husband again."

Fletcher gives Callum's shoulder a squeeze as if to remind him he made it out. Callum doesn't react, but his bottom lip wobbles slightly as he sniffles. A lump of emotion grows in my throat.

"I don't know how many countless beatings you took in order to protect our sister," Kellan continues, "How many of your meals you gave her. Or how the Hel you managed to come up with magically bedtimes stories for her when you didn't know what tomorrow would bring."

"It took every bone of hope I had," Callum shrugs, unfallen tears making his eyes glisten.

"And I need you to summon one ounce of that hope for me now. It's hard to understand, but *this*," Kellan gestures to the Soleil gang, "*This* is the only way we can move forward. I cannot undo what happened, gods I wish I could, but I cannot. All I can do is ensure nothing ever happens like that again. I can control the strongest guards we've ever encountered. I can use their training and skills and grow an army...Our army. Now, I'm not expecting you to befriend every Soleil citizen, but we have to try including them in our society, incorporating them into our policies and welcoming them into our home-"

"And you just expect me to sit across from my kidnappers at meals?" Callum snaps.

"Wren's doing it with decorum isn't she?" Kellan retorts with a playful tone.

"Well, I'm not trying to get into Yarrow's bed, though am I?" Callum spits.

"Hey!" I shriek, launching to my feet, my wings fluttering behind me, "You take that back you son of Cyclops, or I swear to the gods-"

"Pie?" Nessa bounces over to the table, carrying a tray heaving with juicy tarts as sweet as her, "I have the old Ostara favourite of blueberry and strawberry pie, but I do also have a Soleil special of peach and honey, that is apparently delicious."

I smooth out my dress, and offer her a smile, hoping she didn't hear much of the bickering. Although, judging from her unwavering, forced smile, I think the bickering is the *exact* reason she scampered over.

"That's very kind of you Nessa," Kellan says struggling to sound level-headed, raking a hand through his hair, "We'll have three of the new peach, and one of the traditional."

"I don't want anything," Callum gripes, but Nessa sets down the requested plates without faltering.

Kellan rises to his feet beside me, handing me two of the peach crumbles. He then hands Fletcher the last remaining peach, before slamming the berry option in front of his brother, "I know you don't like change so here, eat this and sober up. It might even sweeten you up too, you bitter bastard."

Fletcher and Nessa gasp in unison, with Callum spitting a curse at his brother.

Kellan turns on his heel, and gestures for us to leave, "We'll take ours to-go. I'm in need of fresh air."

I want to encourage the brothers to smooth things over, but with them both being Descendants of Ares, perhaps distance would be the best thing for their tempers.

I offer Nessa a thank you before scurrying to catch up with Kellan as he storms his way out of the hall.

FOUR

We wander aimlessly around the town in silence for a few minutes. With most of the candles now nothing but cold, wax stumps, and the citizens either at the feast or retreating to their bed, the streets are abandoned.

Kellan's ambling leads us towards the stone steps. I follow close, unsure whether he's heading towards the castle to retire to his own chambers or if he's retreating to my cottage. Apparently, he isn't too sure himself, deciding to slump onto the bottom step. Sinking his head into his hands, he releases a muffled grunt, halfway between a roar and a sigh.

"Do you think I was too hard on him?" he asks without lifting his head.

Yes. No. A little. Not knowing what to say, and knowing I cannot lie to save his feelings, I sag onto the step beside him and set down the plates, "He's been drinking since before the fleet arrived."

"So, he won't remember me calling him a bitter bastard then?"

"*So*, I think you could cut him some slack. It's a weird day... for everyone," I say softly.

To this, he straightens himself and twists to gaze at me wholly, "Thank you for coming today, I know it can't have been easy for you either. I wanted to follow you when you left the pier, I wanted to make sure you were alright but..."

"But duty called," I offer, with a simple shrug, "I understand. Actually, I'm probably the only other person in this realm to *truly* understand."

"That's the problem with Callum. He'll never fully know what it is to be a ruler. As a Prince, he has boring meetings and paperwork too, but it'll never be him signing off on important decisions. It'll never be him forced to do something he doesn't want to do for the '*greater good of the Kingdom*.'"

I'm not sure which council member he's mimicking, but to be fair they all sound the same anyway.

I gathered Yarrow had not been Kellan's decision, but he defended the new Master's role so well I didn't know he had been *this* against it. Years of gambling has taught Kellan to keep his cards close to his chest.

"I have to do unconventional things sometimes," he adds with a sigh.

A roguish grin pulls at my lips, "Unconventional like going fishing for a syren with a big net?"

His initial groan melts into laughter. He leans over me to reach for his pie, "Cheers to you being the best radical idea I ever had."

I clink my plate against his and lean against his shoulder.

"I left in too much of a hurry to remember forks," he grumbles.

Not wanting his barely contained stress levels to spike once more, I simply scoop the pie into my hands and take a Drakon sized bite, "There are no forks in the Water World."

As I chomp on a mouthful of succulent peach pieces, he brushes a crumb away from the corner of my lips, "Tell me about your world. What's Ostara like there?"

"Well to start with we don't hang painted eggshells off everything. Seeing as we have more crustaceans than chickens, we tend to decorate with shells. My mother never really celebrated anything, but she allowed some spring-time luring, seeing it as good choir practise. To be honest, I think..."

My voice trails off as conflicted emotion strangles

the end of my sentence. Kellan scans my face a dozen times within a single breath, trying to suss out what's wrong.

"I think it's the only source of happy memories I have with her. With Kestrel. I know she is...she *was* a monster, but it was the one day a year where she was genuinely kind to me. We'd all swim out to the furthest edge of the Seven Spikes, over a hundred of us syrens. It was the only time she dared to swim past the Clam Gates. And we'd all line up in our choir groups and release our songs towards the surface. We'd cause the sea to vibrate, shaking the surface water free and allowing it to rise into a fine mist that covered the land for miles on end. Kestrel always egging me on to sing louder, saying it was our rain which helped nourish the land, reawaken the crops and feed the farmers."

My smiling at the memory dims, "But I should have known she never cared about those people. She just wanted to keep them alive long enough to use them as luring bait when the time came."

"There could be some truth to that," Kellan admits, wincing, "But you don't have to tarnish every memory of her back *then* with what you know *now*."

I push away my half-eaten pie, my appetite having faded, "Look at you, seeming all wise and astute. It must be the old age."

He rolls his eyes, and rises to his feet, "I'd hardly call nineteen '*old age*'."

"Almost twenty," I correct.

With his birthday in less than a fortnight, I had preparations in full swing back on Seven Spikes for his arrival. When I asked what he wanted for his birthday, he jokingly said a break from being King. So that's exactly what I've arranged for him.

"There's life in the ol' dog yet," Kellan growls, his eyes now staring at me like *I'm* the bloody dessert.

I roll my shoulders, and lightly flutter my feathers as I push off the step. With a single beat of wings, I rise a foot off ground, so I'm level with his heavy gaze.

"We'll see about that," I tease, "How about we race.... back to the bathtub?"

Kellan flashes a quick wink before spinning on his heel and bounding up the steps two at a time. His sheer speed takes me by surprise.

I try to pump my wings furiously, to get more air beneath me but I'm too busy laughing at his enthusiasm. I rise another few feet into the air, before joining the chase.

I'm halfway above the steps, when-

Whack.

The air is knocked clean out of my lungs before I even scream.

FIVE

My body plummets out of the sky. As I slam onto the stone steps, another *whack* of pain strikes me in the core, blowing me backwards.

I tumble down the steps, my bare arms scuffing and splitting against the rough shale as I roll. The steps end, and so does the momentum. I slam onto my spine, my limbs flopping to my side.

Pain with no end or beginning encapsulates my body, becoming my only existence. My thunderous heartbeat floods my ears, yet I somehow still hear Kellan's roar as he scrambles towards me.

He throws himself off the last step, caging his body over mine like a shield. His eyes are wider than I've ever seen.

"Shh," he soothes in a tone which is very

un-soothing, "You're alright, you're alright."

I don't know why he's lying to me; I am most certainly not alright. And why the Hel is he telling me to *shh* when I cannot speak, and I cannot breathe.

Shit, I cannot breathe!

Lurching upright, I gasp for air, but the tensing of my abdomen muscles releases a new wave of pain.

"No, no, no," he warns, pinning my shoulders to the ground. "Stay down."

He frantically looks over his shoulder, but his gaze keeps returning to my side where the pain radiates.

I remain pinned against the cobbles, but I strain my neck enough to be able to see what is terrifying him so much.

An arrow has embedded in the soft skin between the ribs on my right-hand side, blowing that gill open as a result.

Gods above! No wonder I can't breathe. My gills and lungs can't work at the same time. They're in competition with each other but without water, my wounded gill is damned to fail.... And I'll fail along with it.

"Oh, sweet Zeus!" A faint, faraway voice blurts in, "Her wing!"

My wing? What the Hel is wrong with my wing?

Of course.... I'd felt two *whacks*. I crane my neck

the other way, my head flopping heavily to the left to see yet another arrow- this time protruding from the centre of my wing.

The dark feathered fletching camouflages against my own plumage. It blends in so well it would be easy to overlook the weapon.... if it were not for the pumping blood and ichor leaking from my feathers.

"I'll take care of her," Kellan growls protectively, "I saw movement in the treeline behind us. Send a few of my men into the woods, without causing mass hysteria in the hall. I want this attacker caught...alive."

I faintly hear racing footsteps receding, or at least I think I do. I also think I hear Kellan add *'so I can kill him myself,'* but I no longer know what is real.

My vision blurs, and I'm no longer able tell if the darkness and stars I see above is the night sky or my fading consciousness. My spotty gaze locks onto Kellan. In the dim light, his hair appears almost silver, his pale skin almost milk-white.

Perhaps I'm seeing him through ghost eyes. Perhaps I'm already dead.

"I want to lift you, but I'll have to take the arrow out for that."

Yes! Please!

I muster up as much an enthusiastic nod as I can handle. It's barely more than a dip of the chin but it gets the message across.

My back arches from the mounting pressure within my chest. The lack of oxygen threatening to detonate me into a hundred pieces.

Kellan wraps his fingers around the fletching. The slight movement of the arrow sends shockwaves of fresh pain through my ribs. I flinch away from his touch.

"I'm sorry, *agapi mou*, I'm so sorry."

The way he says *my love* threatens to take away what little breath I have left. But unfortunately, his tender sentiment is followed with him lightly pressing his knee against my hip as he pins me down.

"Three.... two..."

He yanks on two.

I lurch upright, panting short, sharp breaths as my gill slams closed.

"Easy, easy," he says like I am a wild beast, tossing away the arrow as if it burns him to touch it. He slaps his hand over my wound, trying to stem the fresh wave of bleeding.

"I need to get you out of here," he growls, throwing another glance over his shoulder.

Kellan may not have a hundred eyes like Argus the Giant, but he somehow simultaneously scans our surroundings yet never takes his gaze off my wound.

"Your wing will have to wait," he sighs, trying his best to scoop me up tenderly.

Pain rips through me nonetheless. He shifts around my weight in his hold so his hand can apply pressure to the hole in my side.

My head flops against his solid chest. He nestles a kiss into my mess of hair, murmuring, "You stay with me, you hear? Stay with me."

I want to say something sarcastic about having nowhere else to go, but I can't form the words. Maybe it's because I'm too weak, or maybe it's because it's a lie...One can always go to the Underworld.

I brace, preparing to feel the movement of him ascending the steps I just rolled down, but the sensation never comes.

Instead, the gentle crunch of his boots on gravel fills my ears, and the unmistakable scent of night-blooming jasmine fills my nose.

The castle lawns. He's bringing me to the castle.

I suppose there wasn't much competition deciding between a cottage known for having a key under the mat, versus his chambers on the third floor of a guarded and gated fortress, but that doesn't stop a sob catching in my throat.

I need to be further away from the Lunar Lands right now, not in the bloody heart of it. I'd rather he set me down in a rowboat in the centre of the bay, where at least I have the sea to wrap around myself.

My heavy eyelids fall shut, and when they re-open I'm being laid across the end of Kellan's bed.

"I'm going to send for a healer, and then I'll be right back," he says, moving away from me.

"No." My objection is the loudest sound I've managed to speak since falling from the sky, "No healers. Nobody else"

"Wren, I have to get someone. You still have an arrow in you for gods' sake!"

"Please."

To this he pauses. He hovers somewhere halfway between me and the door, but I don't have the strength to sit up and face him, so I'm left pleading with the white-washed ceiling and timbers above me. He backtracks his steps, coming close enough to see tears silently rolling either side of my face.

"Please," I repeat, my voice wobbling more than I intend, "I don't trust these people."

These people. His people.

He swallows hard, appearing as wounded as me. With a taut jaw he asks, "Do you trust me?"

"Yes," I reassure, but sensing an ulterior motive to his question, I quickly add, "I trust you, but you have to trust me. If you won't do as I ask, then...."

I close my eyes as a result from the mounting dizziness, but also not wanting to see Kellan's face as I say, "Then put me back in the sea where men won't hurt me...where at least I know I'm safe."

"No," he says flatly, but firmly, "No, I won't leave you. I won't give you back to the sea. I'll take care of you by myself; I promise, Wren."

He may not have enough ichor is his veins to form a binding oath, but I believe him.

"No one else, okay?" He says as he gets to work locking the door, and shutting the heavy drapes with enough force to almost rip the iron rail from the wall, "Just you and I."

Relief washes over me, melting away the tension barely holding me together. Without it, numbness steeps in. My limp limbs begin to shake uncontrollably, as my blood levels and core temperature continue to drop.

Kellan races around his chamber, lifting armfuls of clothes out of his wardrobe and dumping them on a pile on the floor.

My teeth chatter loud enough for him to hear over his controlled chaos.

"You'll be warm soon," he says over his shoulder, crouching onto his haunches as he gets to work sparking a fire to life. Retrieving his hipflask from his pocket, he begins splashing rum on the pile of shirts and pants beside him, before feeding them to the growing inferno.

In fact, he tosses anything burnable within arm's reach onto the flames. I make a mental note to add *pyromaniac* to my growing list of Kellan adjectives, somewhere in-between *gambler* and *eager with a knife*.

Flames spit and crackle, threatening to scorch the mantelpiece as they're barely contained within the pit anymore. I get the feeling he's willing to burn down the entire castle to keep me warm.

Satisfied his fire won't die, he returns his attention to his syren which might.

He closes the space between us with a single stride, tugging his knife free from his waistband. Without warning, he nestles the pointed tip under the neckline of my dress and rips the seam. He continues to cut away the fabric, until it falls open on either side, presenting my naked and damaged body for his inspection.

"Gods above."

This is the second time today he's seen my bare body, but this time I want to hide myself from him. I want to hide myself from *me*, because the fear in his voice is enough to make me not want to look down.

Sliding his forearms under me, he carefully prises me off the soiled garment, positioning me on the thick, plush sheepskin rug in front of the now roaring fire instead. He feeds my dress to the flames without hesitation.

"Hey." I croak, watching the beading melt whilst the gossamer fabric billows out smoke, "I liked that dress."

"I'll get you another," Kellan says, as he makes his way to the bathroom adjacent to his suite to fetch a basin of water, "Recover from this and I'll buy you an entire wardrobe."

"You'll need clothes. Not me."

My voice barely carries over the sudden *ripping* sound of him destroying yet *another* shirt. This time to make linen strips.

"I don't need anything bar you surviving, okay?"

I nod, or at least I think I do. I don't feel my body move. I don't feel my body at all anymore.

Even with my eyes shut, the dancing flickers and shadows penetrate through my lids. I try to remind myself it's just from the fire, but an ever-growing part of me fears it is Hades stoking the pits of the Underworld in preparation for my arrival.

Kellan tends to the thumb-size hole in my side. There's some pulling and prodding, but no real pain. I've transcended beyond that now.

He uses some of the linen strips to wash my midriff.

A liquid trickles down my side, pooling beneath the small of my back. I pray it is water from the basin. I'd hate for my blood and ichor to ruin such a soft rug.

He tosses the damp, stained strips into the fire, causing an almighty hiss like Hera's serpents as the cloth steams from the heat.

After a few minutes, or maybe it's hours, he wraps a long ribbon of cotton around my midriff. Calloused hands from years of rope pulling on boats, and sword slashing at men means he struggles to tie a small knot in the ribbon. It takes him three attempts and a lot of swearing to finally finish the bandage.

Running his hand through his hair, he streaks his golden hair with my blood. He releases an unsteady breath, before turning his attention to my wing. Carefully thumbing the feather tip, he extends my left wing to its full span.

"It almost went clean through," he says with an edge of disbelief and disgust, "It might be better for me to push it, rather than pull it?"

If he's asking me, I do not answer. I have no bloody preference. His fingers pinch the fletching end of the arrow. With no time to spare, he does not bother counting again.

I'd naively assumed I'd hit my peak of pain, and because I'd now reached numbness, I was safe.

I don't know why the gods get such joy from proving me wrong.

As he slides the end of the weapon *through* me, I reach a whole new level of agony.

I shriek, reanimated as my nerve ending from my wings to my fingertips electrocute me.

"Got it!" Kellan shouts, shifting into my line of view, wielding the feather and blood-soaked arrow in his hand. He snaps it in two, and tosses it onto the flame, "It's almost over, *agapi mou*."

Jerking upright, I vomit.

Every bite of bread and peach pie now lays spewed across the floor.

There goes my attempt of not ruining the rug.

Kellan moves to behind me, sweeping my thick hair away from my face.

"Breathe," he says over and over again, gently rubbing my back as I pant in-between retching. It takes a few moments for my body to stop heaving. When Kellan brings a drink of water to my lips, I threaten to start again but I fight through it. I drink deeply even though I'm a little worried it might leak through the hole in my side.

He carefully places me back on the bed, swaddles me lightly in a large, woollen blanket and asks, "How are you feeling?"

"Surprised you didn't burn this too," I mutter, nestling into the blanket as he props me up with pillows.

"There's my girl," he says, smoothing my hair, "I was afraid a knock of that magnitude might have blown the sarcasm out of you."

"No chance."

Kellan offers a grin, but it doesn't reach his eyes, "Tell me what else I can do. Do you want more water? Food? Do you need ichor? I'll blood share with you."

His hand goes to his knife without hesitation, his sleeve already rolled up.

Gah, no more blood, I think to myself, feeling queasy all over again. Wiggling my hand free from the snug swaddle, I pat the space beside me, "Just sit with me."

"I don't want to hurt you." He crosses his arms, and moves away from the bed, away from me. Instead, he perches himself on the very edge of his wicker chair. He remains there for about four breaths, before lurching to his feet and pacing.

"I don't understand why it's never me getting shackled or shot." He growls, rage taking over as his worry subsides, "Whenever I let my guard down for a night something happens, and those I love pay the price."

Those I love. Although I felt honoured to be

included on his list, he seemed to view it as a hit-list.

"Kellan," I start, waiting until he pauses his pacing to continue, "This isn't your fault."

"Of course, it is? If it weren't for me, you'd be safely underwater with your people. But you came to *my* isle, to see *me* and *I* didn't even protect you!"

"How do you think *I* felt when Kestrel came to destroy *you* and *your* Kingdom?" I ask through gritted teeth as I try and fail to sit more upright.

He ignores me, beginning his pacing once more, "For the love of gods Wren, I even tempted Fate by saying your bad luck couldn't get any worse tonight! It's as if-"

He stops talking.

His focus snaps to the door, and with almost predator agility he moves towards it, one hand gripping his knife, the other the doorknob. The dancing flames of the suite highlight the looming shadows beneath the doorframe as feet creep closer.

SIX

 gentle knock raps on the door a mere five seconds later. Even though he's prepared, the sound takes him by surprise. Murderers don't tend to knock so...

"Who is it?" Kellan growls.

"It's me again, sir." The same faint voice as before comes through the door.

"It's only Nessa," he says to me before opening the door, just a crack. He uses his broad shoulder to block any view of me, "I'm really considering putting a bell on you. You always pop up unannounced."

Nessa? Gods above why must this poor girl always see me at my worst?

"Apologies, your Majesty," she says, slightly out of breath, "I have news regarding..."

Kellan nods to silence her. He scans the corridors

a few times to make sure she wasn't followed before lifting his arm up, allowing her to slip into his chamber.

Her doe-like eyes scan around the room as she takes in her surroundings. I hate how smug I feel knowing she hasn't been in his chamber before. Her gaze trails from the destroyed rug, to the droplets of blood on the floor, before finally landing on me.

She gasps, like an actual gasp, before saying, "It's so good to see you're okay! I didn't think you were going to survive...there was so much blood, and..."

I offer a small, clumsy smile that probably resembles more a grimace before trying to bury myself deeper into Kellan's blanket pile.

"You said you had news," Kellan says firmly, sensing my discomfort.

"Yes," she says, thankfully turning her attention back to her King. "The perpetrator has been caught. He is being held in a room in sailor barracks. He's unconscious and mildly injured, but alive as requested. No *mass hysteria* was caused."

"Good." There's a palpable edge of anger to Kellan's voice, "That's good. How many men did you send after him? I need to know who else knows about this."

When Nessa doesn't answer straight away, Kellan crosses his arms and presses, "Well?"

"I did not send any men. I...I was the one who caught him, sir," she admits, straightening her shoulders.

"What?" Kellan and I choke in unison.

He takes a physical step back, the anger in his voice is swapped for genuine surprise, "You?"

She nods, her blonde hair coming untucked from behind her ear, "Wren seemed to be in a bad way, so I didn't want to waste time trying to discreetly sniff out a non-drunk man from the hall when I could do the job myself. I chased him as he sprinted towards the coastline forest, and that's where I took him down."

"Took him down?" I repeat, afraid that I've slipped into unconsciousness again and this is all a dream.

"I wrapped a rock in my scarf, swung it a few times and then...then I sent it soaring in his direction," she says, tugging her sleeves in a futile attempt to hide the mud and scrapes covering her hands, "Hence the *unconscious* and *mildly injured* part of my account."

"What did you do then?" Kellan asks, a glint of amusement shining in his russet eyes.

"I half carried, mostly dragged the archer from the woods into the courtyard, and that's when Arthur Wellis found me. He helped me carry the man into his barrack room, and he's keeping an eye on him now."

Arthur. The young, slender sailor whose nose I'd

once crunched with a cannonball. I'll have to get him something nice from the agora to thank him for always dealing with the strain of the trouble I summon.

"And what about the archer?" Kellan asks, any amusement evaporating from his tone, "Is it someone we know?"

Another stark difference between Kestrel and Kellan as rulers was their desire to know their people. My mother always wanted her creatures under her control, but she had little interest in knowing anything about them. Whereas Kellan takes knowing his citizen's seriously. Even if he doesn't know every individual by name, he would know of their family name. I've committed myself to take after Kellan's style of leadership, promising to get to know all of my own citizens, especially those of the Seven Spike mainland which was neglected for so many years.

Nessa glances between me and Kellan, before her azure eyes fall to the floor. Clearing her throat, she says, "It wasn't one of our men, your Majesty. It was one of the visitors.... from Soleil."

Ah. Of course.

An unspoken sense of clarity and understanding flows throughout the room, though Kellan won't insult me by admitting it out loud.

A heavy sigh erupts from his chest as he steps

towards me, "I will take care of this."

Take care.

I don't know who he's trying to fool. I knew there would be no *care* shown to the archer.

He drops to one knee and slides out the Armour of Ares from beneath his bed.

"You keep a gift of the gods under your bed?" I ask with a raised brow.

"It keeps the monsters away," he offers, setting the hefty shield beside me, "You won't need this, but I'll feel better knowing you have it."

He lightly kisses the top of my crown, and brushes a loose piece of hair from my face, "And Nessa will stay with you?"

He asks over his shoulder, despite my tightening grip on his hand. She nods instantly and enthusiastically, "Of course!"

She's so helpful it's sickening.

He gives her a pat on the shoulder as he walks by, "Change Wren's dressing every few hours. I'll arrange for clothes and food to be dropped at the door, but don't let anyone in. Lock the door after I leave, but feel free to launch another homemade discus at anyone you feel gets too close."

"Yes, sir," she nods, although she cringes at the mention of her assaulting skills. Perhaps we'll bond over our shared guilt of hurting Soleil men.

"Thank you, I'll send word to your mother as to your whereabouts," he says to Nessa, before moving to the doorway. He gives a last glance in my direction, "Rest. I'll be back as soon as I can."

Without a second glance, Kellan blasts out the door, barrelling down the corridor with his knife in his palm.

Nessa clicks the door closed, twists the lock, and turns to face me with an awkward smile, "Can I get you anything?"

"I just want to sleep," I say wearily, suddenly exhausted from the day and far too tired to make small chat with her.

"Of course," she says again. I get the feeling she rarely objects to anything.

Without prompt she helps me twist onto my non-injured side, sliding a pillow behind me to stop me rolling before she quietly retreats back to the wicker chair in the corner.

I feign sleep for so long I eventually succumb to it. Between the pillow wall, the blanket swaddle, and the hefty Shield taking up a chunk of bed space, I wake up in the exact same position I fell asleep in. For a girl who normally sleeps like an octopus throwing a temper tantrum, it's a weird sensation to see the sheets unruffled, and not a single pillow having been thrown onto the floor.

Daylight seeps through cracks in the dense curtains. It streaks across the bed and warms my face. Actually, the whole chamber is warm, surprisingly so for an early spring morning. I twist to see if the fire is still burning. The action causing me to hiss loudly as the bandage, stuck to me from dried blood, peels away.

"Careful, your Majesty," Nessa yelps, springing to her feet in an instant.

Gods above, I'd almost forgotten about her. I'm beginning to second Kellan's idea of putting a bell on her.

"You don't have to call me 'your Majesty'," I grate through gritted teeth as I swing my legs over the edge of the bed, "You're not one me my citizens, and I'm not even your Queen."

"Well, how about I call you Wren whilst the King isn't here?" she offers, as if it's our little secret, "But he would be very upset with me if I didn't keep my word and freshen up your bandages. So, stay still."

"I don't have anything else on under this.... toga,"

I admit, pulling the woollen material closer to me.

"Clothes and a whole bunch of other things were dropped off shortly after dawn, but I still need to clean your wound," she says simply yet firmly, "You might be a syren, but we're both women, Wren. It's nothing I haven't seen before."

"I highly doubt you've seen gills and wings before," I quibble, feeling lightheaded as I wobble onto my feet.

She purses her lips into a pout, throwing a hand on her hip, and arching a blonde brow. She keeps her stare on me, waiting, unprovoked by my words.

Not wanting to give her the satisfaction of fainting in front of her, I concede and offer her a stiff nod.

Dropping her hand from her waist, Nessa helps me shuffle to the bathroom, before filling the deep stone sink with warm water.

"You didn't have to clean up my mess," I say, noting the rolled-up rug now discarded in the corner, "I would have done it."

"I don't mind," Nessa says with a shrug, and although she has the human privilege of being able to lie, I don't think she is. She unravels the blanket from my shoulder, lightly pushing it down to my hips, "Besides, it's my job."

I stand before her, bare from the waist up and fighting the urge to wrap my wings around myself.

"What *is* your job anyway? Nurse by day, pie server by evening and a rock slinging vigilante by night?"

A small smile finds her lips, "Something like that. I like being busy."

I nod, trying not to move too much as she peels away the stained linen from my side and carefully begins washing.

"Actually," she adds, without taking her gaze away from my wound, "If I'm being honest, I would just rather not be at home, and the more I work the more coin I get, the less pressure my mother puts on me to marry."

"Huh. My mother always wanted me to find a man too. Granted it was for different and more... murderous reasons, but the same pressure I guess," I admit, finding myself offering her a small smile of sympathy.

She returns the smile, whilst wrapping fresh gauze around my midriff. It's actual gauze this time, not a shredded shirt. It must have been dropped off with the rest of the supplies. Although it's softer against my skin, and easier to move with, it doesn't hold Kellan's scent which matters more to me right now.

Speaking of Kellan....

"So," I start, trying to sound casual but it is hard to sound off-hand when I've been wanting to broach this topic for a while now, "I guess your mother wants you to marry a Master....or maybe even a royal?"

I try not to wince at my own words as they hang in the air. Nessa continues to focus on fastening my dressing. Her nimble fingers tying a dainty bow effortlessly.

She moves to the sink, pulls the plug, and over the gurgling of the swirling water asks, "Is that why you... dislike me?"

My face blanks with surprise. My lack of subtly reminding me I have very little experience in talking to female humans.

"I never said I disliked you?" I offer.

It's true. I never *said* I disliked her; I've apparently just failed to hide my immaturity.

"I can just tell," she says with a shrug, bouncing her way out of the bathroom towards the awaiting crate of goods, "I keep a mental note of those who aren't overly fond of me in the hopes I can make it up to them the next time. At the moment there are five on the list. My three sisters have always positively loathed me, then there is Bevin Doughal, he's Master of the Judge, but to be honest he doesn't hold any women in high esteem so his dislike might not be as personal. And then you're the fifth. Although I should probably add the Soleil archer to that list. I doubt he is very fond of me this morning."

She unfolds a long soft tunic which has two slits in the back, and gestures for me to come closer, but I do not. I can't. My knees are somewhat locked with the weight of a hundred questions rushing through my mind.

Nessa gapes slightly, and raises a hand to her mouth, "I'm sorry. I've spoken out of turn. I didn't mean to make you uncomfortable or anything-"

"*That*," I vent, with a point as I move towards her, "That is why I find you hard to tolerate at times. Why are you so bloody apologetic all the time? You're so poised and perfect, it's infuriating. You're always saying '*of course*' and trotting around following orders."

Nessa swallows hard and remains silent. Her cheeks flushing to a rosy hue. Good gods, I truly am I monster if I make her cry. She tilts her narrow chin away from me and blinks rapidly as her eyes become glassy. *Gah*, she is about to cry.

"Look, I'm more jealous of you than anything," I admit, softening my tone, "And I'm a syren so you know I'm not just saying it to be nice. That's one of the reasons I'm envious of you. You say nice things to people. You're kind. Whereas I'm...I'm more likely to insult and hurt people. Nessa, if I had five or six people on this whole island who *liked* me, I would consider it a win."

"I like you," she offers with a simple shrug, sniffling slightly.

Of course she does, I think to myself. Not out of ego, but because I doubt Nessa has ever disliked anyone. She's the type of woman who would feel rude for not making eye-contact if talking to Medusa.

As I take the tunic from her, I also take her hand, "I'm sorry for being cold to you. I know it's no excuse, but Kellan is the only person who treats me like I'm normal. He doesn't fear my power, and he understands my crown. To him, I'm just Wren. He accepts me as I am which is rare, because I'm not a perfect girl like you...Hel I'm not even a girl!"

Nessa opens her mouth to protest and reassure me, but I wave her off, "But that's beside the point. The point is, I let my possessiveness cause us to get off on the wrong fin, I mean foot, and I'm sorry. Can you forgive me?"

"Of course!" Nessa beams, squeezing my hand, before she cringes at herself, "Ugh, I do say that a lot, don't I?"

"You do," I nod, laughter causing my bandaged side to ache from the movement. Nessa shakes her head at herself and helps me get back into bed.

"For the record, I've never even had so much a

Kairos

school-girl crush on Kellan. I find him quite imperious and arrogant. Also, I partook in numerous races with him as a teenager, and he's such a sore loser!"

Laughter rolls through me once more, and I find myself gripping my side, "He is such a sore loser. Maybe that's where his love of betting comes from? Maybe he's hoping if he gambles on himself he has extra motivation to win."

"You've got him all figured out," she grins, pulling the blanket over me once more. She sobers a little saying, "Please don't mention to my King that I called him arrogant."

I swat away her concern as if it were a fly, "It's just between us, like our little secret. Although my syren side might make secret-keeping quite difficult."

Nessa grins, "I appreciate your attempt nonetheless. However, we both know Kellan will ask *you* directly if you ate whilst he was away, and no amount of truth-evading or squirming will get you out of that."

She ignores my groan of protest, as she prances over to the awaiting crate and retrieves a tray full of food.

A lavish spread of fruits, loaves of breads and even some left-over pies and phyllo from last night are piled high on the tray. There's even a small ceramic dish brimming with fried seaweed and mussels, with a note attached.

I thought some comfort food might help- I'll be back soon.
There's no signature, but I recognise Kellan's curved handwriting after hours of staring at his letters. My heart swells at his consideration, but the memories of my retching across the rug are still too fresh in my mind.

"Tell you what," Nessa offers with a small smirk on her lips, "If you eat eight whole bites, I'll tell you the story about the time my mother tried to set me up on date with Prince Callum."

"Callum?!" I almost knock the tray off my lap.

"The one and only," she shakes her head, her cheeks blushing once more, "Eight bites, and the story is yours."

I groan, but slowly pick up a mussel, "This better be worth it."

SEVEN

I become so engrossed in Nessa's story I manage to eat far more than eight bites.

Four years ago, on a late summers evening, Nessa's mother decided her daughter had to seize her opportunity to catch the Prince's eye before he was married off to some rich man's daughter. Dressed in her best cornflower blue dress with a matching ribbon braided into her hair, Nessa was flung out of her house and sent towards the dock where Callum had taken to spending his evenings.

The Princes' growing fondness for the docks became abundantly clear to fifteen-year-old Nessa when she spotted him passionately locking lips with Fletcher behind a boat.

Not wanting to face a plethora of questions from her mother for arriving home early, yet not wanting to stay by the pier either, Nessa found herself wandering into the West Wing hall. Growing up in a house where she constantly picks up after her sisters, she began aimlessly straightening chairs and dusting shelves out of habit. Once enough time had passed that her faux date with Callum would be believable, she made her way out of the hall, only to run into King Lachlan. Rather than chastise her for being in castle grounds without permission, he admired her efforts. Handing her a coin for her efforts, he asked her to come back the next day and wash the stained-glass windows.

She'd be a royal run-around since then.

"And you truly never told your mother about Callum and Fletcher?" I ask, adding the last empty mussel shell into the bowl.

"Oh, I never told anyone," she says, "I simply told my mother someone already held Callum's heart and I wouldn't make a fool of myself frolicking around in that puffy dress anymore. It took her months to give up. She constantly asked me what this 'other girl' had that I didn't. It took everything I had to not answer '*a deep voice, stubble and an extra foot of height!*'"

I dissolve into laughter once again, the spasm causing my side to pulsate with pain but it's worth it.

Nessa moves away the tray, satisfied I've eaten enough, and gestures for me to lie.

73

"Rest some more. I'll tell you another tale when you wake up," she offers, fluffing a pillow to rest my wing upon.

I think about protesting once more, but even the minimal effort of eating has left me jaded again, "Alright, you have yourself a deal, but it better be as good a story as what you just told me."

"Of course," she grins, "I already have one in mind."

I wake up later that afternoon to firm knocking. Nessa and I lurch to our feet in an instant, though I grip the bedpost to stop myself collapsing from the head-rush.

"It's only me, *lígo poulāki*," Kellan's deep voice rumbles through the wood effortlessly.

Though his voice is distinct, and he's the only one to ever call me *little bird*, I would not be me if I missed an opportunity to taunt him a little.

"Hmm, how do I know if it's really you?" I tease, making my way towards the door, battling off dizziness with each step, "You better tell me your favourite thing about me so I can be sure."

His eye-roll is almost visible through the sealed door.

"I have far too many favourites to list, but I find it

amusing the Queen of the sea is *fishing* for compliments from me."

"It's him alright," I say, giving the nod to Nessa to open the door.

"I've been worried about you. It's a relief to see you on two feet." He says with a smile that doesn't reach his eyes. Eyes which are heavily shadowed. He leans against the now open doorframe but doesn't come into his own chamber.

"Are you alright?" I ask, concern thickening my voice as I notice my dried blood still streaked on parts of his arms.

His hair is dishevelled from his hands running through it a hundred times. He most definitely hasn't slept or bathed since leaving me, but I doubt he has even sat or eaten anything either.

"Yeah," he lies, "It's just been a...challenging night."

"You should rest. I'll arrange for more food and ask Shelli to arrange more clothes for you seeing as you charred everything." I announce, tugging lightly on his sleeve. But he does not budge an inch.

"As amazing as all of that sounds, I unfortunately have to decline." He takes my hand and squeezes it lightly, "I'm here primarily to check on you, but also..." His voice trails off.

Nessa awkwardly nods to both of us before attempting to slip past Kellan and make a silent getaway.

"Wait," Kellan says, "This applies to you too."

Nessa backtracks and waits obediently, though confusion crumples her face.

"There has been a...complication with the archer."

"Complication?" I ask.

He nods firmly, "I'll explain to you on route to the courthouse, we're needed there in a few minutes. But Nessa, you should be aware that as of this moment he's still breathing."

The way Kellan grates out *this moment* makes the man's living status sound very, very temporary.

"There's a guard at the end of the corridor waiting for you, he'll accompany you home and stay at your side until further notice," Kellan explains.

"But the archer is being shackled and imprisoned somewhere right? He doesn't know it's me who got him in all this trouble, right? He won't find me?"

Nessa's somewhat high-pitched voice spikes to a barely controlled shrill.

"I'm taking care of it," Kellan says flatly.

Nessa's mouth flies open to ask another question, but Kellan's unsteady sigh stops her.

Instead, she nods rather reluctantly, "Of course,

your Majesty."

Nessa bows lightly towards Kellan and then me.

"You still owe me a story, Nessa," I call after her as she makes her way down the corridor.

She throws a slight smile over her shoulder, and it's almost enough to mask the nervousness painted across her face. *Almost.*

Kellan normally bounds ahead of me, his long strides forcing me to trot to keep up. But not this evening. Eight guards flank us as we make our way towards the courthouse. Kellan remains glued to my right-hand side, his forearm wrapped around my waist, acting as a human shield whilst also keeping me upright.

As much as I despise being the centre of attention, I'm grateful for the slower pace of movement. The guards and Kellan step in perfect unison.

Having never seen the courthouse before, I have no idea where we are headed, but there's no hope of me getting lost with a box of muscle and boots herding me along the way.

I'm guided through the heart of the town square.

We stick to the main streets which are brightly illuminated with even more lanterns than usual. I guess Kellan's previous desire to be discreet has since vanished.

"Does everyone know about...?" I ask, trying to keep my voice low enough for the surrounding entourage not to hear.

Kellan shakes his head subtly, "No, not yet anyway. I'm not in the mood for an *'I told you so'* lesson from Callum. He'll be sickeningly smug when he hears it was a Soleil man."

I wish I could disagree, but he's right. This will only add fuel to Callum's Soleil-hating fire.

"I don't wish to sound like my mother, but is there a reason why this Soleil man is still breathing? What's the *complication*?"

"Trust me, no one wants to end him more than me, though I'll give you the pleasure if it would ease your pain. But you'll have to wait," Kellan mutters, his tone souring with each step we take, "I ran to the barracks, kicked in Arthurs door, and grabbed the archer by the scruff. The only reason his jugular is still intact is because of Arthur. He knocked the blade from my hand, and stood in front of the archer, pleading with me to listen. I almost killed the sailor just for the inconvenience."

A wince flashes across my face. *Okay, now I'll have to get Arthur at least two presents from the agora.*

"Before I arrived the archer was drifting in and out of consciousness. I guess in the depth of confusion and the dimly lit room, the attackers mistook Arthur for someone else. He started rambling about how he could *only* get two arrows in you before I blocked his shot." The rising anger in Kellan's voice raises his volume.

Although none of the guards peer in our direction, it's obvious they are all listening, ears almost twitching as if they were Panotti elves.

"The Soleil bastard started saying the assassination had most likely failed, and they'd have to roll out Plan B instead."

"And what the Hel is Plan B?" I shriek. Apparently, it's my turn to give the guards something to listen to.

"I don't know yet, hence why he still draws breath," Kellan sighs, stopping at the imposing double mahogany doors before us, "Are you ready?"

The guard's fan into a crescent shape behind us, defending our backs as we face the door.

Typical, when I would actually appreciate a wall of muscle to hide behind, they decide to give me my space.

"No, not really," I grumble, tugging at my sleeves

and flattening my uncombed hair, "What am I even meant to say in there? Why am I needed?"

"There's nothing you need to do or say. Your presence is more to provoke the archer into saying something stupid. Hopefully spitting out the details for whatever attack is next planned."

"And whose bright idea was it to use me as shark-bait?"

Kellan pounds on the door twice with his fist, rolls his shoulders and stares straight ahead, "Mine."

EIGHT

essa was right.

Bevin Doughal, Master of the Judge, holds no women in high esteem and being a syren ranks me even lower on his receptive scale.

Both his bones and chair creak as he sits behind a well-worn wooden pulpit. I wonder which is older.

Directly in front of the podium stands Yarrow. The new Master of the Guard is in deep conversation with a younger, plump man who sits slumped in a chair. Upon seeing me approach, the man lurches upright. Yarrow twists to see us and places a firm, grounding grip on the young man's shoulder.

"Your Majesty," Yarrow grovels, bowing to Kellan and me respectively, "Thank you for agreeing to a trial."

"Think of it as less of a trial and more an

interrogation," Kellan says flatly, "Fynbarr's innocence is not up for discussion."

Wait. This Fynbarr man is the archer?!

My gaze locks on the unshackled, relatively comfortable looking young man. He's rather plump. At least double Nessa's weight. *Huh.* I guess all her carrying of hefty trays and constant elbow-grease cleaning makes her stronger than she appears.

A raised bump swells out the left-hand side of his forehead. Bruising and scratches marble his temple where Nessa's swinging rock scarf made contact. I guess she has a better aim than I give her credit for too.

Yarrow nods, before turning to me, "How are you feeling?"

I fight the urge to twitch my wing. Truth be told, this is the first time I've remained upright for longer than a few minutes and my body is feeling the brunt of it. I juggle words in my mind, trying to find a loophole, a way to say I'm fine and avoid looking weak.

"I'm feeling grateful the archer hiding behind your legs like a scared child has such a weak aim."

Yarrow gapes like a coy. Before he can say anything else, the Master of the Judge drops a hefty leather tome atop the pulpit. With stiff, knobby fingers he leafs through the yellowed pages until he finds a blank one.

Kellan releases a sigh through his taut jaw, "Must we bother will all this bureaucracy?"

Bevin doesn't say anything. He just withdraws an inkwell and flamboyant quill from under this desk and scribbles something on the page. Holding out the dampened quill, he nods towards Yarrow and the archer. As they rise to the pulpit, Kellan positions himself between me and the archer, not allowing the men to even look at me.

The men sign and Yarrow hands Kellan the quill before resuming his tight grip on Fynbarr's shoulder.

"It's just a register of everyone present. It's a silly old tradition." Kellan mutters an explanation to me as he takes the quill.

"A tradition which has been upheld for over a century," Bevin says, shaking his head so hard at Kellan's remark his jowls sway, "This record dates back to before the castle was even built. It's the oldest thing on this isle, and a tremendous example of the upholding of justice throughout the decades."

Kellan bites his tongue, but his eyes betray any attempt of neutrality. I knew he would like nothing better than to light a bonfire in the heart of the town square and burn the tome. His growing disdain of paperwork has also begun to extend to those who enforce it. The older men who deem their young King too...volatile. Kellan cannot see it as well as I, but I can tell when people act as if there is a monster in the room. Granted it's normally me, but I've seen their occasional glances towards Kellan too. These men are terrified of his Descendant side. They try to cage him in, holding him back with regulations and policies, but they shouldn't. They should unleash their King, for Kellan could reign over every mortal realm if he was given half the chance.

He signs his name with more force than necessary, pressing his signature so hard it marks the two pages beneath.

Then it's my turn. I step up to the pulpit, twirling the quill between my fingers.

Bevin Doughal, Master of the Judge.

Fynbarr Odim, the accused.

Yarrow Hillington, Master of the Guard.

Kellan Lunar, the King.

I write *Wren* and then pause.

"Kellan," I say quietly, but the nosey Judge peers down at me from his pulpit, "I...I don't have a family name."

Confusion knits his eyebrows, before realisation dawns across his face. Most magical creatures don't.

Some of the nymphs attach their birth river to their namesake, such as Lower-Bank or Mountain-

Creek. And some forest dryads use their nesting tree as a form of clan heritage like White Oak or Silver Birch. But syrens do not live in rivers or trees. And we most certainly don't have fathers to pass on their surname.

"Of course, you don't," the Judge says in a tone I cannot decipher as understand or condescending, "You don't have families do you? Is it true the spawn of your kind are laid in eggs and then left to their own devices to survive? Rather like fish?

Fynbarr snorts behind me.

Condescending, I decide, *definitely condescending.*

"I'm sure Wren would be happy to teach you all about the survival of syrens and their sheer capabilities, once we've dealt with the man who tried to assassinate her," Kellan says, his tone flat and threatening.

He keeps his hard stare on the Judge who feigns elderly confusion as if him being as ass was an innocent mistake.

The judge is so elderly I think my mere sneezing in the right key could lure him into death. I wiggle my nose and toss him a death stare, as Kellan gives my shoulders a light squeeze.

"Write whichever name you want. Hel borrow *Lunar* if you wish or leave it blank. I've grown weary of paperwork the past few weeks."

Borrow Lunar?

I don't know who his casual words stun more, me or the Judge. I consider leaving it blank when a better idea comes to mind. Swallowing a grin, I write, *Wren, Daughter of Poseidon, the Queen of the Seas* and slide the tome away from me.

Ha! Take *that* tradition.

The judge reads my signature and thumps the book closed before the ink is even dry. My name would be a smear in their otherwise perfect record.

"Good evening gentlemen," Bevin says, not even bothering to include me in his greeting, "Let us begin, I would-"

"Yes, lets," Kellan interrupts, pushing away from the pulpit to face Fynbarr, "Do you deny attacking Queen Wren of Seven Spikes?"

The archer blinks a few times, processing, before shaking his head, "No, sir. I do not deny shooting *the syren.*"

"What is your defence?" Bevin asks.

"There is no defence." Kellan growls.

Yarrow takes a half step forward, shielding the archer behind him, "Your Majesty, I've known this young man all his life, and half of mine. I trained with Fynbarr's father for almost a decade. He was a good man. He never would have raised his son to do this."

Naomi 👑 Kelly

Was a good man?

Fynbarr's gaze drops to his scuffed boots, and he sniffles ever so slightly.

"His father perished last winter," Yarrow continues, his gaze drifting past Kellan and landing on me, "He was commanding one of the naval fleets which were.... sunk."

Sunk.

The irony of my heart sinking the moment I hear the word doesn't go unnoticed. The gods have always had an extraordinary sense of humour. I knew some, if not *all*, of the citizens coming would have lost loved ones because of me, but it still floors me like a herd of centaurs to hear it.

Bevin offers a sympathetic head bow, "I'm sorry for your loss, son."

"That's no excuse," Kellan says flatly, crossing his arms, "I lost both my parents; you don't see me trying to assassinate people."

Thankfully, Kellan isn't bound to tell the truth like I am, so he's his throat doesn't convulse in a fiery burn as he says the statement. Everyone in the room is aware he decapitated Prince Alistair of Soleil Island, but thankfully no-one brings it up.

"*People?* She's not even human," Fynbarr spits.

"No, I'm not," I say, shrugging, letting the acid of

87

his words roll off me, "But at least when I put my mind to killing someone I don't fail."

It's a cheap shot, but he already views me as a monster so I might as well work it to my advantage. An angry mind makes for a loose tongue. Maybe I can provoke him into telling me his plan, "So what else do you have planned? Maybe I can give you pointers, so you don't *fail* this time?"

Fynbarr lunges to his feet, and it takes all of Yarrow's strength to slam him back into his seat.

"You're a monster," Fynbarr roars, twitching under Yarrow's hold.

I roll my eyes, trying my best to seem bored as I step away from Kellan's side, "Yes, yes, you've already said that. So why don't you say something useful? Like what else do you have planned?"

Ignoring me, he twists to face the Judge, "She killed my father, four of my cousins and three of my neighbours. Along with countless others. Those fleets had at least forty men on each vessel! She should be on trial, not me!"

Kellan also twists towards the Judge, and simply says, "I want him hung for treason."

The archer is *finally* stunned into silence, his face paling.

"Th-there hasn't been a hanging here in...well, it

must be almost two decades!" Bevin splutters, finally looking somewhat alive.

Dampening his stiff fingers, he begins thumbing through the tome.

Kellan nods simply, "It was my father ordered the last hanging, so I'd say we're overdue one?"

Of course, it was Lachlan, I snort to myself.

Yarrow doesn't dare step closer, proving he's at least somewhat smart, but raises his arms out slowly, "Your Majesty, I could enlist him in the guard. I would keep him out of trouble, out of the way. We've already lost a lot of men."

"I want loyal soldiers in my army and navy, not traitorous scum like him," Kellan says without hesitation.

Having gathered himself, the judge pipes up, "The boy cannot be tried for treason because he never aimed or injured you, Your Majesty. Fynbarr waited until he had a clear shot of the syren.... I mean, Wren."

Bevin corrects himself for his own safety, not for my happiness but I throw him a forced smirk anyway.

"So, unless she wishes to extradite him and trial him on her own isles, treason is not an option. I don't know if they even have a judicial system but..."

"No, we don't," I say truthfully, "We have no need for one. I have never had to punish my citizens.

They are loyal to me. Come to think of it, my army of centaurs would be most furious to hear about what happened."

Granted I'm mostly boasting, but Aengus would be livid to hear what happened. He already has trust issues with mortals, and I doubt this would help. Perhaps I shouldn't tell him...

"I'd rather die than go to an isle full of monsters," Fynbarr says. He spits on the ground. His lump of frothy saliva landing halfway between Yarrow and I.

Kellan blasts past me, moving so fast a gust ruffles my sleeve. Hooking his boot around the leg of Fynbarr's chair, he drags it away from Yarrow. A deafening scrape echoes through the courtroom.

Grabbing a fistful of the archer's grubby tunic, Kellan hauls him halfway from his chair, only to punch him back down by the jaw.

I hiss under my breath as blood gushes from Fynbarr's nose. It floods the front of his tunic and drips onto the cobbled floor. Yarrow turns away, scratching his own jaw with either phantom sympathy pains or sheer relief it wasn't his face at the end of Kellan's fist.

Bevin bangs his hand off the pulpit repeatedly, "This may be your Kingdom, your Majesty, but this court-room is mine! Control yourself!"

Kellan releases his grip on Fynbarr but does not move away. He keeps his face mere inches from him, "This is pointless. Nothing but slander and spit has come out of his mouth. If I cannot get the truth of out him, then..."

"Wait!" Yarrow and I call in unison, us both sensing another blow coming.

No one speaks.

No one moves.

I doubt anyone breathes for a moment.

"I might have an idea on how to get the truth out of him," I offer.

Fynbarr drags up his gaze to stare at me over his bloody hands which nurse his face. He looks at me with pure hatred. I wish his stare made me enraged, or upset, but no. It just makes me feel pure and utter guilt. It's my fault he loathes me.

"The ichor within my blood is what compels me to speak the truth. Maybe if I could get a concentrated dose of it, we could finally get to the bottom of this?"

"You can't inject a mortal with magic! You could kill him," Yarrow exclaims.

"I'm a mortal with ichor in my veins, and I am very much alive." Kellan shrugs, finally moving away from Fynbarr to return to my side.

"But you were born with the condition, your

Majesty. Who knows what effects it could have on this boy?" Bevin gasps.

Condition?

Gods above they really do have an issue with anyone slightly different or more powerful than them.

"He's dead either way in my book, so what's the harm in trying?" Kellan says flatly, in a tone not to be questioned. Turning his attention to me, he offers a proud smile, "I think it's a wonderful idea."

"My own ichor levels have not recovered yet, and I think the amount needed would be too great for one person alone to give. It would be less strenuous if a dozen or so of my citizens helped contribute-"

"I told you I am *not* stepping foot on that monster isle," the archer declares, somehow feeling braver now Kellan has stepped away from him.

"Well, you aren't bloody invited," I snap, "I don't want you anywhere near my people. I'll have the vial made up and brought to you."

Sage, a young dryad, had a knack for creating potions and tinctures from various herbs and oils. She would be the fae to know about gathering ichor, that's if it can be done at all.

Kellan nods, looking reasonably content for the first time all evening, "Good idea. Until then I want him kept away from the rest of my people, both Lunar and Soleil. I do not want his toxic views being spread."

Judge Bevin draws breath to protest something, but steely looks from both Kellan and I seem to change his mind. He shuts his mouth and tome in silence.

"Fynbarr," Kellan calls as he guides me towards the door, "Know you're only alive right now because Yarrow beseeched me to act as your patron for your father's sake, and because Wren is more capable of forgiveness than you. Remember that."

I do not bother glancing in Fynbarr's direction, nor does he bother to glance in mine.

Kellan pounds his fist once on the mahogany door, and it instantly yawns open to show the guards standing to attention and eagerly awaiting us.

"And Yarrow," Kellan says over his shoulder as an afterthought, "You heard yourself how my brother holds you in such high esteem as the cruellest guard he's ever met. I'm sure you could use some of those techniques on Fynbarr. You did ask for him to be your ward after all. His welfare, or therefore lack of it, is now completely in your hands. Do not disappoint me."

Fynbarr may be the one on trial, but it was obvious Yarrow was also being tested. His new King wanted to test where his loyalties really lay.

Yarrow swallows hard but gives a tense nod. With the three men silent, Kellan turns on his heel and vacates the room. I remain quiet as I follow, but I cannot hide the slight smirk pulling at my lips.

There is something rather alluring about a man who wears his streak of wickedness with such authority. And although pain still twinges through my body, I stand a little taller and sway my hips a little wider as I turn my back on the stunned men.

NINE

urrounded by the guards once more, we return to Kellan's suite in silence. With his anger subsiding, tiredness takes over and now only his frequent yawns move his taut jaw.

Exhaustion commands every inch of his body, yet once we are inside his chambers, he begins filling a basin and gathering clean dressings without being asked.

"How do you feel about going to Seven Spikes a few days early?" he asks, unwinding the gauze from my midriff.

My wound is transitioning from the weepy stage to the itchy phase and it takes all my limited self-control to not scratch the stretching skin as my wounds knit themselves closed.

"I'm happy to go home as long as you're still

coming with me."

Home. Less than a year ago the thought of returning to the Queendom was nightmare inducing.... literally. But now it truly is my home.

"I will still come if you'll have me. There's no fear of me not accompanying you, if anything there's a fear I won't come back here," Kellan sighs.

He shifts his attention to my wing. With the injury being in the centre of my plumage, the area is impossible to bandage. I must keep the wound clean, and impatiently wait for the thin membrane of skin to close over, and the feathers to regrow.

"You're always welcome on my isle, but I do have one condition," I tease over my shoulder.

"And what would that be?" he asks, sinking into his bed and kicking off his boots.

"You have to bathe before we leave," I taunt, scratching his chin to emphasise the scruffy blond stubble shadowing his face, "Otherwise I'll have no option but to tie you to the front of the ship and let the sea wash you."

"Darling, I think out of the pair of us, *you* would make the better figurehead," Kellan smirks.

With a slight groan he tugs off his grubby tunic and tosses it aside. The thin gold chain which houses his mother's broach swings around his neck. I've yet to see him take it off.

"I'll bathe in a moment, just let me rest my eyes for a few minutes," he mutters as he stretches out, wrestling a pillow under his head.

His breathing turns deep and rhythmical as he succumbs to sleep instantly.

Quietly chuckling to myself, I pull the blanket over him and use the basin of warm water and leftover gauze to dab clean his face and hands. He doesn't stir once.

I blow out the candle, slip off my shoes, and nestle into the far side of the bed to avoid disturbing him.

I lay there for a few minutes before Kellan's sleepy hand pats the space between us. Once he makes contact with my side, he tugs me in close.

Tucking me into the grove of his body, he mutters into my unbound hair, "*Zoi Mou.*"

My heart soars like Pegasus.

I expect the sudden pounding in my chest to wake him up, as it pulsates beneath his strong arm, but he does not flinch. His breathing remains deep, occasionally releasing a light snore. Maybe I imagined his voice? With the lower levels of blood and ichor within me, I wouldn't be surprised...But I decide to believe in my possible delusions.

"You're my life too," I whisper into the darkness.

It turns out when Kellan said, '*a few days early*' he actually meant '*in a few hours.*' Needing to obtain a vial of ichor and wanting to put as much distance between me and the Soleil men, Kellan starts preparations to leave as soon as he wakes. We split up, but Kellan insists on all eight guards following me everywhere I go. It takes me three attempts to convince them I'm safe within the walls of the cottage as I gather my belongings.

Granted I've been looking forward to going to my home with Kellan since first arriving, but since the attack and equally as painful trial, I would travel back to Seven Spikes inside Charybdis' belly if it meant getting there sooner.

The sentries and I step foot onto the dock at midday as planned. Leaving in the middle of the day, in the middle of the week without any official announcements meant the piers were relatively free from crowds. I spot a few nosey spectators walking slower than usual as they mill about their daily chores, but thankfully no large gatherings. I knew the lack of people was not a plan Kellan implemented for my comfort. The speed and secrecy of our departure could not be mistaken as anything other than a safety measure.

Crates containing food and water are traipsed onto a boat which I have not seen before. It is not as colossal as the usual vessel Kellan opts to use, but it's still ridiculously big for the two of us, unless...

"Good morning!" Arthur cheers from behind, causing all my guards to pivot towards the sound.

"Oh," he chuckles, setting down a small trunk by his boots and showing his open, weapon-free hands to the guards, "Don't worry guys, the last time I got too close to Wren, it was *me* who came out worst for wear, not her."

I wince slightly, but nod for the guards to stand down, "Morning Arthur. Is that your trunk?"

"It sure is! I even packed some playing cards to keep us entertained," he beams, "And thank you for letting me come to your isle again."

"Emm..." I start, fighting to keep confusion from twisting my face. Glancing around, I try to spot Kellan to figure out what's going on. But when I finally spot him, he is deep in conversation, kneeling before a very upset Aveen, "Em, yes of course. You're most welcome."

Arthur scoops up his case, grinning as he bounds up the boarding plank.

Once Arthur has boarded, I sigh and make my way toward the sobbing Aveen, my guards following wordlessly. Kellan's hair is slicked back, still damp from his thorough bath this morning. He runs a hand over his clean-shaven jaw and tries his best not to sigh as Aveen stomps her little foot against the dock.

"But you promised," she cries.

He brushes a raven hued tress from her face, "I know I did, but as King sometimes my duties call me away. You'll understand when you're Queen someday, *mikros.*"

"I've already told you I don't want to be Queen," she huffs, crossing her arms tightly, "Ever."

"For someone called *little one*, you have an awfully big pout," I tease, crouching down beside Kellan, "What's wrong?"

Upon seeing me, she unfolds her arms and throws herself into my hold instead, "Kellan promised he would come to my spring songs show, but now he won't be here."

I drape my arm over her shoulder, trying not to over-stretch my damaged side, "It's not your brother's fault he has to leave. If anything, it's mine."

Both Kellan and Aveen slam their eyebrows down.

"How is it your fault?" she asks, wiping her tears with the edge of her sleeve.

"It's not," Kellan mutters.

I lightly pull away her hand, and she begins twirling a strand of my hair around her finger instead, "Remember I told you about the election taking place on my island? The one where everyone casts a vote?"

Aveen sniffles slightly as she nods, but her tears finally cease, "Uh huh. I remember. I said I would vote for you."

I flash a grin, "Well, the votes are being tallied and I would like to be there for the results."

It might not be the actual reason behind our unscheduled departure, but it's still true and a valid reason.

"Oh," Aveen says quietly, "I guess that's okay then."

She steps out of my arms, but before she can begin her sulking once more, I offer, "How about you get Callum to hold open a shell whilst you sing? And then after your performance you throw it as far as you can into the sea."

She spins on the ball of her foot, a gasp separating her petite mouth, "And then Kellan will be able to hear my performance!?"

Theoretically, yes, if she skimmed the shell correctly, but it's a long shot. Unable to lie, I give Kellan a wide-eyed gawk.

"Eh, yeah? Yes, of course. But you better find a big shell if you want me to hear the whole song, otherwise it won't all fit," Kellan says, struggling to keep a straight face, "And it would capture the sound better if you asked Callum to stay completely quiet and stand right beside the stage for the whole evening."

I cover up my laugher with a feigned cough. Kellan rises to his feet and offers me his hand. Even with his help, pain stabs my side. I cover up my wince with a small smile to stop an onslaught of questions from Aveen.

Beaming ear to ear, she gives both our legs a quick squeeze hug, before skipping her way toward the beach. I'm sure her search for the perfect large shell will keep her out of trouble for at least...ten minutes.

"You're good at that," I say to Kellan, once she's out of earshot.

"Lying?" He asks with a grin.

"That too," I laugh, "But I meant being a big brother. She idolises you."

"Sometimes. Though I doubt she appreciates me being her brother, guardian, and King all at once. Her patience for my pushing of extra lessons is wearing thin. She would much rather spend her evenings running around the rope bridges with the other children than learning about the art of warfare."

"The art of warfare? Kellan she's not even eight!"

"And?" he asks with a shrug, "I started when I was five. I'm already too soft on her."

Rolling my eyes at him, I sigh, "I feel guilty taking you away from her. Maybe you should stay here. I can swim home alone and fetch the ichor needed-"

"No," he says more firmly than I'm expecting, "I went almost three months without seeing you Wren. A mere week or so with you isn't enough. Forever would not be enough. You aren't *taking* me away; I want to go. And don't let Aveen's sad puppy-eyes make you feel bad. She inherited them from my mother, and it seems she was born with an innate understanding on how to turn them on and off at will."

I batten down the sense of guilt within my core. We knew splitting our time between isles and thrones would be tough, but I didn't think it would be *this* tough.

We turn towards the boat, and every guard spins with me. *Gah!*

"I've already gathered Arthur is coming, but please tell me my eight shadows are staying behind?" I mutter under my breath.

"Don't worry the guards are staying here. I know you're protected once you're upon the sea," Kellan declares loud enough for the guard to hear. With a dismissing nod, the sentries finally leave my side. I roll my shoulders, feeling lighter without their presence.

"As for Arthur," he adds, guiding me towards the plank, "Daughter of the sea or not, we need someone to take the wheel overnight and I figured he could use the break after me almost stabbing him in his own barracks. But if you don't want him here just say the word."

"It's not that I don't want Arthur here. I just...I thought we might have some...alone time," I admit, hating how selfish I sound.

In the background Arthur whistles a merry-little tune as he unpacks his trunk into the smallest of the cabins without being asked to. His humility only highlights my greed.

"Ah," Kellan says with a hint of remorse in his tone that he didn't think of it first.

His gaze turns heavy, and I suddenly hate that it is morning time and I'll have to fill an entire day of tasks and talk before nestling into his arms once more.

Scowling at himself, he adds, "Well even if I did dismiss Arthur, I have already invited someone else I thought had been through a tough couple of days. She too has grown weary of guards following her every step."

As if his mere words summoned her, the plank

sways beneath our feet as someone else begins boarding behind us.

"I hope I didn't keep you waiting, your Majesty," Nessa says, "It was harder to get away from my mother than I expected."

She bears a basket of her belongings, meaning she cannot use her hands for balance- yet she walks delicately up the plank without so much as a wobble.

"What did you say to get away from her?" Kellan laughs as his boots hit the deck. He reaches back to offer a helping hand.

"I guess I didn't *say* anything," Nessa explains, "I left a note on my bed and climbed out my window whilst she was scolding to my sister."

"Nessa Shay, you continue to surprise me. I think spending time with Wren is rubbing off on you," Kellan jokes, flashing a wink at me.

"Is that such a bad thing?" I ask, lightly shoving Kellan's chest, "Besides, I can't have had too much of an influence on her yet. She packed silverware."

Burrowed between her woollen blanket, and a handful of books lies a shiny fork and knife.

"I...I wasn't sure if your citizens used cutlery," she says with an awkward smile, "I didn't mean to insult you."

Before I can reassure her, Kellan shouts over his

shoulder whilst retracting the anchor, "Oh, don't you worry, her people have tons of knives. And sharp teeth. Talons and hooves even!"

Nessa pales before my eyes.

"He's not wrong," I admit, giving him an edged look, "But he's only trying to scare you. And if he's not careful he could be on the receiving end of my arsenal."

Kellan releases a deep chuckle before he and Arthur busy themself with ropes and sails.

Nessa doesn't seem fully convinced, but she swings her basket and hips towards the cabins.

She would be the first human female to ever set foot on my isle, but I had no concerns for her safely. There would be no arrows or dirty looks fired in her direction. Although my isle brims with diversity and differences, all my citizens have one thing in common: acceptance.

Whether you have scales, wings, hooves, horns, or just plain ol' mortal flesh, everyone was welcomed and celebrated, unless you have prejudice in your heart. The only trait not tolerated is intolerance itself.

Ever-polite Nessa and happy-go-lucky Arthur would be warmly welcomed, and probably the centre of attention.

But if Fynbarr were to step foot on Seven Spikes

soil, well...I doubt the archer would get as far as the Temple grounds. The same frosty reception would be extended to the Master of the Judge, Yarrow, or anyone else would harbours hatred or bitterness in their heart.

Centaurs have an accurate sense of smell, especially when it comes to sniffing out bullshit.

TEN

ver the next few days, we fall into a routine. Arthur and Nessa take control of the deck during the day, with our communal meal signifying the shift swap. They would have dinner, whilst Kellan and I had a make-shift breakfast before taking over for the night shift.

Or at least that is the plan Kellan wanted. Ironically, he's the only person *not* sticking to the schedule, constantly finding reasons to fuss around on deck during the day instead of sleeping. For the first two days, I woke alone in the cabin, only to find Kellan micro-managing the deck hours before he should be.

When Arthur asked him why, Kellan reassured the young sailor his presence was nothing to do with a lack of faith in his abilities, quietly adding he was keeping an eye out for any threats heading my way.

But when I asked Kellan why, he told me he had no real safety concerns for me, but quietly added how he wanted to keep an eye on Arthur's abilities.

Thankfully on the third day, having put some distance between Fynbarr and me, and Arthur now having gotten into the swing of things, Kellan begrudgingly agrees to sleep.

Having caught up on some much-needed rest, Kellan awakes the following evening with far too much vitality and vigour.

"Good morning," he greets in a tone *much* more awake than mine. His open-palmed hand splays across my belly and tucks me in close to his warm frame.

"Good *evening*," I mumble to correct him, stretching cautiously beneath the sheet. Thankfully, no twinge of pain tugs at my side.

Warm sunset light floods through the circular cabin window, drenching the bed and wooden slates overhead in an array of tangerine and peach hues, "It seems late, did we over-sleep?"

He begins nuzzling kisses against my neck, and mutters, "Oh, I think we have time."

Even with my back to him, I can tell his eyes are heavy-lidded though not from the same tiredness weighing down mine.

Leaning into Kellan's solid frame behind me, I melt into the pool of sunlight and the warmth of his lips. He leaves a trail of kisses from below my ear to towards my collarbone. Each touch lingers longer than the last.

I rub against him like a stray cat in desperate need of touch. He responds by lightly slipping his knee between my legs to spread them apart.

"Lest we forget the bath incident," I offer breathlessly, but make no real effort to move away from him or his ever-lowering lips.

"I see no bath here," he mutters against my shoulder. His gravelly tone pebbles my skin with goosebumps.

"No bath," I admit, "Just an entire ocean filled with waves and marine life I could accidentally lure onto the deck. Arthur has impressed me with his skill level, but I doubt wrestling a shark is something Fletcher prepared him for."

Kellan opens his mouth, either to kiss me once more or protest, but I do not give him the opportunity to do either.

Untangling myself from his arms and the blanket, I force myself to move away.

Groaning his disapproval, he rolls over and buries

his face into my pillow. He inhales my scent off the still-warm fabric.

"Besides," I add, pulling a fresh tunic on, "It's rude to keep people waiting."

"I'm their King," he says, flopping onto his back, "And you're a Queen. I think that grants us certain liberties don't you think?"

"Don't pull rank for trivial things, it's unbecoming."

"Me wanting to have my way with you is never trivial, Wren."

I roll my eyes but find myself biting my lower lip.

"With the vote happening as we speak, I won't even be Queen for much longer," I add, tearing my eyes away from the outstretched body, waiting for me in the sunlight.

Despite what I said to Aveen, arriving earlier than expected means the results of the first-ever Seven Spike election won't be fully tallied yet. It will be another few days before candidates from each faction are chosen, but knowing that doesn't stop the growing sense of nervousness in my core.

When I announced to my citizens that I wanted to dissolve the crown and implement democracy in its place, I didn't exactly receive the round of applause I had been hoping for.

I want to ensure no Kestrel-like tyrant ever single-handily rules and ruins our isle and Queendom again, a concern I assumed they would share too, but apparently not. Although I have yet to understand why the citizens have decided to put all their faith in me. Declaring that I would never follow in my mother's footsteps and that they are content for me to rule for forever. Quite literally *forever*.

A life underwater.

Ageing slower.

Kellan growing older without me on land. The feeling of drowning without water which Callum referred to as a panic attack begins to sting my chest once more.

Releasing a shaky breath, I shudder, only to find Kellan watching me with an attentive gaze.

"No-one asked you to give up your throne, Wren," he offers gently, "You've become increasingly contemplative about the whole thing. Cancel the vote if you wish. They sure as Hel won't find a better ruler than you."

"I've made my choice already. I chose you."

"This isn't a question of me and you because that topic is not up for debate. This is about what you want. Your life. And how I'll stop at nothing to make sure you get everything you desire."

"As valiant as you sound, there isn't a way for me

to have everything I desire," I say, shaking my head.

"Don't tell me what can't be done." Kellan wraps a strong forearm around me and hauls me back into bed, "It only spurs me on."

A yelp escapes my lips as he bounces me off the thin mattress. I land on my back, with my hair fanned out around me and Kellan caged over me.

"As if you need *any* spurring on!" I say, grinning so much it causes my cheeks to slightly squint my view.

Kellan cranes his head back an inch or two to study my face, "Gods above, I love that smile."

Although my cheeks flush lilac with embarrassment, I don't pull away as I might have before. Instead, I allow him to relish in the smile he caused.

His look of pride turns to annoyance as his gaze is snagged towards the door. Following his line of sight, I notice feet shadowing the thin strip of light around the doorframe. And amongst the constant drone of waves and distant seagull cries, I faintly hear the floorboards creak.

Noting our sudden silence, Nessa's awkward voice comes muffled through the door.

"Eh, sorry to interrupt, your Majesty. It's just the meal I prepared is starting to go cold and Arthur gets intolerably grumpy when he is hungry. But I can wrap up two dishes if you would rather eat later-"

"Yes." Kellan cuts off her rambling instantly, "Later."

"No," I counter, scrambling to my feet before Kellan stops me, "We'll be right with you, and we can all eat together."

"Of course," Nessa says before her shadow lowers to the door before toddling off. Gods above, did she bow to a closed-door?

I turn to find Kellan glowering at me. Rolling my eyes, I pick his tunic off the floor and chuck it at him, "Here, you can't go onto the deck wearing nothing but a scowl."

He rises to his feet, and before he can drop the bedsheet to show me how undressed he is, I scurry out of the cabin.

Thankfully once I'm on the deck, sea spray mists my face, quenching whatever fire Kellan threatened to ignite within me.

I find Arthur and Nessa sitting around the sawn barrel table, patiently waiting to feast. I rather admire their control. As much as my citizens respect me, there's no way a herd of Centaur colts would display such self-restraint.

Kellan emerges a few moments later and gives a

silent nod to Arthur who eagerly dives into his food and of course, yet another story.

And although my interest in the football games the men play around the barracks is rather limited, I nod along and ask questions.

It stops me noticing Nessa's inability to look Kellan or I in the eye. It also stops me catching a glimpse of Kellan's wolfish gaze which watches me like I'm the next thing on the menu.

The following evening, we wake to someone as the door once more, but this time it's Arthur.

"Apologies to wake you, sir, but I require your help. A fierce gust has undone the jib sheet."

Kellan groans under his breath but rises to his feet to go help without hesitance.

I pad after them, watching the men wrestle with the front sail. Shivering, I tug my cloak up close around my neck. Syrens are normally immune to feeling the cold, but the transition from cosy cabin to the bare deck is enough to make the hairs rise along my arms.

With a northern breeze like this sweeping across the deck and unrigging the sail fixtures, there's no doubting we're close to the Seven Spikes now.

"You've made great progress overnight," Kellan admits, once the jib is back under control, "I thought I'd be the one sailing through this part of the sea. It's known as a wind trap. Even Fletcher struggles with it at times."

I know that isn't true. Fletcher has sailed this sea corridor many times without so much as breaking a sweat, but the way Arthur grins with pride makes me wish I could lie to people sometimes too. I offer a silent thank you to Zephyrus for his aiding wind which could have just as easily blown us off-course had the god been in a foul mood.

"At this rate, we'll arrive by tomorrow afternoon," Kellan adds, casting a calculating eye to the sun and his compass, "I think a make-shift feast with all of our rations is due as a celebration."

Arthur nods enthusiastically, "Yes sir!"

The sailor flashes me his beaming smile as he goes about dividing up the leftover food whilst whistling one of his merry tunes.

"Where's Nessa?" I ask, noticing a lack of movement around me. At this time of the evening, she's usually spinning a dozen times a minute as she completes tasks.

"She's been in and out to her cabin most of the

day. She looked rather peaky. I think the rockier seas are getting to her," Arthur suggests, seeming rather proud of himself for having a tougher stomach.

I leave the men to their food prep and sail wrestling and make my way towards the cabins. When I reach the end of the wooden corridor, I pause to hear the muffled sound of retching through the door on my right.

I don't bother knocking as I let myself into Nessa's cabin. Clinging to her circular window, Nessa pants short, sharp breaths as she tries and fails to keep her heaving at bay. A wave of motion writhes through her midriff as if she were a snake before she vomits into an old bucket by her feet.

"Are you alright?" I ask gently, stepping further into her cabin.

She pirouettes on the ball of her foot, wiping her mouth with the back of her hand and attempting to straighten her skirt, "Oh, hello. I didn't hear you knocking."

"Sneaking around outside doors seems to be the norm on this boat," I tease, but noting Nessa's ashen colour and the way she crosses her arms tightly across her stomach, I doubt she's in the mood for humour. "Arthur said you'd been in and out of here most of the day."

"I'll work through the night shift to make up for it," she offers, her fists curling subtly as pain cramps through her once more.

"You don't have to earn your keep all the time, Nessa. We aren't going to toss you overboard for needing to rest," I say with a slight eye roll, "I've never been afflicted with sea-sickness myself, but I've been told it's horrible-"

"It's not sea-sickness," Nessa interrupts, releasing a weary sigh, "I simply told Arthur that to avoid the awkward stupor on his face if I told him it's my monthly cycle. Although the sea *definitely* isn't helping."

Her cycle. Of course.

"Ah. Well, I've never been afflicted with that problem either," I admit, feeling unhelpful, "Wait, did you say monthly?"

"Unfortunately, yes." She sits on the edge of her bunk, tucking a bucket with her vomit in it under the bed, "Every month, every year since I turned twelve."

"Twelve? Good gods, Aveen isn't far off twelve."

Nessa offers a small nod, before wincing slightly once more. I cross the room and scoop up the pail containing the contents of her stomach.

"Oh no, you shouldn't-

"You cleaned up my vomit, so I will clean up yours," I interject, "Isn't that what friends do?"

She cops my use of the word *friend* straight away, seeing it for the thinly disguised olive branch which it is.

If my mother were still around, and still could torment my mind, she would tell me it's selfish. A kind-hearted and hard-working girl like Nessa doesn't need *me* as a friend. She would taunt how everyone around me ends up dead and I am unworthy of friendship. Kestrel's voice rang through my mind for so many years I still hear an echo of it. It's sometimes hard to tell where the memories of her torment end and the reflex of my conditioning begins.

"I would very much like us to be friends, Wren." Nessa beams, her tired eyes glinting.

I release a breath I didn't realise I was holding. Since Dove's death, there's been a shadow within my soul I've been trying my hardest to ignore. And although I'm experienced at running away, loneliness has a way of always catching up to you.

Between their similar hair and caring natures, it's easy for my mind to forget in the dimming light that the person before me is not my *adelfi*. I would never again see my soul sister again, not in this lifetime anyway. And even though I still feel a pang of deep guilt for Dove's passing, perhaps it's a greater honour to allow myself some friendship whilst I wait to see her again.

As a Queen, I'm incredibly grateful to be surrounded with loyal people who would defend me, fight in my honour and serve me until their last breath. But Rhea is busy with her daughter. Aengus isn't exactly one for small talk. And Kellan most certainly has no interest in shopping at the agora with me.

But Nessa was proving to be something of a tonic for me- although she left a sour taste in my mouth at the beginning, she seems to be soothing my soul now.

"Right then," I say, giving her a nod. I make my way onto the deck grinning like an idiot carrying a bucket of vomit.

"Is she alright?" Kellan asks, with an arched brow as I slosh the contents of the pail overboard.

"Uh-huh," I offer, now chucking a selection of the rations onto a thin plate, "You said you brought playing cards, right Arthur?"

The sailor nods enthusiastically, digging the pack out of his pocket, "I did indeed, we could play *Go Fish*?"

Carefully prising them from his fingers, I cut him off, "I need to borrow them actually."

"Oh." Although Arthur does his best to not look disappointed, I still feel as if I'm punching a pup in the gut.

Gah. I can only deal with one hurting mortal at a time.

"You boys will be having dinner without us this evening. Nessa and I are having a girl's night."

Kellan chuckles, "*You* are having a girl's night? With Nessa Shay?"

"Yes," I say flatly in a tone not to be tested, "You know where I'll be if you need help with the seas."

"And you know where I'll be should you need saving," Kellan offers with a grin.

Sticking out my tongue, I return to Nessa's cabin armed with an empty bucket, food and playing cards.

"I believe you still owe me another one of your tales," I taunt as I step back into the room.

"Luckily for you, there is no limit to the number of embarrassing stories I have," she laughs whilst sighing at herself, "But you'll have to close the door to hear the one I have in mind. And there is no way Arthur, or the King are ever allowed to know this one."

"Deal."

With my arms full, I kick the door shut beside me and nestle in beside her on the bunk.

For the rest of the evening and long into the night we trade tales in hushed tones and burst into laughter loudly.

ELEVEN

A s Seven Spikes looms on the horizons, hippocampi begin breaching the waves around us. No longer driven to relay Kestrel's taunts, their days of being messengers of death are over. Using the boats powerful bow-wave for momentum, the creatures rear up into acrobatic spins.

Arthur leans so far overboard watching, he risks falling into the sea headfirst.

"They must like you. They're putting on a show," I say, shaking my head at their playful antics, but deep down I'm glad to see the hippocampi happy.

My previous disdain for the creatures has faded in the months since becoming Queen. Without my mother dictating them to bellow tormenting taunts, they were somewhat placid...loveable almost. I felt an odd sense of connection to them, knowing if my mother had not been defeated, I too would have been used as a vessel for destruction.

Overhead harpies begin to circle. Using one hand to block out the bright white sun, I wave with the other. Nessa casts a glance towards the winged women, and although she too offers a wave and says hello, her bewilderment is poorly veiled.

"They don't speak," I explain to her, "Not in a way you or I would understand anyway. The harpies have language and social structures more avian based. They roost in the treelines by the coast, so you won't see much of them, but you never need to fear them."

"Do they understand?" Nessa asks, clearing her throat but keeping her wide eyes locked on their orbiting movements, "When you speak to them, do they understand?"

I nod, to which she simply replies, "Then I'll always say hello."

A mere half an hour later, Kellan slings the anchor into the bedrock below and the boat is berthed into the bay.

Trailing from the dock all along the coastal front are seashell garlands and fresh bunting made from ivy and flowers.

"All for me?" Kellan gasps sarcastically from the helm, "You shouldn't have."

I roll my eyes over Arthur's loud chuckle to say, "It's not every day an island's first-ever vote, Ostara and yes, a visiting King's birthday all coincide around the same time. There's a lot to celebrate."

Creatures from every faction gather along the docks as we disembark. As I walk off the boarding plank, the entire island seems to bow to me.

"I've missed you all," I say honestly, smiling back at the wide grins welcoming me home. As ready as I am to give up my throne, I will miss feeling solely responsible for this much happiness.

"Is that why you returned early, your Majesty?" A deep voice carries through the crowd.

I recognise Aengus's voice immediately, but it isn't until he rights himself from his bow and stands almost two foot above the dryads surrounding him, that my eyes spot him.

But his dark eyes are already locked on me. On my midriff, and then my injured wing.

His nostrils flare as he draws a deep breath, and in an instant, he knows. Not who injured me, or what happened, but he knows in a single scenting breath I came to harm on Kellan's island. And suddenly, my right-hand Centaur's face is the only visible storm on this perfect spring day.

"I came back for many reasons," I start, choosing

each word carefully as to not trip up and give him further ammunition for whatever lecture Aengus is mentally preparing, "And yes, missing everyone was one of those reasons."

Looking incredibly unconvinced, Aengus casts his gaze towards Kellan as the King takes his place beside me.

The two men give each other a slight chin dip out of respect for me but make no overt attempt at small talk.

Arthur yelps as a harpy descends, wrapping her talons around the handle of his travel trunk and silently taking off towards the guest house.

His high-pitched screech causes all the dryads and fae to burst into giggles immediately. Arthur's cheeks burn a scarlet hue as he jogs down the plank, into the clan of the winged who are as enamoured with him as he seems to be with them. I try not to audibly groan as a river-nymph runs her fingers through Arthur's windswept hair.

Though judging from the awkward grin on his face, perhaps this confidence boost is a greater gift than anything I could have purchased him at the agora.

Nessa clutches her wicker basket full of blankets and cutlery as if it were a shield. She carefully weaves her way through the crowd, acknowledging everyone she passes with a modest hello.

"Where is Rhea?"

I had been hoping to leave Nessa in her care but glancing around I don't see the crimson-haired syren amongst the crowd.

"She's down below in the nursery," Aengus replies simply, as if she were just downstairs in a house, and not in an underwater world.

I smile to myself, incredibly grateful that despite all the differences within the Queendom, it is more combined than ever. A lesson which the Soleil and Lunar Lands could learn.

"And where is Sage?" I pose my question to one of the few dryad's who isn't currently fawning over Arthur.

"Last time I saw her, she was in the main kitchen gathering ingredients for one of her potions. Do you want me to fetch her?"

"No, but you can bring her a message," I start, "And could you also bring..."

My gaze falls to my guests. Nessa, upon hearing the word *kitchen* takes a half-step forward.

"-Arthur. You can bring Arthur with you. I'm sure some extra cooking skills would be no harm for the journey home."

The dryad nods enthusiastically, taking Arthur's

hand as she skips her way towards the kitchen.

"And Nessa, you can go with Aengus."

I don't know who is more shocked.

"I have colt training," Aengus says with sudden relief in his voice, and feigned sympathy on his face, "Perhaps one of the nymphs could bring her swimming?"

His reluctance is only highlighted by the fact I've never heard him object to anything I've asked before.

"Oh, but I think she would enjoy watching Centaur jousting, right Nessa?" I ask, battening down a mischievous grin as her bright azure eyes grow wide.

To her credit, she manages to nod and even give a somewhat convincing, "Of course."

Aengus clicks his tongue, before clearing his throat, "Whatever you deem best, your Majesty."

His onyx hued tail swishes slightly as he plods towards the sand arena. Nessa silently follows, having to jog to keep up.

"Was that pairing for Aengus's benefit, or Nessa's?" Kellan asks once the two are out of earshot.

"It was entirely for my own amusement," I admit with a wicked grin, "Why, do you find it *unbecoming* when I pull rank?"

Kellan chuckles a deep laugh, "No, not even for *trivial* things like your own wicked amusement. I

127

actually quite enjoy you when you're bossy."

"Good," I smirk, shifting onto the balls of my feet to kiss his forehead, "I must visit Rhea, but I want you to have a relaxing bath with a glass of rum and be waiting for me when I get back."

"Is that a promise?" Kellan asks playfully as I make my way towards the sea.

As I submerge myself, I throw a quick wink over my shoulder and call, "Oh, it's a direct order."

Once I've swum past the Clam Gates, I paddle to the right, opting to swim past the main fortress all together having no desire to see the vacant coral throne.

"*Eisai ekeí*," I sing lightly.

My call echoes through the craggy tunnels freely. As someone who spent most of my life loathing the thought of using my song and magic, I never thought I would enjoy the feeling of singing freely. But I cannot deny the sense of fulfilment which comes over me when I access my magic. Nor can I deny how much I've missed my home or my people.

"*Eímaste edó.*" Rhea's soprano tone calls back. *We*

are here. We. Granted Rhea rarely leaves her daughters side but knowing baby Robin is so close makes me swim a beat faster.

Deep within the tunnels, nestled into the bedrock of Seven Spikes itself, is the immense circular grotto which acts as a nursery.

Luscious seagrass acts like carpet, covering the entire floor of the cave, whilst dense kelp clings to the cave walls. Stalactites descend from above. Each one so heavily decorated with shells and gemstones, it's hard to recognise their original form.

Fissures in the rocky roof allow sunlight to stream through from above. The light casts a teal glow and shines directly onto the large shell in the centre of the cave.

The last time I was near a shell of this magnitude, it had been belched up by Charybdis. But thankfully only gentle coos emerge from within, and no messages of terror.

"I was wondering what all the commotion was about," Rhea muses as she emerges from the shadows, "The hippocampi have been going ballistic since they felt your unexpected presence arriving."

"I've always known how to make an entrance," I offer with a coy smile, hoping she doesn't question our early arrival too much.

Granted Aengus had about a hundred pounds of extra muscle over Rhea, but it's her reaction to the archer attack I fear more. With her heightened maternal instincts and overwhelming desire to make the world a safer place, who knows what she would do if she found out. And all mortals, not just Fynbarr, would be at risk, seeing as she deems they all look the same.

Rhea drifts towards the shell-cot and tenderly scoops up Robin before handing her to me, "Well we're always glad to have you back home."

Although I've held Robin a hundred times, I still find myself tensing slightly as I take the weight of her kelp-swaddled body into the crook of my arms. Knowing I'm not always the more gracious of women, I'm terrified I'll fumble and drop her. At least here if I drop a new-born, they will float. I can't imagine the stress of holding an infant on land. *Gah.*

"I swear she's grown even more in the short time I've been away," I gasp, shaking my head in disbelief.

Robin's little feet had comfortably fitted within the bend of my elbow just over a fortnight ago, but now she's spilling out.

It's common knowledge syrens often resemble their mothers, but even knowing this doesn't make Robin's mop of scarlet hair any less surprising.

"I have only left her side for a few hours to help with the count, and I think she had stretched by the time I returned!" Rhea chuckles.

The count- Of course.

"I'm probably too early to know the voting results," I say, "But how is the tally faring so far? Any clear favourites yet?"

Rhea blows air through her lips, allowing a stream of bubbles to rush outward, "Emm.... The votes are still being counted, but yes, there is a clear winner."

"For which faction?" I ask, rocking Robin in my arms.

Rhea reaches out for her daughter and pops her back into her shell crib.

"Finned," she answers, spinning the stone-carved mobile above her daughter. The intricate design is shaped to resemble an octopus, with a different colour shell floating from each crafted tentacle.

"But you didn't just win the finned faction," Rhea adds after a beat, turning slowly face me, "You also won the fae. And the hooved. The closest contender is Aengus, but you still have at least triple his numbers."

Suddenly I understand why she took Robin out of my hold, "What the Hel do you mean I won the fae and hooved faction? I wasn't even a contender for those bloody votes!"

"*Shh!*" Rhea chastises, throwing a glance at Robin who doesn't even stir, "Everyone is aware you weren't an official contender, but they chose you anyway. You gave all your people a choice, and they still chose you."

"And who did you chose?" I ask, keeping my voice low like she wanted, though I doubt she desires the quiet growl I send her way.

"For the finned?" she asks innocently, "I voted for you."

"And the other factions? Who did you choose for those?"

She hesitates for a moment, her eyes pleading with my weighted stare for understanding as she sighs, "I wrote your name in every category possible."

"Why?" I gasp, sending a stream of bubbles crashing into the stalactites above.

"Because there is no-one else I'd rather have governing over Robin," Rhea says simply, "And like many other of the syrens and merfolk, we feel like a vote against you is a vote against the gods. You wield the Trident. You're the only syren to have wings, Wren. If you're favoured by Poseidon, you will obviously be favoured by the sea creatures too."

"But..." My voice trails off as questions cloud my mind.

"Is it such a bad thing to have your people love

you?" Rhea asks with a shrug, "We chose you. Now it's your turn to choose us."

"As if I haven't put this Queendom ahead of everything else my whole life. I almost *died* because of that throne. It took everything I had to defeat the last Queen."

"*That throne* which you have yet to sit in since it became yours," Rhea counters, showing no fear of my temper. Unlike Aengus, Rhea doesn't let respect and restraint control her tongue.

"I have not sat there because I do not ever want to be like her," I grate out through gritted teeth, my patience wearing thin as my frustration grows. I cannot help but feel cheated by my people instead of honoured.

The nightmares I used to have about my mother have now been replaced with dreams of Kellan. So many hopes and plans fill the nooks and crannies of my mind, and yet all those plans will never come to fruition should I remain as Queen.

I do not know if it makes me a worse syren or worse ruler to want to put a man before certain elements in my life.

"I believe it's that fear, that very wish to never be like your mother, which is a strong reason you won so many votes. No-one else knows the horror of a tyrant as well as you. That's how we know you'll never turn into one."

The burden of faith and trust of an entire Queendom weighs on my chest and suddenly even though I'm underwater, an overwhelming need to get fresh air itches in my lungs.

Drifting towards her, I begrudgingly give Rhea a light hug and blow a bubble kiss towards snoozing Robin.

"I'll see you in the Temple for the official results," I sigh, swimming my way towards the cave entrance, "Try your best to not tell others of the outcome until then. Mermaids are notorious gossips, and I'd rather not have this news *surfacing* to the King before I can tell him myself."

Rhea nods, giving me her word, and as I begin my swim home, she adds, "We all voted for you because we love you, not because we wish to punish you, Wren."

TWELVE

oo busy overthinking to swim, I simply drift my way back up. The surrounding current lightly tossing me from side to side, but it continues to do all the work for me, pushing me upward.

When I finally reach the surface, I twist onto my back and just float for a while. Waves and serenity gently wash over me as I watch the night sky.

Without the glow of the mainland lanterns, the constellations always seem to shine brighter here. The crisp, cloudless sky lets me easily identify the familiar scattering of stars.

As my eyes trace a path from Taurus' horns to Pegasus' tail, I remember the last time I was here.

My stargazing whilst drifting didn't last too long before my binding oath to Kellan panicked every inch of me. I'd almost died racing to get back to him, the ichor in my veins heaving me towards him. He had released me from his oath, but although I'm no longer tied to him through his promise, I feel more bound to him than ever.

But this is no vow he can release me from. It is no longer just my ichor which yearns to be near him. I fear it something much worse. I'm a syren who's come down with a mortal infliction. Love.

"Wren."

Yep. I am most definitely a fool in love because I swear I hear Kellan's voice amongst the gentle lapping of waves. You know you've got it bad when you start bloody hallucinating their voice in your mind.

Whenever we're apart it's from this location I skim my song shells. I've spent so many nights watching my shell hurtle into the distance, wishing I could follow it, that maybe part of my mind is permanently *Kellan-ified* in this area-

"Wren."

Gods above! I twist, my damp hair whipping around my shoulders.

As if my thoughts could summon him, Kellan bobs towards me in a narrow rowboat.

In disbelief, I swim a few strokes, needing to close the distance between us and wanting to make sure he wasn't a trick of the light.

Setting down his wooden oar, he offers me his outstretched hand, "It's cold out. I thought I'd show my gallant side."

With a wide grin, I open my mouth to ask where he was hiding this gallant side the first time he dragged me into a boat, but no sound comes out. A stream of bubbles gurgles up beside me.

Of course. My gills.

"I know, I know. My chivalry has left you utterly speechless," he jokes, noticing the bubbles all around me. I roll my eyes with extra flare just to get my point across.

As he hauls me in, I try to keep my distance as the cold water runs off my skin. Wind ripples through his blond hair. His jacket is tucked up close to his neck. A drenched syren dripping all over him is probably the last thing he wants. Or at least that's what I assumed. Yet as soon as I'm fully in the boat, he lightly shakes the excess droplets from my wings, before draping a towel over my shoulders and pulling me in close.

It's a tight fit for both of us in the slim boat. He lays me against his chest, my legs nestling on top of his. Even with the drying cloth, I'm leaving a Wren-shaped puddle across his jacket and slacks, but he doesn't seem to notice nor care.

As his warmth seeps into me, he absentmindedly strums his thumb over my gills. Between his soothing repetitive motion, and the gentle sway of the boat, I fight the urge to sleep. Instead, I tilt my face upwards and gaze at him. Even if I could speak at this moment I wouldn't.

He lightly kisses a droplet off my nose, before reaching for the oar. Rolling his shoulders, he sits up straight in his seat and begins the row home.

Feeling his powerful muscles work beneath me bats away *any* sleepiness I felt. I consider lying against him the whole way home to savour the way his torso tenses and eases as he cuts through the water. The sheer strength of his strokes.

Shaking my head at myself, I snap out of my Kellan muscle trance and decide to help. I am the Queen of the sea after all.

Reaching towards the waves, I let my hand skim through the water. I cannot lure whilst in transition, but I don't want Kellan to spend another five minutes bobbing along in the cold whilst I wait for my voice to return. Thankfully, I have other means.

Snapping my fingers beneath the water makes almost no sound. At least no sound a mortal could hear, but I have no interest in summoning humans.

My near-silent clicks are loud enough to draw the

attention of the nearby hippocampi who rove outside the Clam Gates. Upon hearing my call, a herd of eight gallops towards me. Their collective charge drives a bow wave before them, propelling our boat forwards with great speed.

A curse explodes from Kellan's mouth. He grabs a side of the boat with a white-knuckle grip as the wave threatens to topple us.

"How is it even when you can't speak you're able to summon trouble?" he asks, surprise audible in his tone spotting the hippocampi rumps breaching the waves.

Summon trouble? Oh, he's lucky I have about three minutes left transition, otherwise, he'd be getting an earful.

Withdrawing my hand from the water, I dismiss the hippocampi and flick my wet fingers towards Kellan.

He watches the creatures descend, and lightly shakes his head, "As much as those overgrown seahorses creep me out, I wish I could follow them. I'd love to explore the other half of your life. I want to know where you grew up, where you slept for almost eighteen years. To see your throne, meet Rhea's daughter. There is this whole part of your life intangible to me."

A weird sense of guilt seeps into me as his tone

turns more and more defeated. I nod a small nod. There's no point in denying the obvious. I was not created to lie.

"I'll commission my oil painter to recreate the scenes for me," he declares. Even with my back to him I feel his beaming smile at the idea.

I'd seen the painter's work. His detailed portraits of Iseult and Lachlan hung throughout the Lunar Lands, so I knew the artist would capture the essence of my world well if I were to describe it to him. But it would never be the same.

Kellan would never experience the weightlessness of underwater life. The constant yet soothing background hum of creatures in the distance. The chorus of giggles emerging from the mermaid quarters each morning, and the harmonising notes of a hundred syrens singing together. He'd never experience the rush of riding of hippocampi as it rapidly descends, nor the sensation of being able to talk without having to pause for breath. I spent so long trying to escape the Queendom, I had never noticed all the good things about it. It's only now that I think about the experiences Kellan will never have I realise how wonderful my world can be.

"How are Rhea and her baby?" he asks as he eases his rowing, the shore now just ahead thanks to the bow wave, "Does she have any update about the vote?"

Dread drops like an anchor in my gut.

I'm surprised the weight of my conscious doesn't sink the boat into the shallow water. I can't tell him. Not now. Not when he's just arrived on this isle to get away from regal duties for a few days. And it's almost his birthday for gods' sake.

With the last few strokes of the oar, the rowboat bites into the grit below us. Rising to his feet, he spears the paddle into the silty sand and halts our movement fully.

I hop overboard, splashing my feet into the water and walking briskly ashore. He follows suit, dragging the boat further ashore behind him.

"Your gills should be closed by now, shouldn't they?" He asks gently as if to remind me...as if I wasn't aware.

Walking ahead, I try not to make my breathing through my nose and mouth obvious. I take shallow breaths to avoid moving my chest too much, anything to buy me a few more seconds. He asked about Rhea and the baby, so I'll just answer that part. I'll talk about Robin and how adorable she is, and then I'll ask about Aveen when she was a baby. That will definitely keep him talking, he has such a soft spot for her and-

"Wren," he says, catching up to me easily. One of

his strides is about four of mine. Snapping me out of my own chaotic world, he repeats, "Any news on the vote?"

I remain quiet, continuing to walk towards home, somehow feeling like if I make it there everything will be better.

He lightly bumps his shoulder against mine, which wobbles me, "Someone's awfully quiet. Catfish got your tongue?"

I manage an eye roll and a small smile, but it's off. And he notices.

Stepping in front of me, he blocks my path, "Your gills are shut, so not talking to me is just rude, love. What is it you don't want to tell me?"

"I just want to get home," I offer, going to step around him. But he grips my arm with a single hand, and easily holds me in place.

"Do not make me abuse your truthfulness, Wren."

I sigh and mutter a curse under my breath.

How can he see straight through me?

Perhaps I've spent so long in the sea my soul has become transparent as the water I live in.

"The vote isn't working out the way I hoped," I offer, snagging my arm away and continuing my walk, "My citizens are choosing a fool. But I'd rather not talk about it until all votes are counted, so let's-

"You shouldn't call yourself a fool."

I freeze.

Slowing looking over my shoulder, I see Kellan hasn't moved at all. He stands firm, with his arms crossed and a waiting expression.

"How do you know?" I ask, my voice raspier than I'm expecting.

"That your people would choose you? Because I would too. And because I know damn well what the desire to keep you feels like."

Tears I don't even have a chance to fight off, spring freely in an instant, "I don't know what to do..."

"Yes, you do," he says flatly, "I doubt Poseidon crafted the perfect syren, giving her wings and his Trident, helping her to the throne only to watch her walk away from it. Be the Queen you're meant to be."

He strolls past me without pausing, without reaching out for me as he normally would.

"But...but what about us? What about all of our plans?" I ask after a beat, stumbling as I try to keep up with him and his stupidly long legs.

"Your people will come first, they have to. As a Queen, it's your duty."

He spits the word *duty* as if it were dirty in his mouth.

Reaching home, he lets himself in without

hesitation. He's the only other person in all the realms who can enter without an invitation. Although he is always welcome, I wish for once he needed to wait for my words to cross the threshold because the way he almost rips the door off its hinges makes me wince.

"Why are you mad at me? And my door? Kellan, I don't even want to be Qu-"

Queen.

A burning cough rips through my throat. My ribs morph to kindling, my lungs replaced with chunks of coal as my insides ignite because of my words. Bracing myself against the doorframe, I stagger for shallow breaths and wait for the burning to subside. After a few moments, my internal inferno dies down. Managing small, hitched breaths, I run my tongue over my lips to make sure they aren't charred. How the tears rolling down my cheeks have not turned into steam I'll never know.

When the Hel did I start wanting to remain Queen?

"Lies aren't very becoming on you, *lígo pouláki*," Kellan says with a small, sad smile.

He moves to the foot of my bed and slumps down. Hanging his head in his hands, he mutters, "I'm not mad at you, Wren. Or your door. I'm just pissed-off with the gods and the future they've planned for you and for me. How much responsibility must they shoehorn into my life? Can they not leave any room for simple happiness?"

I cringe a little and throw an uneasy glance through my window towards the seas. Thankfully, there are no looming thunderstorm or tsunamis, so I doubt the gods took his snub to heart.

Wait. Responsibility shoe-horned into *his* life? Confusion furrows my brow slightly. I'm the one who found out I'll be a monarch for the rest of my life, he only has to rule for a decade or so until Aveen is old enough.

"We can continue splitting out time between isles. I know it's been hard, and far from perfect, but I'm sure Persephone had an adjustment period too. We'll find a way to make this all work, okay?"

"We won't." He snaps, snagging his arm away, and launching to his feet again, "Because I have to remain King as well. Indefinitely."

If a Chimera had crawled out of his mouth and waved at me, I would have been less shocked.

"What?" I barely ask, no louder than a whisper. Now I'm the one deflating onto the bed.

Huh, so that's why he's irritated at the gods over responsibility.

"I wanted to give my sister a legacy, but I realise now what she needs is a life. A somewhat normal life," he says, as he paces around my tiny home, "Unfortunately I'm not like you, I *can* lie to myself. I kept telling myself I wanted to step aside to give Aveen the crown because she deserved something good in her life. I know now I just wanted to step away from something bad in my life. She has no interest in the crown. None. And yes, that might change as she gets older, but I won't ruin her childhood and turn her against me by constantly forcing her to prepare for the weight of this bloody crown. A crown which was thrust onto my head when I was barely a man. How selfish would I be to do the same thing to her?"

I don't know if he's actually asking me, but I don't answer. I wouldn't even know where to start.

He pauses his pacing to look at me, really look at me. As if he needs to capture every detail of my face like I'll soon be a memory.

"I promised you *'Together, or not at all,'* but I fear the latter part is creeping closer by the minute and I don't know how to stop it."

"No," I say firmly, "Don't say that. Even if we remain ruling over different isles, we can figure something out. We can keep visiting and-

"I will not destine you to a life of letters by your bedside instead of me in your bed."

He throws a wide arm towards the stack of well-

146

thumbed letters waiting on my bedside locker, "I won't condemn you to a half-life, Wren. That's all we would have, a half-life. Half our time between isles. Half our time together. And when I come here, I can't even go beneath the waves to your Water World, so that's half again! You deserve so much more."

"I would rather a half-life with you than not having you at all," I declare, reaching for his hand but he begins pacing again, "I want you. Any and all of you, to whatever end."

"Haven't you heard? Despite the fairy-tale stories, royals rarely get what they bloody want!" he spits.

His handsome face now full of rage and bitterness. His russet eyes glisten as they well in anger.

Lurching to my feet, I close the gap between us in an instant. I shove him in the chest with everything I have. He doesn't budge an inch, but it snags his attention.

"You're a Descendant of Ares, Kellan! You're meant to have war in your veins, not self-pity!" I snap, "Where the Hel is the man who takes what he wants, huh? Where is he gone? I've seen you fight. I've seen you take what you want. You took an entire island! You took *me* for the love of Zeus! But what? You suddenly don't want me anymore?"

"Don't you say that." He rumbles, stepping into

my space. His chest heaves as his breathing turns uneven, "You don't *ever* say that."

"There's no part of you wanting to chuck me back in the sea now you don't need me? Do you wish you'd chosen a syren who was less hassle for you?"

I spit the question at him to provoke him, but a small part of me is afraid to hear his answer.

But he doesn't answer.

Not really. He just snarls.

I don't move my wings an inch, yet I seem to be flying anyway as he scoops me off my feet.

"Hey!" I yelp, as he moves me, setting me against the wall.

"You think I don't need you? That I don't want you?" he asks, shaking his head as he holds me in place between the wall and his body. He grips my chin with his calloused fingers and forces me to look at him.

"I. Want. You."

He puts emphasis on each word, his eyes pinning me under his hold, "I want you. I want us. I want to be your consort. Mate. Husband. Everything. I want to bind myself to you in every way possible."

Butterflies explode within my stomach. My heartbeat picks up to gallop as if a herd of Centaurs were set free within my core.

Consort. Mate. Husband...

"What about being my *King*?" My words are little more than a whisper, but they blow him back.

"What?" he asks, startled into calming down a notch.

"I...I think we're going about this the wrong way." I start, "We're trying to rule separate thrones and separate isles. Our time is divided. Our travelling doubled. You said you don't want to give me a 'half-life', but for us to be together, one of us is always away from their people, their home. But what if..."

For once in his life, Kellan stays quiet.

He remains waiting, watching. Unable to take the tension of this limited space anymore, I duck under his caging arm whilst he's stunned.

"If we were to merge our isles, we would always be home. They wouldn't be my people, or your people, but *our* people. We could be together and still be rulers, Kellan. Maybe there is a way we can get everything we want."

"Are you suggesting we form an empire?"

I wince at the word, "No not an empire. Empires tend to fall. I'm saying we should merge your Kingdom with my Queendom and form a.... Crowndom."

Crowndom? Is that even a real word? It just popped into my head.

"You dreamt of me for weeks before you ever laid

eyes on me. You said it was like no dream you'd ever had before. An omen, that you were Fated to find me. You knew of my wings before Poseidon ever gifted them to me. I doubt the gods went to all that effort only for us to go our separate ways."

A low rumble echoes in his chest when I say *separate*. He steps closer once more, grasping my upper arm as if to claim his hold on me for the gods to see.

I prise his fingers off my biceps and lightly squeeze his hand, "Most people spend their lives figuring out who they want to be, and what they want to do. Our lives were decided for us. Maybe we need to stop seeing it as a burden so much as a blessing."

Kellan cocks an eyebrow, "Don't you sound awfully wise."

I shrug, struggling to hide a smile as I say, "Must be old age."

He smirks, finally, and then releases a sigh so large his chest sags. "Fate has caught up with us. We cannot run away from our crowns. Or *swim* or *fly*. If you are Fated to be Queen of the magic, and I, King of the mortal, then you are right. But I only wish to rule if you are by my side."

You are right. I bite back the urge to comment on his rare use of the words, and instead nod, "Well, you always say, '*Together, or not-*

"No," he interjects firmly, "No more "*not at all.*" Just together. Always."

Between one breath and the next, he withdraws his blade.

"What are you doing?" I ask, my eyes growing wide.

"What do you think?" he asks, rolling up his tunic sleeve until it gathers at his elbow, "I'm making you my Queen, *lígo pouláki.*"

"Wait, what?! You want to do this *right now?*" I shriek, stepping away from him to check his face for signs of insanity, "But...But what about your Masters and councillors? Don't you need to run this by them?"

"A beautiful woman reminded me I am a Descendant of Ares," Kellan says playfully, "I'm thinking I should do as I wish more often. So, I'm done seeking the unattainable approval of Masters, council members, Hel even my brother. I am their ruler. They follow my leadership, not the other way around."

Tucking a loose piece of hair behind my ear, he leans closer and quietly adds, "Besides, I'd rather we didn't have an audience for everything I'm about to do to you."

Tingling ripples through my whole body, racing

down my spine until my toes curl. *Oh.*

He cups my face, lightly brushing his warm lips against my forehead, "This is our time, Wren. Can't you feel it? This is our *Kairos.*"

My heart skips a beat.

Kairos.

I hadn't heard the ancient term in an era. I almost forgot it existed. It's not often one declares *this* moment has been crafted by Fate. That this instant must be seized...or lost forever. For the Weavers will not cross their twines, our lives, in this pattern or flow ever again. This is our fleeting moment to decide- it's now or never.

"I believe you," I announce, nodding.

The air crackles with electricity. I feel it in my being, in my very soul, that this is right. "Let us seize our Kairos."

Pride flashes across Kellan's face.

Like always, he does not hesitate.

He makes a small incision on his left forearm without blinking. The area is already so battered I doubt his shredded nerve-endings even feels the cut.

Blood wells across his skin. He dampens his thumb, before marking a circular shape on the centre of my forehead.

"I, Kellan, anoint you Wren, as Queen of my

people, Queen of my isles. I mark you as my equal, I claim you as my mate. I bestow you with half of my land, half of my throne, but entrust you with the care of my entire heart and soul. I vow to honour you, protect you, and absolutely adore you in this life until you take your last breath, and then I'll find you in the next life."

He strokes his fingers down the side of my cheek, and gently cups my face, whispering, "I love you."

"And I love you," I whisper back, before rising onto the balls of my feet to kiss him. I need to feel his lips, I want to taste every word he pledged.

He wraps his arm around my lower back and tucks me flush against him. He deepens the kiss, occupying my mouth fully.

"Wait," I mumble, trying to catch my breath, "It's my turn."

I hike up my skirt on one side to reveal the knife identical to his, strapped to my thigh. I had secured the leather holster this morning with the sole purpose of spotting the glint of delight in Kellan's eyes when he'd see me with nothing else save the blade.

But alas, I have been Fated to wield it for a different reason.

I mirror his action, though I struggle to maintain

the same deadpan face as he when the knife meets my skin.

"You don't have to say the words," he says gently.

We both know any vow I utter carries a different weight to his. Magical creatures are picky with their words, and even slower to make life-longs oaths.

But I'm not your standard magical creature, and Kellan...well, Kellan is the only person in the realm who I would ever bind myself too.

"I want to," I say honestly, dampening my thumb with my ichor rich blood.

He lowers his forehead against mine.

"You won't regret it. I'll prove myself worthy of you in every way. I promise."

I nod, whole-heartedly believing him.

"I, Wren, anoint you, Kellan, as King of my people, King of my isle and Water World," I say, emotion catching in my throat, as I streak my thumb between his brows, "I mark you as my equal, I claim you as my mate. I bestow you with half of my land and throne, but I give you my entire heart and soul. I swear to honour and defend. I vow to love you in this life until you take your last breath, and then I'll find you in the next life."

The ichor in my blood bubbles to attention as the binding words rip through me. My core tightens as my magic realises the magnitude of my vow. It's as if my very soul swells. I've never sworn an oath like this before. Come to think of it, I doubt anyone ever has.

I worried a promise of this scale would negatively affect me. When I vowed to return to Kellan on Soleil, my words immediately made me feel ill. But there is no wave of nausea this time. The magic in my veins doesn't lurch towards him, for I am not bound like my life depends on it.... he *is* my life now.

I shiver like I've stumbled through Arachne's web, as my ichor settles back down.

"Are you alright?" Kellan asks with a steadying hold, worry burrowing his brow and smudging my barely dried blood mark.

"I've never been better," I offer, without sarcasm.

He tilts my chin upwards. "Prepare to feel a whole lot better. I haven't finished with you yet...my Queen."

His lips meet mine again, this time with a kiss more tender than I thought he was capable of. There is no haste or urgency to the way his tongue plays against mine- for once we have time, and he's going to make the absolute most of it.

Sliding my arms around his neck, Kellan scoops me up without breaking our kiss. He lays me down gently on my bed but maintains his caged stance above me. His russet eyes turn molten as desire courses within him.

I reach up, draping my arms over his nape to pull him towards me. There might only be a few inches between us, but it's too great a distance. Despite my best efforts, he doesn't budge. Not even slightly. He remains towering over me watching me from under a heavy-lidded gaze.

"Sometimes I can't believe you're real," he rasps, shaking his head in disbelief, "And you're mine."

Growing impatient, I raise my legs up, hooking my feet behind his back and try again to tug him towards me. He doesn't concede.

"I ensure you I'm real. And I'm very much yours," My voice sounds slightly gravelly, thick with lust, "So take me."

Shifting his weight onto one fist, he uses his free hand to pull his tunic off. He tosses it to the floor, before lowering his body until he is flush against me.

"I plan on taking all of you, and giving you all of me too," he vows. The serious edge in his voice causing my lower abdomen to flutter, "I'm just considering fashioning my tunic into a syren bridle. I can't have you luring half the coast with your beautiful noises."

Heat rushes through me, my cheeks blushing instantly, "That won't be necessary."

"Oh, it will," he growls, kissing me senselessly.

"My cottage is magically enchanted, remember?

Nothing enters or leaves without my permission. The rule extends to my.... sounds."

He laughs beautifully against my neck, sending shivers down every inch of me, "Let us test that theory."

He flips me over in an instant, pulling the blanket over both of us as if to shield us away from the outside world.

THIRTEEN

etween the bright sunrise and the blaze of birthday candles atop the cake, my little bungalow had never contained such a warm glow.

Light streams through my window, spilling across Kellan's bare, toned back as he lays strewn across my bed, barely covered in a tangled sheet. His arm which bears the symbol of last night's ritual drapes over the Wren-replacement-pillow I swapped places with an hour ago.

Tidying away the pile of letters occupying my bedside locker, I begin blushing intensely. Now I have actual memories and experiences to pair with all his words and promises. Promises which he most definitely lives up to. I shove the letters into a drawer before distraction threatens to ruin my plans.

Afraid I'll drop it, or possibly singe my eyebrows off, I gingerly move the two-tier cake to my bedside table.

I make a mental note for next time to move first, set it on fire later. It's times like this my lack of mortal experiences really shines through.

I position the specially crafted bottle of rum beside the cake, making sure the ribbon tied around the neck of the bottle is straight. Having the drink crafted turned out to be quite a community effort. The river nymphs sourced the freshest, sweetest water, whilst the woodland fae harvested molasses from the eldest oak tree on the isle. Sage then added an array of crushed herbs and spices, before handing the corked bottle over to Rhea.

Beyond the Clam Gates, the liquor had the opportunity to mature faster than it would on the mainland, giving the drink a rusted hue and rounded flavour. Or so I'm told. Rum, pickles, and any other sharp flavours are Kellan's forte, not mine. Growing up on a raw fish and cold crustacean diet, left me with a muted palette.

"Can I stop pretending to be asleep now, or do you have more fussing and fretting to do?"

I turn to find Kellan propped up on his elbow, grinning widely. His golden hair is as dishevelled as the bedsheet, which is now pushed down low, dangerously low...

"Happy birthday," I announce, tearing my gaze away from his hips and stepping aside so he can admire the cake.

"Citrus cake?" he asks, spotting the lemon and clementine peel used for decoration along the bottom of the plate, "It's my favourite. How did you know?"

"I asked Callum. He was surprisingly helpful actually. He even got a hold of Iseult's recipe. He said she made it for you every year, and a citrus cake wasn't worth baking unless it was hers."

Kellan looks at me with complete admiration.

"I didn't make it," I quickly add, trying to manage expectations, "Baking is not my speciality, but the cooking fae are wonderful and I know they did their utmost best. Be warned though, lemons tend to be more astringent up north and I don't think anything can rival what your mother made. Childhood memory is not an ingredient easily sourced."

"It's perfect, my love," he says, sitting upright and scooting closer, "It's kind of on fire, but it's perfect."

"A candle for every year. It's not my fault you're old," I joke, sitting beside him, "I don't really understand the whole candle idea, but Aveen told me it's *very* important."

"You've never blown out candles on a birthday cake?" He sounds genuinely shocked. I say nothing, waiting for him to figure it out.

His furrowed brow rises with realisation, "Ah. I guess birthday candles aren't really popular in the Water World, huh?"

It's an effort not to laugh in his face, "No, not particularly."

He carefully plucks a lone candle from the top tier, "Well, here. I'll share with you. As you said, I have enough bloody candles to give Hephaestus a run for his money."

"I don't know what I'm meant to do," I admit, cautiously pinching the candle between my fingers. Whereas Kellan looks like he wants to snub it out with his fingers just for the Hel of it.

"I'll go first. Follow my lead," he says, closing his eyes and leaning towards the cake. I shut my eyes too, but mainly so I don't have to see his face so near the bloody flames. *Gah.*

"Dear gods, thank you for granting me the past twenty years. If I could ask one thing this year it would be that I see the Water World," he says, before blowing out all the candles in one big huff. He opens his eyes, shrugging, "See, it's simple."

"I don't want to be downbeat on your birthday,

but you visiting the Water World is impossible."

Kellan rolls his eyes, and lightly shoves my shoulder, "It's a *wish*. Therefore it's up to the universe to find a way to make it happen, not me. But if you're right, and it is forever impossible, I won't complain. I'm a lucky man, who already has everything he could want in the world. Including a thoughtful, beautiful wife at my side."

"*W-Wife?*" I splutter, almost dropping the candle into my lap.

Tilting his head back, he laughs a gorgeous, deep chuckle, "So you'll bind yourself to me forever, but cringe like a school-girl when I call you my wife?"

"I just didn't realise you slipped marriage into the ritual last night," I say, before closing my eyes and making my wish before the wax can melt onto my fingertips.

"Wren, when I told you I wanted to bind myself to you in every way, I did not say so lightly," he says, "I'm happy to give you whatever sort of ceremony, party, or vow you wish on any isle, seeing as they're all *ours* now. I know you probably had a vision for the wedding you wanted and-"

"Do you honestly think *that* is what I'm worried about? Syrens don't exactly swim around dreaming of what they'll wear to their wedding. My kind are not exactly the matrimonial sort, Kellan. *That* is what's taking me by surprise. Last year I didn't even know what a brother-in-law was, and now I apparently have one?"

"And a sister-in-law," he adds just to watch me squirm.

Sweet Zeus, Aveen!

I didn't even think about her. I wonder how she will take the news. I have no idea how she'll feel having me for a big sister, but there's no doubt she'll be thrilled about fewer history lessons and more time to sing and play now Kellan is willing to remain as ruler.

He plucks his slacks off the floor, and hauls them up his bare thighs, before rooting out his knife from the pocket, "Would my *wife* like some birthday cake for breakfast?"

I'm in the middle of dramatically rolling my eyes when a hippocampi whinny drifts through the window with the morning breeze.

The merfolk had embraced them as a sort of pet, and the hippocampi were flourishing with affection. Each morning the creatures circle outside the Clam Gates, neighing and whinnying until the merfolk and syrens wake up to play.

Kellan is busy hacking an uneven slice out of the

bottom tier of his cake with his trusty knife when I hear the hippocampi neighs again. Granted they kick up a fuss during their morning rituals, but these cries sound ...worried?

Kellan notes the slight change in my posture immediately, "What's wrong?"

"It's probably nothing, I just thought I heard-"

A blood-curdling scream rips through the town.

Kellan drops his knife, his gaze snapping to the window in an instant, but I am already on my feet and moving. I dash out my door, barrelling towards the sound before I even gather my thoughts.

Someone by the bay is crying out for a healer, but the plea for help barely audible over the wailing.

As I sprint past Poseidon's Temple, Aengus appears out of nowhere, almost knocking me off my feet as he canters around the corner. His hooves kick up a cloud of dust as he barrels ahead.

Kellan's longer strides mean he catches up easily, as he tugs his jumper over his head without pausing.

Although we all rush our way at our own pace, the three of us skid to a halt at the same time when we finally see it. When we see her- the young, dead mermaid being nuzzled ashore by a frantic hippocampus.

With flared nostrils and the whites of his eyes bulging, I can tell the beast is injured. Badly. And that's before I even notice the harpoon spears protruding from his withers, flank, and rump.

"What happened?" Aengus demands, but no-one answers. No-one in the gathering crowd responds to him or even glances in our direction.

Either they do not hear him over the growing commotion of the bay, or else they do not have answers to give. Questions rush to my mind, but I cannot form the words.

A merman bursts his head above water, hauling an injured body in his arms, "Help! She's hurt."

This mermaid is alive, but barely.

A spear, lodged firmly through the thickest part of her tail, protrudes from the water. A sea of merfolk hands rush to support her. As she is cautiously turned onto her side, I recognise her.

"Maeve?" I say shakily, but she doesn't respond. Instead, her eyelids flutter like butterfly wings. Her head lolls backward as it becomes too heavy for her to hold.

A dryad healer bursts onto the scene, eyes scanning both mermaids instantly. She winces upon seeing the ashen skin mermaid, knowing there is nothing she can do. Like a true healer, she shudders off the death and focuses on the living, turning her attention to Maeve.

Regardless of species or island, it's a universal

known truth a healer tutting and shaking their head is never a good sign.

"What are her odds?" Kellan asks.

"She's been struck through her tailbone." The healer sighs, her hands now covered in blood, ichor and silvery scales, "If I can remove the harpoon and stem the bleeding, she could survive. But I'll have to act...now."

For some reason, everyone looks to me. I don't know if they're expecting me to leave or grant permission, but I say nothing.

I simply step forward, kneel on the water's edge and lean forward to take Maeve's limp, damp hand.

The dryad nods once before taking a deep yet incredibly unsteady breath. She grips the base of the spear. A deep voice mutters a curse behind me as the healer braces, but I cannot tell if it is Aengus or Kellan. My ears are muffled with my own racing heartbeat, and I cannot look over my shoulder to check. I do not remove my eyes from the paling mermaid. I wonder if it's too late to change my candle wish.

"One.... two..."

Like Kellan, she never says three. Or perhaps she does, but the Banshee scream which erupts out of Maeve drowns it out.

Her hand clenches into a fist around my fingers

as she lurches upright, jumping out of the merman's hold.

"Hold her steady!" The dryad cries, trying her best to pack the wound with moss and kelp, but it's no easy feat. Reanimated with the fresh wave of pain, Maeve twists and turns frantically.

"Easy lass!" Aengus bellows harshly from behind, though I hear the fear in his voice, the concern he often masks with discipline.

Sage bursts onto the scene, twisting a branch into her hair to keep it out of her face as she leaps into the water without hesitation.

"Saoirse and I were riding our hippocampi out early to see the sunrise," Maeve sobs, trying to twist and see her friend. Her wide eyes snag on her injured hippocampus beside her, causing her to cry harder.

Although I hate the distress which seeing her pet injured causes her, I am glad the beast was too injured to move. His body blocks her from seeing her dead, floating friend on the other side of his rump.

Sage uncorks a small vial from her dress pocket and encourages Maeve to drink deeply, "This will take away the pain."

"Where were you swimming?" I ask, moving out of the healer's way but still holding onto Maeve's hand, giving her an encouraging squeeze to answer. I need answers.

"We didn't even see them coming," she sobs, her previous hysteria turning to despair as Sage's potion takes it's hold. The healer continues to pack her wound with moss, before tightly binding her tail with long strips of seaweed.

"Who? Who's *them*?" I demand, reminding myself not to shake her as my anger builds, the need for retaliation growing greater in my core. Maeve wince's her eyes closed as the dressing is sealed snuggly with an old lobster claw, but then her eyes stay sealed.

"Maeve," I call louder than I intend, and with more desperation than I would like to admit, "I need a name, if you can tell me who, or where-"

Though her voice comes out no louder than a groggy whisper, there is no denying she says, "Lunar Lands."

I drop her cold hand into the water as if it had burnt me.

"What do you mean *Lunar Lands?*" Kellan demands, striding into the water in an instant. But Maeve does not respond. I'm not even sure she's conscious anymore.

"Kellan, she's probably confused," I say, for myself to hear as much as him, "She's lost a lot of blood, so-"

"White boats carrying the moon, stars and sun,"

Maeve croaks without opening her eyes, without parting her lips, "They're coming for us..."

"She needs to rest," the healer blurts out firmly, sensing the onslaught of questions about to implode from Kellan, "The worst is over for this mermaid, but she'll need to recuperate. Lots of sleep, no swimming, and no resurfacing for at least a week. That laceration needs to be in the saltwater at all times to avoid infection."

No resurfacing is the polite way of saying *no more questioning* to Kellan and me, although we don't challenge her. He doesn't say anything as he wades out of the water, ignoring Aengus's stare.

I do not follow him, at least not immediately. Instead, I watch as Maeve's limp body is carefully positioned onto a driftwood stretcher.

The spears have been removed from the hippocampus, though I do not know who by. As the creature limps his descent below the waves to rest, four strong stallions appear. They flank their injured stablemate on all sides and offer reassuring nickers as they disappear out of sight.

The dead mermaid is gently tied onto another driftwood stretcher to prevent her from floating away.

"Wait." I call, swallowing the lump of emotion swelling in my throat, "Maeve said Saoirse was her name, right?"

"Yes, your Majesty." A young merman replies, meeting my gaze with unfallen tears in his eyes.

"Mermaids rarely see fresh blooms," I say, forcing myself to take a step away from her body. I snag part of the flower garland the drapes along every inch of the pier, and pull it down, "Let her have this small piece of spring."

The merfolk carefully weave an array of white and yellow blossoms into Saoirse's floating, deep juniper hued hair. Sage and I wiggle a single white tulip between her stiffening fingers.

"I don't have my coin purse on me," I sniffle, over my shoulder. Aengus nods understanding and retrieves a lone golden penny from his pocket.

"A Charon coin for her voyage." He says, handing it to the merman beside her.

I'm not sure if Hades' ferryman would turn away a soul for not having the fee, but I didn't want to take the chance. Not when an ever-constricting knot in my gut is telling me it's my fault she's sailing the Styx.

I give a single, solemn nod and then Saoirse is carefully lowered towards her home, never to resurface again.

I wait until the last ripple of their descent dissipates completely before I turn around.

Kellan ceases his pacing, twisting on his heel to meet my gaze. His attempt at bridling his inner rage seems to tighten everything else about him too. His face and form are taut. The dripping saltwater from his lower half is the only movement.

"The Lunar Land boats were all sanded and painted over winter in preparation for the new crest. The only ships which remain painted white are those of the older vessels of the Soleil fleet."

Soleil.

The island coined the name for its solar shape, but as of late whenever I hear the name, I feel no warmth, no correlation to the sun at all. I just feel utter dread.

Coldness spreads from my wet hands and feet. It travels through my limbs and captivates my core until my heart itself feels frozen.

"So, this is the Plan B which Fynbarr spoke of," I say, but my own voice sounds far away from me. Guilt, anger, and a growing need for vengeance muddle my mind.

"I don't understand," Kellan says, "I got you away from there, you're meant to be safe! Your people are meant to be safe!"

"Chaos follows me remember," I laugh without a drop of humour, "And you were right, Fate has a way of catching up."

I stumble and scramble my way onto the bank, ignoring the outstretched hands waiting to aid me.

My body wants to sit, but I do not. I cannot. Unlike tensed Kellan, I must move to at least feign productivity as my mind whirls to catch up.

"She said *they're coming for us*," Aengus rumbles, watching me pace, "I don't know what that entails but I can have the hooved army ready with-in the hour. My colts and I will guard the coastline against all angles, and-"

"No," I snap, "I won't let them hurt anyone else. I won't let them near my home. I'll take care of this."

"You sound like me and I don't like it," Kellan grates, "You can't take care of this alone, Wren. We have no idea what we're up against. We don't know how many boats, how many men, or when they're arriving-"

"Which part of not letting them near here did you not understand! Those bastards are *not* arriving," I exclaim, throwing my hands up, "I will meet them at sea where I'm strongest."

I don't know who says what, but a collective clamour of "*Not a hope in Hel,*" and "*Are you completely crazy?*" explodes from Kellan and Aengus.

"Sage," I call out, ignoring them both.

She trudges out of the water, the bottom half of

her dress dripping. "Yes, your Majesty?"

"I know this is short notice, but do you have the ichor vial ready yet?"

"I have a small amount prepared, but not an entire dose yet."

"That will do." My firm nod sends her jogging to fetch it.

Aengus looks confused, but Kellan.... well, Kellan's face is darkening by the second, like clouds rolling in before a thunderstorm. At times I find it hard to believe Zeus doesn't have a direct claim to him. I guess Ares is a Descendant of Zeus so maybe it has trickled into him that way...

"Tell me you aren't about to run headfirst into this with a half-thought of plan, and a half dose of ichor?" Kellan rumbles.

"I'm not," I snap. And it's true. I am not going to *run* into trouble, I'm going to *fly*.

My wing is still healing. The wound has yet to fully close and after being trapped under cloaks and smothered beneath blankets, they're stiff and heavy.

Knowing I'll need a helping hand to get started, I begin marching towards the higher ground of the wooded coastline. At least I can use the cliff edge drop to get some air beneath my wings and glide my start.

Kellan immediately follows. Aengus does not.

"You pledged *'together'* Wren." He says flatly, as he bounds beside me.

Sage catches up with us along the way and wordlessly hands me a vial. It's not much, but it's better than nothing. Sensing the palpable tension, she bows lightly before jogging away again.

"I pledged 'together', and I meant it Kellan, but that doesn't mean I stay fastened to your waist for the rest of our lives."

"If you leave, I can't follow you," he says, looking utterly miserable.

As we near the treeline hugging the steep coastline, harpies descend from their surrounding nests. Glancing up at the feathered females circling overhead, sheer jealously crosses his face.

"My people, *our* people, are in danger Kellan. It's my duty to do all I can to protect them," I offer, glancing out the seas before me.

No boats are visible. I have no idea what direction to fly in. *Great.*

Kellan says nothing. He just rakes his hand through his already messy hair.

"If the situation were reversed, would you stay?" I ask.

He hesitates before forcing a nod, "Yes."

A small smile pulls at my lips, "This is why we

work, because you can lie, and I can fly."

Standing tall, I take a step back, spread my wings wide and take a deep breath.

"Wait." He calls, grabbing my wrist lightly. I pause to see the poorly veiled panic in his eyes. "Just wait."

He steps before me and draws me into a heated kiss.

"I'll find a way to help you, a way for us to be equals," Kellan mutters against my lips.

Before I can ask what he means, he adds, "The men on those boats think you're a murderous monster. They couldn't be more wrong, but I want you to prove them right this time. Be what they fear. Show them no mercy."

I nod, blinking back emotion and kissing him once more.

He forces himself to drop my hand and takes a step back. "You bring the chaos to them, *lígo pouláki*. Rattle the stars and ripple the seas."

FOURTEEN

eeping my eyes locked on the horizon, I break into a sprint. I run until the ground disappears beneath my feet. Throwing my arms wide, my wings catch flight.

I soar.

Harpies flock to the skies, following me out of instinct. They were once devoted to my mother, but now their loyalty lies with me. With a silent jerk of my chin, I disperse them across the skies to look out for the boats below.

With my initial glide losing momentum, the time comes for me to flap my wings. I tuck my wings inward with a closing beat. And then they do not reopen. I begin plummeting downwards. My clothes flap wildly against my skin. I begin kicking my feet as the sea rushes up to meet me.

A cry bursts through my lips as I force my wings to expand against the gust of my descent. Sleepy, stiff muscles jolt awake as agony rushes to every feather tip. Whatever thin membrane of skin my body had managed to heal was now being torn away.

I pump my wings furiously, demanding short, frenzied beats to avoid slamming into the water.

My feet skim across the waves before I start rising. Each beat sends a new paroxysm of pain through my left wing, but I continue to push. Slowly but surely, I climb back into the skies, silently praying Kellan couldn't see my near failure from the distant coastline.

Every wing beat hurts, but I find counting them helps. It distracts me. It convinces me I am moving forward even though I feel as if I'm getting nowhere.

I'm on beat one hundred and ninety-seven, when a harpy squawks loudly to my right. She hovers mid-air for a moment, extending her long, avian legs to points her talons at something on the horizon. It takes me twelve more beats to catch up to her side, and then I see it too.

The boats. Three of them. White painted wood with billowing sails as Maeve described. And they're hurtling through the waves towards Seven Spikes.

Tucking our wings, we begin our downward dive.

Making the most of our stealthy speed, we aim headfirst towards the vessels. The faster harpies, swoop wide, encircling the boats from behind.

"Starboard side!" A sailor bellows, as we get closer. We can no longer be mistaken for a flock of large crows, although it would still be accurate to call us a murder.

"They're coming in stern-side." Another voice calls, quickly followed by, "And port-side!"

We surround them effortlessly. There is no escape.

Harpoons and bows point at us from every direction.

"Disarm." I order, landing on the wooden mast of the central boat. I don't expect the men to listen to me, but I know my harpies will.

They dive, talons-first, towards the deck. Some men are knocked off their feet by the sheer force of the creatures landing. Others scramble backwards in fear. The few who manage to stand steadfast, brandishing their weapons with a white-knuckle grip are quickly introduced to the harpies' four-inch talons. They each wrap their black hooks around the bows and harpoons, either snagging them away or breaking them in the process.

A yelp burst out of a sailor on the boat across from me. He made the grave mistake of holding onto his weapon. Blood runs down his forearm which is sliced to the bone.

"I meant disarm as in take their weapons, not take their actual arm," I holler, allowing a light yet heinous laugh to pass my lips. I do not let the relief of my now still wings show. Instead, I wear a mask of bravado and indifference.

Swinging from the mast, I use the height to my benefit as I have a clear bird-eye view of the entire fleet. There is about a dozen men on each vessel, though the harpies have rendered half unconscious. At least I hope it's just unconscious...for now.

The harpies back down, perching themselves on the edge of the boat. They keep their pinpointed pupils darting from man to man. Their wings out-stretched slightly, like hawks guarding freshly killed prey.

"One of my girls was murdered this morning," I shout from the mast as an introduction, "And another severely injured, along with one of my hippocampi. I do not take that lightly. Tell me who-"

"Make sure you cannot hear her!" An older man yells over me, fidgeting with his ears, "There once was an evil crow..."

"Who sung like a strangled cat!" Another sailor replies.

"Ugly from head to toe, with wings like an overgrown bat!" The rest of the crew join in the chant.

They recite it again. But louder this time. And as they begin their taunt a third time, the rest of the fleet join in. Each boat starting at a different time to form a deafening round that echoes across this small corner of the sea. The stomp their boots on the deck to the beat. They clap their calloused hands as the begin yet again.

Some sailors crane their necks up to watch me as they roar. Others spit in the faces of the harpies. My creatures hiss back, glancing at me, waiting for my order to attack. But I do not give it. Not yet.

Swinging off the mast, I drop to the deck. I land hard on my knees, an ache jolts through me, but I'm far too angry to be concerned with something so trivial as pain.

"Look boys, the crow fell out of her nest!" A sailor missing half his teeth guffaws. My hands curl into fists. An urge to knock out his remaining teeth bubbles inside of me.

One word from me could end this. How easily I could kill them all. Too easily- and worse still, I don't think it would bother me.

I find myself grateful for the scuffed pine deck beneath my feet, for if the sea was beneath me then I could see my twisted reflection. And I know without needing to see it, that I would resemble Kestrel.

With this much fury behind my eyes and bitterness on the tip of my tongue, I truly look like my mother's daughter.

Be what they fear. Show them no mercy.

With Kellan's words ringing through my mind, I lunge towards one of the men. He stumbles backwards and a circle of space clears around me. The harpies guarding the boat ledge hiss loudly as the men creep closer to them. There is not enough room of all of us. Especially with all the men's animosity and poorly veiled fear taking up so much room.

The guard who initiated the chant is growing flushed in the cheeks. He bellows his tune, over and over again. As I step closer, he drops his gaze as if I'm Medusa.

Thick wads of cotton protrude from his large ears. Glancing around, I notice the rolled-up buds shoved in every sailor's ear. Some have even soaked the cotton balls in sticky honey to stop them being blown away with the sea breeze.

Imaginative, I admit to myself, *but useless.*

I once joked with Kellan that he was too full of anger, and he should replace it with benevolence or graciousness. He replied that anger, if harnessed correctly, was one of the most beneficial emotions we have. It's our intuitive response to being wronged. Our way of ensuring we are treated correctly.

I must think like him.

I must harness this rage.

I must be smarter than them.

Holding my head high, I parade past the sailor. I somehow manage to look down my nose at him even though he is at least ten inches taller than me.

My eyes go hunting through all the sailors surrounding me. I glance past the rowdier men who roar the loudest. The hateful ones egging on their comrades to sing. They're not a good fit for what I have in mind...

But he is, I smirk to myself as I spot a timid teen alone at the back of the boat. He quietly words along with the chant, but I cannot hear his voice. Feeling the weight of my stare on him, he looks up from his tattered boots.

His wide, walnut hued eyes are only a fraction darker than his skin. Skin which is stretched too thin over his cheekbones. His gaunt stature is magnified by the fact he's wearing at least four layers. I cannot bear to imagine how thin he truly is beneath all his coats.

As I approach him, five harpies move from the ledge to the deck. They stand behind me, spreading their wings fully to block me and the boy from the others.

Unfortunately, the harpies cannot block their voices, and the roar of, *"The sea-witch is going to turn him into an eel!"* is perfectly received by both me and the teen.

His eyes grow wide as he scrambles to the edge of the boat. He peers overboard with trembling hands trying to grip the ledge.

"I wouldn't jump if I were you," I advise. When he doesn't immediately move away from the edge, I add, "Besides, I will always be able to out swim you so don't waste your energy."

The boy twists, keeping his back firmly glued to the edge, and guarding as many inches between us as he can.

He flinches as I raise my hand towards his face. If this were a mere reaction to me, to being touched by a syren, then I would naturally feel hurt, but I would accept it.

But as my fingertips graze his swollen cheek, I notice the subtle mauve bruising shadowing his left eye. He is not just afraid of me touching him, but anyone. My anger burns a little brighter as my imagination paints a picture of this boy's life.

I carefully pluck the cotton wool from his ears. Well, his *ear*. He only has one. Where his left ear should be is almost completely flat. Still healing scars took its place instead.

"Can you hear me?" I ask, having to almost shout over the taunting chant which grows in verses and volume behind us.

He nods, tilting his ear towards me. His head looks far too big for his body.

"And do you know who I am?"

"You're a Queen." He drops his gaze either out of fear or respect. His quiet answer takes me back.

"Well, yes, but I'm also a syren. Which means you can fully believe me when I say I have no intention of hurting you. But I'll need you to co-operate, and answer my questions, okay?"

He doesn't respond.

The harpies behind us hiss as the crew go bolder and inch their way closer. They won't be able to hold them back for much longer. And I doubt the crews attempt at breaching the feathered wall has anything to do with checking the teen's welfare so much as to get a clear shot at me.

"They will kill me if I say anything."

"You will speak," I say firmly as I reach into my pocket to retrieve the vial of ichor, "But this will make it easier for you to spill your truths. Now, drink."

Uncorking the vial with my thumb, I raise it to

his cracked lips which quiver slightly. With some reluctance they part, and he sips every drop.

It's only half a dose, but he's only half a boy.

I've never used ichor in this way before, though I doubt anyone ever has. I have no idea how long to wait or if it will even work. But there's only one way to know.

"What's your name?" I ask.

"Pip."

I start with that question as it feels the most natural, but I have no way of telling if it's true or not. Thankfully, like most sailors he dons a signet ring on his middle finger. It brands the initial *P*, so I take it as a positive sign.

"Alright, what colour eyes do you have?"

"Brown."

True. Time to try for something bigger.

"What happened to your ear? I mean, your *lack* of ear?"

To this, Pip shakes his head. He stays mum until the ichor begins choking the truth out of him.

"It never worked real' good," Pip admits, fighting off a cough as he adds, "Fynbarr said I could join the crew as a deckhand, that my deformity could be handy for them if we were going against syrens. I was only allowed on the boat if they could ensure I was useful."

Deformity. Apparently, Soleil's smear their disapproval on anyone that is different, not just magic creatures.

"Let me guess, Fynbarr selected you from Omphalos Stone Orphanage?"

"Yeah," Pip shrugs, "I've lived there the past few months since my father died last winter. He was a naval officer aboard the fleet which sunk during the.... attacks."

Both Pip and I wince as the truths come tumbling out. I was responsible for his father's passing. This child ending up in Omphalos Stone was my fault. Hel, the orphanage becoming crowded because so many children lost their parents last winter is my fault. Pip losing his ear was my fault.

My fault. My fault. My fault.

A familiar tug of guilt threatens to unravel me.

"I'm sorry," Pip offers, his wide, brown eyes searching mine, "I didn't mean to upset you."

If I wasn't fighting off the urge to cry, I might have laughed at the ridiculousness of his apology. Something about him reminded me of Nessa.

A harpy squawks as a sailor throws a punch at her. The rest of the flock hiss loudly, some looking to me once again for the order to attack but it doesn't come.

"Was it Fynbarr who organised this attack?" I ask,

clearing emotion from my throat as I continue to push for answer.

Pip nods, "Well, Fynbarr arranged the Lunar part of the attack. Galli and Paxson oversee the Seven Spike side of things. But they all answer to the Master and the True Prince."

"And who the Hel are they?" I ask through grated teeth, growing impatient at this drip-feed information. I need more time. I need more answers.

"Master Yarrow, and the late Prince Alistair's cousin."

Yarrow.

Alistair.

Shit.

A sailor barrels into a Harpy. Feather and blood fly as the two drop the deck and begin fighting. Whatever wall of defence they had been maintaining is now shattered.

I need more answers and more time, but I will get neither upon this boat.

Snapping a curse, I grab Pip by the scruff of his threadbare coats. Bending my knees, I force myself upwards into the sky. I groan loudly as I tow Pip with me. He may be an emaciated teen, but he's still an entirely separate person. The added weight threatens to undo my damaged wing entirely.

It takes three colossal wingbeats to retreat to the mast. The strain on my wings feels as if I'm flying through cold honey.

Scrambling for grip on the wooden beam, Pip looks terrified. Though more from the height than of me which I guess is a small victory.

"Is there anyone down there worth saving?" I yell, over the growing chaos and commotion.

Sailors who aren't too busy loading up bows or punching harpies, are now at the bast of the mast, shaking it violently. Pip cries out, pleading with the men to stop, but they do not. They would rather kill the both of us, than risk losing me.

"Well?"

Pip barely mumbles, "No. I don't believe there is."

The old me might have offered a chance of redemption to the men. I might have granted these sailors a second chance to prove themselves. But if Yarrow is anything to go by, he showed that some men use forgiveness as a Trojan horse to creep in further only to destroy you more effectively.

With a single command, I summon all the harpies to retreat. Some must fight their way to freedom, and others limp their way into the sky, but thankfully they all rise. As they ascend, a cloud of arrows and harpoons being to follow. Pip yells as a spear skims past us.

"Take him."

I snap the order at the harpies as they make their escape. With stronger wings and strength in numbers, the trio of creatures who heed my call easily scoop Pip into the sky.

Without instruction, the harpies know to head home. Poor Pip has no idea where the creatures are taking him, but at least I know he will be safe. At least he won't have to bear witness to what I'm about to do.

Ducking to diving to avoid the spray of weapons now solely focusing on me, I begin to sing.

The men don't hear it, not over their *twanging* bows, their stomping boots and ridiculing riddles they spit in my direction. They do not hear it, but they see it.

A wall of sea water rises to the right, then to the left. The waves I summon grows larger still, shadowing the men and boats beneath it.

"*Óneira glyká*," I call to the men as the wave hits it pinnacle strength.

Sweet dreams.

As if I were a messenger of death, I fold the waves in around them like an envelope.

There is no escape. They will all be delivered to Hades.

I go limp as the waves come bearing down, allowing the wall of water to drown me too.

FIFTEEN

 waited for the last straggler to sink to their watery grave before I started the swim home. Even though I survived attacking the fleet, the journey home threatens to kill me all over again.

Swimming most of the way allows my wing to get some rest. But knowing Kellan will be pacing the shoreline and waiting for my arrival, I opt to fly the last leg of the journey. If I stay quiet for a few minutes whilst transitioning, I fear he'll start a never-ending lecture before I can draw breath to talk.

Relief floods my core as the land of Seven Spikes comes into view. The release of tension almost causes me to drop from the sky. The sodden bandages around my mid-riff have slipped, now chaffing against my wound with every movement. And my wing...Well,

I'm trying and failing not to even think about my wing.

Fatigue, pain, and a racing mind make for a distracted landing. I slam the ground hard, barely having time to tuck my wings before I roll clumsily.

Landing on my back, my limbs flop beside me.

"Wren!" Arthur calls, as he sprints towards me. He throws himself onto the muddy ground beside me in an instant, "Are you hurt?"

Groaning in response, I shake my head, "Nothing new."

Slipping his slender arm under my neck, he quickly helps me onto my lead-heavy feet. My body cries out with aches as I stretch my stiffened limbs.

Shifting from swimming, to flying, to walking takes its drain on my body, and although I would be quite content to lay on the soil for a few hours and watch the world go by, I know I cannot. Every second that passes is another that Yarrow digs his claws deeper into the Lunar Lands.

"I need to skim a messenger shell to Callum, to warn him as soon as possible. Gods above I hope he isn't drunk when it arrives. And I need parchment and a quill. And Kellan. I need Kellan."

"He hasn't come back yet," Arthur says, "He must be catching up in the boat I guess."

"What boat?" I cease my stiff walking, halting

under Arthur's supportive shoulder.

His eyebrows slam down, "You didn't see him? He left just after you?"

"I didn't see him at all," I say, snagging out of Arthur's hold to face the sea.

I scan the horizon a dozen times in a single breath.

It's a clear day. Calm waves. Bright skies.

I should be able to see him. And if not from here, then definitely from my wider field of vision when I was up in the skies.

"Are you sure he was heading towards me?" Panic heightens my tone, "Tell me exactly what he said."

"He didn't really *say* anything. He grabbed some things from your house, demanded a boat and headed out that way."

Arthur jerks his chin to the East.... not the West. *East?*

"Are you sure?" I ask.

Arthur nods confidently. The young sailor might make mistakes with his jib sheets and sails at times, but to give him his credit, he had an in-built compass which had never proved faulty.

"But he has his own ship here, why would he not utilise that?"

Arthur kicks invisible dirt from his boots to avoid my scathing gaze as he replies, "Like I say, the King didn't say much, but he implied he needed a smaller vessel. Once which he could sail single-handily."

I shriek loud enough to give a Banshee a run for her money, "And who the Hel handed him over a boat and let him sail, *alone?*"

"I did, your Majesty."

Aengus appears beside me.

He looks as unflappable as usual, but there's extra tension in his folded, corded arms.

"You?" I say with a mix of shock and mild disgust, "You honestly thought on the day where my people are washing up on the shoreline dead, it would be fine to allow someone to sail out alone!"

Aengus remains silent, but his tail swishes slightly.

Spinning on my heel, I turn my back on the sea and although Aengus towers over me, I still manage to look down my nose at him as I spit, "Look, I know you have this weird testosterone, '*my horse is bigger than yours,*' complex going on, but I expected more from you."

Before he can say anything, I half run, half fly towards my home.

My gut begins to piece things together before my mind.

I'll find a way to help you, a way for us to be equals.

I wish to see the Water Worlds.

East? Why would he sail East?

Twisting and tighten knots sink in my stomach, splashing acid into my throat.

Battling the urge to retch, I swing open my door.

Everything looks the same. The bed is still unmade from this morning. Our sheet lays disregarded on the ground. His lemon cake and gifts remain on the bedside table. I cannot see anything moved or taken.... until I drop to my knees and scan under the bed.

The Armour of Ares is gone. He took his Shield.

My gaze flies to where my Trident normally hangs, only to find the space vacant.

No...No. He wouldn't...He couldn't....

The gentle clop of Aengus' hooves alerts me to his presence at the doorway, but he does not enter. That would require my invitation and I'm not feeling very hospitable.

"He left..." I say, my voice breaking.

Aengus clears his throat behind me, "I didn't hand him over a boat because I hope for misfortune to find him. He can be as arrogant as Aphrodite at times, but I do not wish harm on him. Your Majesty, I had to do as he asked.... because it was a direct order from my King."

My King. Not *a* King, or *the* King.

"He told you?" I gape, turning to face him, "Did Kellan use that information as....as leverage to get his own way?"

Apparently, it's Aengus turn to look at me with a mixture of mild disgust and shock, "Did your mother's deceit scar you so deeply you assume everyone wants to use you for their own personal gain?"

The sting of truth causes me to wince. It's a sorry day for the realms when Aengus of all people needs to reassure me of Kellan's good nature.

I wish I was not like this. I wish my distrust and my need to run could be banished from whatever shadow of my soul my vices hide. But I had already used up my wishes for today.

When I blew out that candle I asked for the same intention as Kellan, that he would someday see the Water World. I am a daughter of the gods, with ichor and magic within my veins. I should have known better than to wistfully hope for an impossible thing, especially when I bonded myself to a man who likes to test the possible.

"King Kellan didn't tell me anything," Aengus finally says, softening his tone, "I saw the symbol of Kairos on his arm for myself, and well...I'm a centaur so..."

"So?" I press, with an arched brow.

For the first time in my life, I see Aengus grow.... uncomfortable? He rocks his weight between his front and back legs, before muttering, "So I can scent you have bonded with him."

My face blanks with surprise. Heat rushes to my cheeks and ear tips, blushing them lilac in an instant. Of course. Centaurs scent everything.

And now, probably smelling my growing embarrassment too, he adds, "I cannot stop you from flying into the face of danger, and now I cannot stop him either."

"Aengus, I'm sorry for what I said earlier-

"Queens do not apologise to their attendants," Aengus scolds, sounding more like himself again.

"Maybe not, but I certainly apologise to my loyal comrades," I say firmly, crossing the room to place a gentle touch on his tense, tattooed shoulder.

"What do you need me to do?" His tone is firm, and ready for action, but I do not know what orders to give.

I want to give the order for everyone to leave me alone. I want to close the door, crawl into my bed holding Kellan's smell and let someone else deal with everything.

And maybe if I were merely Wren, I could. But I have grown to carry many more names than just Wren.

But as Queen Wren Lunar of the Seven Spikes, Water World, Lunar Lands and Soleil Island, I can no longer hide, or runaway, or wait for Kellan to make the first move.

With staggered sigh, I ask, "Where is the boy I sent home before me?"

"He is in the Temple with Nessa," Aengus says, and with a subtle eye-roll adds, "He is rather terrified of anyone non-human. Ms Shay is calming him and ensuring he eats. Can I ask who he is?"

I nod but pause after opening my mouth.

I doubt Aengus hearing, "*an orphaned teen who lost an ear to gain a place aboard the ship which harpooned Saoirse to death. Oh, and also he was recruited by the archer who attacked me which I still haven't told you about,*" would instil a lot of confidence.

"His name is Pip, and I'm hoping he'll have the answers to whatever the Hel it is that those bastard Sol's have planned," I offer instead, to which Aengus immediately tenses.

"Should I gather the colts?"

I nod stiffly, "Yes, I'll need at least a dozen of your best. Arrange rations and armour leathers for each of them. I'll question Pip in the Temple, and when I emerge, we set sail. I've grown tired of tolerating other people's intolerance. It's time to teach them a lesson."

Eastern Acropolis

SIXTEEN

Four Days Later

Kellan

ost people have never heard of Eastern Acropolis. The few who have believe it to be a myth. And the even smaller minority of those who considered the ancient citadel to indeed be real, stated it was impossible for mortal to access. But never one to take 'impossible' at face value, Kellan hoped Fate might make an exception. He only needs permission to *enter* the isle as a mortal...for he hopes to leave as something else.

Kellan had been so furious when he left Seven Spikes days ago, he hadn't thought about what he would do if Eastern Acropolis wasn't real, or if it were real but he cannot gain access.

Wren would most likely chastise him yet again for his lack of forward thinking. His inbuilt nature to strike first, think second is a lingering birthmark from Ares. Kellan silently prays his bloodline connection is enough to not get him *immediately* exiled from the isle.

For the hundredth time since setting sail, he finds himself aimlessly running a hand over the Armour of Ares. The shield bestowed to him last winter has become something of a worry-stone which Kellan thumbs whenever he finds himself questioning life decisions. He is rather surprised the decorative rivets haven't been worn smooth over the past week.

Resting on the deck, between his boots lays the Trident. He tries not to touch it, for it feels as if he's disturbing it when he does. There is immense power within its metal which he is not designed to wield.

Poseidon gifted his cherished weapon, this tool, to his syrens. The Olympian created the original syrens an era ago and granted he is responsible for all songbirds of the sea, but he *crafted* Wren himself. Poseidon bestowed Kestrel with her own demise, whilst he gave Wren his Trident to wield and her own wings to soar.

"And here I am, sailing to the city of the gods to the Olympian that I have anointed myself King of all syrens, hippocampi and merfolk.... *Oh*, and I'm eternal bound to your greatest creation." Kellan half laughs, half sighs at himself as he mutters the words aloud just to hear another voice.

The odds of this going the way he hopes are slim, but the great thing about slim odds are the higher pay-outs.

Rooting around in his cloak pocket, Kellan digs out two coins. He raises one up to the sky to show the gods, before placing it above the lip of the cabin door. He mutters a silent bet and places a gamble on himself. That this is right path for him, a journey that Fate has deemed him to make. If he is right, then the gods will reward Kellan with the pay-out of a lifetime. But if he is wrong?

With a staggered breath, Kellan nestles a lone coin back into his deep pocket. Well, if he is wrong then he has his Charon coin ready in case he is Fated to take a different journey.

Kellan rises before the sun. Opening his cabin door, he finds the deck bathing in faint pre-dawn light. A pale navy hue tints the world, making everything seem colder. He stretches his stiff muscles in the doorframe and considers returning to his somewhat warm bed for another hour or two. Gods know he could use the rest.

A week of sleeping on a boat with far too many creeks, and far too little Wren, has meant Kellan's quality of sleep has been dismal. But the idea of getting into bed without her by his side sounds colder than anything he could imagine, so he opts to brave the bleak, bitter deck, and get an early start on the day. Any extra hour of progress he can make is vital, especially when he knows she is following. He knew she would. He also knew Wren would be furious with him for leaving, but he had to.

Kellan throws a watchful glance over the stern side of the boat yet again. He has yet to see any sign of her behind him, but it would only be a matter of time.

He crosses the deck, gathering the anchor chain so he can continue his journey...but something is wrong. The chain falls slack within his hold. The anchor drags freely along the sea floor, kicking up a storm of silt and bubbles in its wake.

Any trace of sleepiness evaporates in a split second, as Kellan snaps his attention to the sails overhead. It's a rather windless morning. Not a hair on his head moves. Yet a mere dozen feet above him, his sails have caught wind. The creamy sheets billow as a silent gust glides the boat forward. It's as if Zephyrus stands behind him breathing life directly into the sails.

Kellan flips open his bronze compass, laying the instrument flat across his trembling palm. Granted he may not be as iconic a sailor as Fletcher but allowing your boat to drift off-course whilst sleeping was a rookie error. A grave mistake reserved for novices and idiots. Neither of whom would ever be worthy to step foot in the city of the gods.

The compass needle oscillates a few times before locking onto the delicately painted '*E*'. Kellan frowns. He wiggles his palm, not believing what he sees. But the needle holds steadfast.

East.

He hasn't floated off-course at all. He is soaring directly to where he wants to go as if being reeled in by some greater force. Kellan swallows hard as he figures out that is *exactly* what it's like. He's overnight progress is less of an unexpected bonus as much as a calculated beckoning forth by those whom he seeks an audience with.

With a slight scowl, Kellan perches himself upon the wooden bench. He is more a passenger upon the vessel than a captain now.

A few hours later, with the sun now high in the sky, Kellan spots the atoll surrounding Eastern Acropolis coming into view upon the horizon. The atoll, once known as the Saturn Reef, is a coral and rock ring encompassing the mainland.

From his years of marine life, geology lessons as child and having a living, breathing textbook for a brother-in-law, Kellan understood what atolls were made of, and knew they were a natural occurrence.

But his information doesn't stop a growing sliver of him believing the old legend. The sailor myth that the jagged ring around the isle was in fact the bones and skulls of those who never made it to the isle within. It's because of this atoll that the forgotten isle is referred to as the *Land of Mortal Death* in the textbooks Fletcher loves so much.

"It's just a myth," Kellan mutters to himself, ignoring the fact syrens and centaurs were once said to be a myth too.

As the hull of the boat inches into the jagged ring of rock, the sails suddenly fall limp. The ropes flail with the abrupt slackness.

The lack of speed and stillness allows Kellan to nimbly navigate his way through the reefs and shallow sand mounts which dot the uninhabited island.

It's a slow, and delicate procedure which quickly beads Kellan's forehead in a thin mist of sweat. As much as he focuses on the task at hand, he cannot help but think of home, and the similar perilous entrance to bay of Crescent Cove.

Is this what Lachlan felt like when he gained access to the Lunar Lands for the first time? Striving his way through the rocky teeth and jaws of an isle, not knowing what awaited him on the other side?

When Lachlan stepped foot on Lunar Land soil, he had claimed the isle as his own by nightfall, but there would be no such commandeering occurring here. Kellan might be ambitious, but he's not stupid.

It takes over an hour at sea-snail speed for Kellan to inch his way through. He's aware he's not as skilled a sailor as Fletcher to risk going any faster, nor is he as strong a swimmer as Wren if he were to sink his vessel.

The thought of Wren causes him to grip the wooden wheel a little tighter. Since watching her soar off the cliff, Kellan finds himself scarcely thinking of anything else, yet simultaneously banishing every thought of her from his mind. He'd seen her sink an entire naval fleet with a single tone. He'd watch her siphon the gods power through the Trident to obliterate her mother. He knew as he set sail from Seven Spikes, that Wren could tackle whatever she was flying towards. She didn't need his help, not when she had the sea surrounding her.

But Kellan vowed to honour and protect her as his equal. He intended to keep his vow, but first he would have to become Wren's equal. Or at least try to.

After an hour of weaving his way around rocks and coral, Kellan finally cruises into the shallows. The barnacle covered keel bites into the dense silt below, grinding the boat to a halt. Before him looms the small yet intimidating, mountainous isle. Dark shale and dense moss stretch upwards, with the highest rocky tips hidden under a blanket of cloud.

As Kellan cranes his head upwards, a gentle yet persistent wave tilts the vessel to the right, threatening to topple it.

"Alright, alright," Kellan mutters, taking the not-so-subtle hint to hurry the Hel up.

He braces the Shield onto his forearm, before lifting the Trident and hoisting the forked end over his right shoulder. Splashing his boots into the shallow waters, Kellan trudges his way towards land. The water is warm.... surprisingly so for early spring. He supposes it isn't too far of a stretch to assume normal seasons and weather don't apply here. Perhaps normal rules of the realms do not apply here at all.

Nestled between two of the highest peaks glistens a sun. Not the real sun, but a pantheon gilded with gold and ichor. The colossal temple reflects every drop of light which hits it. It guides the way like a lighthouse for Kellan, calling him forth like a beacon.

It may not be the real sun, but Kellan cannot help feeling like Icarus as he begins his upward hike. It remains to be seen whether he too will crumble and burn for trying to soar above his post.

SEVENTEEN

ventually the steep, sharp shale beneath Kellan's boots eases into soft moss and the incline flattens into a vast grassy plain on either side of him. The plateau is home to an open meadow, lined with mature evergreen trees and drenched in a fine mist.

Kellan slumps onto a damp, fallen log. Casting a calculating glance toward the gilded pantheon, he figures it at least another hour of trudging. His calves are burning from the constant uphill trek, so he lets the cramps pass and enjoy the eerie silence, until-

"Did you hope carrying the Trident and Shield would act as some sort of invitation? That perhaps we wouldn't throw you off our isle straight away if you came bearing our weapons?"

The voice booms from behind Kellan, but he

recognises it even without turning around.

"Dad?" Kellan croaks. His voice more fragile and childlike than he'd heard in years.

He swivels on the log to find Lachlan leaning against a pine tree behind him. Kellan wants to hug his father, to feel his solid frame and warm skin and know he is real. But this cannot be real. Kellan goes to stand, but his legs fail him. He doesn't budge an inch.

"Not exactly." Lachlan gives a slight smirk which tugs at his infamous scar stretching from brow to jaw. He pushes off the lichen covered trunk to close the space between them. As he steps into the light, confusion dawns across Kellan's face. His father looks.... younger?

His eyes are not as shadowed as they were before his passing. And his hair shines raven black, instead of being peppered with silver streaks.

This is what his father looked like almost a decade ago. How the paintings captivated him. How Lachlan looked before he lost Iseult.

"I am glamoured to appear in a form you find less... intimidating." The young Lachlan figure offers, "You tend to get defensive around males you feel inferior to. I know the fragility of your ego for it's my bloodline which fuels it."

Ares, Kellan realises with a breathless gasp.

Whatever attempt at standing he hoped for vanishes as shock floors him entirely.

Kellan clears his throat, "Thank for you for the Shield."

Ares nods once, "It is not yours indefinitely, though I was glad to lend it to you on that fateful day. You gave us quite the showdown to watch. We had not been that entertained in...a while."

A while.

Kellan had no idea how long a while was to a god, but he figured even if he asked, his mortal mind wouldn't comprehend it. Especially not when Ares' grandfather is the bloody god of time itself.

"I doubt you came all this way to say thank you, so tell us, what is it you desire?" Ares says with a gesture towards the rest of the meadow.

Tell us?

Kellan casts a glimpse behind him. He doesn't see anyone else, but the pasture comes alive with activity of a different nature.... with *actual* nature.

Subtle rusting from a hydrangea bush, grabs Kellan's attention. Between the bright bursts of blue blossoms stands a young, wild boar.

A mottled serpent slithers its way around the trunk behind Ares. And an owl perches itself delicately on the edge of Kellan's log.

The bird looks like any other of its species with cream and tawny plumage, pointed claws and a tidy beak. But its eyes captivate Kellan completely. Instead of the rounded amber eyes one would expect, he finds himself staring at wide, slanted eyes beneath the feathered brow. The eyes of a human...or a god.

Ares clears his throat and releases a slow sigh. The gods may have infinite time but that does not mean they enjoy wasting it.

Dragging his attention away from the bird, Kellan starts, "I'm in love with a woman, a syren, named Wren and-"

"We know Wren." Ares says simply, "And we know of your connection to her."

"Well, I want Wren and I, and our Crowndom to never be separated," Kellan says, and when Ares doesn't react to the news of their Kingdoms merging, he guesses the gods know that too, "I vowed to protect her and I cannot fulfil that if we are parted by the seas, or sky."

Ares steps forward, picking up the Trident resting against the log. He says nothing as he bounces its weight within his hands, turning in a circle absentmindedly. When he turns around to face Kellan once more his appearance has changed. He still bears Lachlan's resemblance, but he's much older now. His stature more imposing. His face more formidable.

"And what about time?" His voice has changed too. Deeper. Prudent. "She intends to live a mortal life because of *you*. She sacrifices her immortality because of *you*."

It takes every fibre of resistance within Kellan's being to not flinch as the Trident is jabbed towards him. Between his sheer familiarity wielding the weapon and the parental possessive tone in his voice, there is no mistaking this is Poseidon.

"I'm aware mortals have a habit of lying but be honest with yourself. Do you think I crafted the perfect ruler, daughter, syren for her only to rule for a few years?"

Even as a mortal Wren could rule for decades if she chose, but Kellan supposed those would seem like mere months to someone who existed before time had a name.

"She is no pawn in your game," Kellan says before realising he even opened his mouth, "She will live whichever life she chooses."

"A dozen generations later and Ares's temper still breathes fire within you." Poseidon muses, raising Lachlan's eyebrows high. A barely noticeable smirk pulls at his lips, "It is noble of you to want her to live her life as she chooses but being with you limits her.

With you she gets no choice. She gets mere mortality."

"She chose me. I chose her," Kellan challenges, "Why did you send me omen dreams of her if you wished for me not to source her? I called on you to revive her when I enacted the Chant of Life. I poured part of my *soul* into her to save her. If this is not what you want, if you do not deem me worthy of her, then why has Fate led us together, time and time again-"

"No one is worthy of her!" Poseidon booms, "It was not part of my vision to have her sullied by some eager warlord."

"Now, now." A feminine voice sighs, "You promised you would be kind."

The owl has vanished. Kellan instead finds a golden-haired woman sitting beside him. Iseult.

He knows this isn't his mother. Taking this form is their way of seeming less imposing, to give him a form his mortal mind can comprehend. But that doesn't stop his heart lurching forward, or his bottom lip from quivering ever so slightly.

It has been almost eight years since Kellan last saw his mother. The day of Aveen's arrival was the day of her departure. The last, and most replayed, memory Kellan has of her is that very day where he gained his sister yet lost his mother.

On that clammy, summer evening Lachlan's

bellowing sent a chill through the entire castle. Kellan sprinted to his parents chambers only to find her mother laying limp and lifeless in the centre of their bed. The air was stale with blood and sweat. Her unfocused stare stuck on the ceiling above her.

"Get it out of here," Lachlan roared at a healer, as he began ripping their suite apart searching for a blade. Any blade. He settled for a decorative sword which he ripped from the wall and sliced his forearm open without thinking. A flurry of healer's rush to calm their crazed King. Someone shoved a small, screaming baby into Kellan's arm before the oak door was slammed closed.

After he stumbled into the hallway, Kellan slide against the wall until he found the cobbled floor beneath him. He didn't trust himself to remain standing, especially with a wiggly baby girl in his shaking arms.

Bare, bar the blood she was covered in, Kellan juggled his sister into the crook of one arm and shrugged off his warm shirt. He tried his best to swaddle her and hold her close to his chest as their father roared the Chant of Life. Through thick tears, he attempted to sooth his sister. Not having a name for her yet, he called her *mikros*. His *little one*.

As their father's roars turned into sobs of despair,

214

Kellan buried his head against his sister and vowed to always protect her. From that day forward, Kellan always carried a blade and a relentless need to safeguard those he loves.

"I am being kind," Poseidon objects, snapping Kellan out of his thoughts, "He is still alive, is he not?"

"Uncle." The tall goddess warns in a clipped tone.

"You're Athena." Kellan draws in a sharp breath, as he realises who is beside him.

Granted Lunar Land children are taught to respect and love all gods equally, but Kellan cannot help but hold Athena upon a higher pedestal. It is to her the Lunar Land Temple is dedicated. And within the marble and stained-glass walls of the Virginal Temple of Athena, Kellan offers his silent prayers and pleas for guidance and courage. It seems after all these years she may have been listening. Her half-brother may have given Kellan his fight and fury, but it was always Athena's ability to implement strategy amongst the chaos that he aspired towards.

"Quite right," she smiles.

Kellan's heart swells at the sight. It may not be his mother, but he would be forever grateful for this moment, for this illusion. It has been so long since he last saw Iseult's golden smile he had almost forgotten about it. His memories of her had faded. They'd become foggy in his mind, as if he were seeing them through oil covered glass- but this smile refreshed his memories. Kellan can't help but grin back, completely ignoring the pierced prongs pointing in his direction.

"It was *I* who deemed you worthy, not my Uncle. He deems nobody worthy of his singing syrens, but he can be particularly tetchy about Wren," Athena explains.

"Well, she's extraordinary so..." Kellan offers with an understanding nod to both Athena and Poseidon.

With a great reluctance, Poseidon lowers the Trident an inch or two. Athena nods in silent approval as if he has passed some unannounced test.

"Yes, she is quite special alright, but so are you. Granted, I had my fair share of suitable males to choose from. Ares and Zeus have bedded enough mortals over the years to lend themselves to *many* sired Descendants. I had no shortage of men who could withstand her song, but the Weavers of Fate showed you were the only one who could truly love her for all she is."

Kellan scowls slightly. Confused as to how the whole damn world couldn't love her, yet silently glad he is the chosen one.

"There is a reason why the two of you have been brought together," Athena adds, "Without sounding indifferent to your happiness, I did not put you both on a collision course to meet each other for the fun of it. I am not Aphrodite. I'm not a lover, I'm a fighter."

To this Poseidon huffs a weak laugh.

"What is the reason?" Kellan ask, not sure if he wants to know the answer.

"To prevent a war," she says simply.

"A war?"

"Yes, and quite a substantial war at that," Athena says, an undeniable glint in her eyes at the thought of it, "A battle between mortal and magic which we could not allow to happen. We try not to intervene or meddle, but when we receive word that the River Styx would be bottlenecked with the number of corpses from both sides, well, we could not ignore it."

Swallowing hard, Kellan grates out, "Is this to do with Kestrel? All her scheming and attacks?"

"She was part of the problem, yes," Poseidon admits, "A rather large part. But this war has been brewing for years. Before you or Wren ever drew breath. Fixing the future began long ago in the past."

"We've known for a few decades now that Soleil would become...a problem. But thankfully the Weavers came to us almost twenty years ago saying they caught glimpses of the golden headed Descendant ruling Soleil. We naturally assumed your father would seize the island and you would inherit it, but once Lachlan reached the Lunar Lands, he married your mother and gave up his raiding days."

Athena's mild disappointment at Lachlan is palpable. A goddess of war would never understand giving up glory for something as trivial as marriage.

"When Lachlan suddenly died which was inconvenient, but it made way for you. But then Alistair decided to ruin our plan by stealing your siblings. Mortals are the ficklest of creatures at times," Poseidon sighs loudly, "That is when little Miss Optimistic here saw an opportunity. Athena fed you an omen dream after you prayed to her for days on end. She gifted you with a vision of my daughter. A syren to resolve all your woes."

"You were not meant to see her wings during the dreams," Athena admits, "That was a mistake on my behalf. The Weavers had shown me the outcome of the Kestrel battle and I let it slip. I was too excited at the possibilities."

"I don't understand. We defeated Kestrel. And now I rule over Soleil. There was no death," Kellan says, before remembering the gods would have had a prime view of everything, "Well, there was *minimal* death. Not enough to clog the Styx. So, whatever the Weavers envisioned has been defeated, right? It's all in the past?"

"In a way, yes. But in another way, no," Poseidon says, for once offering Kellan a kind sympathetic look, "Fate is as fickle as mortals it seems."

Athena nods, "I would suggest the course of action has been *changed* more so than *defeated*. But it would be easier to show you."

Between one breath and the next, three women appear. An elderly woman with hunched over shoulders is held upright by a middle-aged woman, whilst a girl of about sixteen fidgets beside them.

Kellan knew there was a strong resemblance between himself and Callum. Granted he never really saw it himself, but he had been told often enough to know it was true. But these women...

He had never seen any relatives look this similar. From under the large shawl they all share, he spots the same silver tresses, dark eyes, and slender bare feet across all the women. With so much ichor running through their bodies, their veins appear darker. These near black branches are a stark contrast to their ashen, almost grey skin. Like bare winter trees under undisturbed snow.

The trio do not appear to be goddesses, but they

most certainly are not mortal. Kellan does his best not to blanch as Athena and Poseidon offer a head bow to the women. Kellan didn't think the gods bowed to anyone.

It isn't until the women step towards him in unison that Kellan makes the connection. These women don't just look similar.... they move as one. They are one. One woman, the Weaver, in three separate stages of her life.

The Maiden. The Mother. The Crone.

Between their fingers, *her* fingers, are long, winding threads from the shawl draped over their shoulders. An array of threads intertwines and connect them all, yet the shawl does not seem frayed. The cloth is not shabby and unravelling as Kellan first assumed...it is unfinished.

"Your past cannot be unravelled," The Mother says to Kellan, gesturing towards the woollen strands within the Crone's hold. The strands are as twisted and knotted as the fingers which wield them.

Jerking her narrow chin towards the Maiden, she adds, "And your future depends on what you chose in the present."

The Maiden holds two threads in her constantly moving hands. She criss-crosses the threads, then straightens them. Ties them in a bow, only to loosen it immediately. Twists them between her thumbs. Over and over again. Always fidgeting, and staring off into the distance, as if she were watching the realms most interesting yet invisible play. It's exhausting just to watch her.

And somewhere in between the lock tight threads of the past and the chaotic cords of the future, stands the Mother. She holds her strings relatively straight but the small motions she does make sends the Maiden into a fresh wave of movement.

"I rarely show my Tapestry. My duty is to stitch the narrative of lives. I weave what has been, what I see and what will soon be. I do not design the pattern, nor can I cut certain strings," the Mother explains, "Do you understand, King?"

Thankful he does not have half as much ichor as the Weaver become him, he can manage a dishonest nod. Truthfully, he's never been more confused.

"To show my work before it is completely can alter its course entirely," the Mother continues, "But when I saw a hole forming in the fabric, I had no choice but to show the gods," the Mother says with palpable sorrow. She nods to Athena, who clears her throat and takes over.

"The Weaver came to me and showed me the war, the hole forming in the fabric as she put it. You won't need reminding how deep Alistair's hatred ran for you. You caught a glimpse of this when the Soleil princeling stole your siblings, but what you didn't see is the future we prevented. Alister was gathering troops. A collection of sailors and soldiers he called the Trojans. He planned to infiltrate your Kingdom and take seize power. You, your brother, and all your men fought back. It quickly turned into the War of the Moon and Sun. A bloody battle which only a handful survived."

Poseidon releases a weary exhale, and plants the end of the Trident into the mossy ground, "I may have been able to remove Kestrel's song in an attempt to quell her ambition, but I could not take away her hunting skills. Her innate ability to sniff out a weakness and dive on it. She was quite the creation."

"She was a monster," Kellan snaps.

"Monsters can still be exquisite," Poseidon says firmly, "But alas I digress. Kestrel, like her namesake, was a creature of prey. She would have sniffed out the war and been drawn to the bloodshed. Gathering any scraps of men she could, she would have used them for that wretched Luring Lullaby she created and then seized every isle in her wake. It would have been the end of mortals as we know it. No one would rival her."

"But Wren could? Wren *did*. She defeated Kestrel," Kellan argues.

To this Athena huffs, and gives a stern look to Poseidon, "Apparently not in this timeline."

He gives a warn growl to her, before admitting, "I seemed to have made a slight flaw when creating Wren. I crafted her to have less hauteur than her mother, but it seems self-doubt filled the void instead."

"She would never have risen up against her mother without belief in herself, without someone to show her she could," Athena offers with a small smile for Kellan, "He does not like to admit I was right but pairing you two worked out wonderfully. We managed to line up the sea queen and hateful princeling along the same trajectory. To kill two birds with one stone so to speak. You needed Wren and she needed you."

"But like I said, to *view* the Tapestry is to *change* the Tapestry," the Mother says, having never taken her eyes off Kellan, "Yes, this ill-Fate of men has been avoided, but the hole in the fabric has not been stitched fully shut. The hatred the princeling Alistair contained did not perish with him. Much like when he kidnapped your family, you have already seen the beginning of this thread."

"The murdered mermaid? The archer?" Kellan says, running a hand through his hair.

Athena gives a solemn sole nod, "With your help, we prevented the end of mortals. But now those very mortals who were saved are now threatening the very existence of magical creatures and everything associated with them. Including you."

"I will permit you to gaze upon the Tapestry," the Mother announces, presenting an inch-wide sliver of the thread between her thumbs, "If you're brave enough to look at it."

Before doubt or hesitation can creep in, Kellan draws a shaky breath before grasping the warm cord. And before he can exhale, the world around him turns black.

EIGHTEEN

pring-time rains drift across Soleil, covering the vast gardens in a fine mist. The high rising sun gleams through the vapour, splashing a faint rainbow across the bright sky.

Beneath the colourful arch, standing on the top step of the stony stairs, is a man who bears a resemblance to Fynbarr. He faces the lawn which is overflowing with sprouting blossoms and eager soldiers in equal measure.

"Good afternoon," he grins, holding up a letter to the crowd, "I've received more news from my nephew."

The crowd falls hush, but their excitement is still palpable.

"To my fellow Trojans.

I'm writing to you from my cell in the Lunar Lands, although to call it a cell would be a lie. The prisoner here

225

is rather opulent. I have my own lavatory, writing desk and a comfortable bed. I believe forcing me to reside in Galli's barrack would be better punishment."

A young guard amongst the crowd pipes up, "Oi! My room isn't that messy."

His comrades dissolve into laughter, giving the man slaps on the back.

With a wide grin, Fynbarr's uncle continues his reading, "*Most evenings Yarrow visits me under the watchful eye of Lunar sailors. Behind a closed door he pretends to beat and starve me, and I feign the wailing victim. We've become rather good faking our scuffles, although it's hard to cry out at the fake punches when I have a mouthful of fresh bread. Yarrow insists my cell door is always firmly shut. Little do the guards know it's to keep my unbruised and pudgy stature hidden. There is little fear of harm finding me unless I die of sheer boredom. I suspect you will receive this letter on the morning of your departure, so I wish you good luck.*

You need not fear the seas. Although I'm ashamed I failed in my duty to rid the sea-witch, I know our brothers in arms will succeed in dealing with her and the vermin isle. An added benefit to the change of plan, means that the demon-blooded usurper has also left with her. With only drunken brother ruling in his stead, us Trojans have never had a clearer view of the crown for our True Prince. We broke Callum once before we can easily do it again.

Yarrow has included various maps and schemes for you to revise on your journey. We both send our regards to the True Prince, and we'll be ready to fight when you arrive. You know the plan.

PS: There's a judge here by the name of Bevin. He's a man of tradition. His contempt for magic and women will make him a simple conquer. Winning him over for our cause will be an easy feat, and I believe he will sign off the marriage."

He's barely finished before the men burst into applause. A few loud, whooping whistles are released and excitement crackles through the air. Like wolves catching the scent of fresh blood upon the wind, they make haste towards the awaiting boats. It's time to hunt.

As the crowd dissipates, Fynbarr's uncle trots down the steps and lightly bows towards the only man who isn't moving. The so called 'True Prince'.

"I feel as if I am the only one who doesn't know the plan," the man sighs, running a hand through his cloud grey hair. Though he is a similar age to Kellan, his receding hairline, and dull shade tresses make him appear older. Much older. Yet something about his insipid appearance is familiar. Nostalgic almost.

"You're our future ruler and soon to be groom. I think you have enough on your plate, True Prince."

The Prince shudders at the word groom, "I would much rather be fighting with the rest of you than having to marry a mere child. Especially one who has the same demon-blood as her brothers."

"The marriage will only be a cert of paper for the first few years. You don't even have to see her. We can carry out the ceremony by proxy if you prefer. As long as we have her in our hold, we have little use for her until she's old enough to secure an heir and strengthen your claim to the throne."

"My claim to the throne is already strong enough," the Prince spits, "My pedigree is greatly superior to that trespassing orphan who stole Alistair's crown. He stole my cousin's whole bloody head!"

The vision begins to fade as anger builds within Kellan's body, drawing him back into the real world.

Alistair's cousin.

He should have known by the unremarkable face. A temperament peppered with hatred, and a face smeared with dullness are family traits after all.

"We will take back what he took from us and so much more, but your control of Aveen is a critical part of this plan. Besides, if she's anything like her whore of a mother, she'll be too weak to survive childbirth anyway. Perhaps she'll die after giving you an heir," Fynbarr's uncle suggests.

There's a brief pause before Kellan hears the Prince's laughter ringing through the darkness, "Well wouldn't that be most convenient."

A feral snarl erupts from Kellan's lip, but he does not release the thread.

"You've seen enough, Kellan." Athena's voice warns in the background.

With the premonition dissolving back into reality, the lawns of Soleil morph into the meadow of Eastern Acropolis once more.

"Not yet," Kellan demands, jerking his hands further up the thread. Squeezing his eyelids shut as he wills himself to see more of the living nightmare.

He feeds the cord through his calloused palms, inching his way closer to the Maiden. Manic movements threaten the tug the thread from his grip.

The closer he gets to her, the more chaotic the visions become. Chopping and changing faster than his mortal mind can understand, but he refuses to give up.

Ignoring the protests around him, Kellan flings himself into the obis once more.

Bursting through the darkness, a stampede of people bolt past Kellan. A crowd of terrified citizens bottleneck into the winding alleys of the Crescent Cove. There is no bowing and scraping before him. Even with their widened eyes they do not see their King. They only see fleet full of soldiers disembarking in the bay. The arrows darkening the skies. The blood flowing between the cobbles.

Blind with panic, a teenage girl barrels straight into Kellan as she sprints for higher ground. As he steadies his footing the ground beneath him changes. Gone are the blood-stained cobbles.

Under his boots, Kellan finds the wooden floors of the West Wing hall. And under his jugular he finds a blade.

"I told you," the knife-wielder spits, slurring his words as he inches closer to Kellan, "I told you one bad apple can lead to an orchard of rot."

"Callum," Kellan says gently, raising his empty hands to either side of his head, "I had no idea this would happen-

"But I did! I knew what those bastards were like and I *warned* you, but you never listen to me," Callum growls, the stench of rum leaking from his mouth.

Twisting the knife-tip further into his brothers'

neck, Callum growls, "My husband is dead because of you."

"Fletcher?"

Fletcher.

The very thought of him changes the vision once more. Now bobbing in his rowboat, Kellan sees the *Iseult* warship defending their seas. Standing at the helm is Fletcher, with young Arthur right beside him. Across the waters, positioning the starboard side of their boat to face us is the Soleil fleet.

As Master of the Sails, Fletcher must know what is coming, but it's too late to react. He winces as a dull *thud* echoes from the enemy ship. Seconds later a cannon soars into the gut of their vessel.

Shrieks and splinters erupt.

As a deluge of seawater begins to rush, Fletcher gives the order for his sailors to escape on the rowboat.

With no time to untie them, Fletcher swings an axe through the ropes which secure the rowboat to the main vessel. As the boat freely drops, he begins ordering sailors to leap overboard.

As the fling themselves over, the second cannon Lands. The blow almost halves the boat, sending debris scattering.

With no time to spare, Fletcher scrambles onto the ledge, glancing around to find Arthur. And that's when Kellan see's the sailor too. Pinned to the deck beneath the shattered mast pole.

Roars intensify all around. Fletcher cries in disbelief. Arthur weeps from pain. And the sailors plead with their Master to leave with them.

Fletcher takes one look at Arthur, another at the Soleil ship reloading, and shakes his head, "No, I'm the captain. If I cannot get everyone off, I will not leave."

"But sir-"

"Leave!"

The sailors reluctantly begin rowing. Fletcher drops to the deck, clasping Arthur's hand as the waters rise around them.

As another iron ball is loaded, Kellan closes his eyes, unable to watch the final blow.

A deafening sound fills Kellan's ear, but it is not the *thud* of before. It's a crack. It's a catapult, Kellan realising as he opens his eyes once more.

Burning barrels soar through the air, exploding into balls of flame on impact as they collide into the coastline. The Seven Spikes coastline. And in between the rocky edge and burning material is Wren.

"No," Kellan sobs breathlessly into the real world. He faintly hears someone calls him back, but he's too far gone. He cannot pull his eyes away from her. At the edge of her cliff, facing the wind and incoming fleet, Wren sings with all her being.

He'd seen her lure a dozen times, but Kellan had never seen this. This war-song, this warning, is not to lure the Soleil men, but to drive them away.

Fýge i chatheí.

Leave or perish.

Granted Kellan knows little of syren songs, but from the blood and ichor dripping from Wren's ears and nose, he gathers repelling is more strenuous than luring.

The Queen maintains an invisible bubble around her citizens, whilst summoning a wave to quell the flames around her. Centaurs file in around her, dressed in fighting leathers and armed to the hilt. They flank her sides, waiting to step in when her bubble bursts. But Kellan knows Wren.

She won't give up easily. She won't give up until it's too late. As Wren collapses onto her knees, Kellan sags onto his.

Dew damp grass soaks through his trousers, but he cannot move. Not when the weight of suffering keeps him grounded.

Grief and mourning builds in his chest. His heart physically aches, as if it's constricting away from all the pain. And just when he his soul cannot suffer anymore another vision begins to materialise.

Kellan braces for another onslaught of sorrow, but this time silence fills his ears instead of screams. He opens his eyes to find himself staring at an oil painting. The setting sun glows through the stain glassed window, splattering colourful squares across the artwork.

Every inch is painted to perfection, but the smiling face in the centre of the canvas captivates Kellan the most. Those eyes which seem familiar yet impossible hold his gaze for so long, his eyes begin to burn with the need to blink. There is no way. How did the artist capture this portrait of a person who is not alive-

Kellan is blown backwards.

"ENOUGH!" Poseidon barks, having shouldered him onto the ground, "Your habit of taking what you wish will not extent to the Tapestry."

The Maiden cries quietly as her hands and fingers flail, trying to keep up with Fate. To see the Tapestry is to change the Tapestry, and Kellan had seen far too much.

"How much of that is set to happen? How far into the future is this?" Kellan asks the Weavers, all of them, each of them, as he scrambles to his feet, "How far?"

The Mother glances to the gods before answering.

"On the current trajectory, the Soleil's set sail on the next new moon."

"No," Kellan protests breathlessly. Bile races into his throat. It's an effort to not vomit on the women's feet, "No, that's too soon. I can't.... What the Hel am I meant to do? Show me that part!"

"You will see no more," Poseidon booms, stepping closer to Kellan again.

But god's presence does nothing to batten down Kellan's rage. And in either the bravest or stupidest move of his life, the young King squares up to the ancient god. Stubbing his worn boots against the Olympian's sandals, the two go toe-to-toe.

"Do. Something." Kellan spits the demand through grated teeth. His heartbeat pulsating behind his ears and out through his jaw, "That future is a kaleidoscope of despair and death. It cannot be allowed to happen."

"Not every element is guaranteed to happen," the Mother says quietly, her voice sounding weary with exhaustion, "Not yet anyway."

The small mercy does little to ease the tension which ripples through the meadow.

"We have done all we can. The game is already in motion, though the outcome has yet to be seen," Poseidon says flatly, his eyes boring into Kellan's, reminding him of who he is talking to.

"*Game?*" Kellan rumbles, causing Athena to quickly step in between the two men.

"I think what my Uncle means is, if this were a game, we cannot change the players nor the rules, Kellan. There is a natural order to the realms and a larger ripple effect which we do not have time to explain to you," Athena says in a stern tone.

Kellan looks past Athena's shoulder towards the sea. With emotion catching in his throat asks, "Will you at least tell me where she is? My wife."

Poseidon holds Kellan's gaze for a beat, before sighing and casting a quick glance in every direction.

"Wren is upon the seas," he says simply, as if he could see her, as if the entire world was just outside a personal window which mortals cannot see.

A sliver of relief allows Kellan to ease his shoulder a fraction. At least Wren is in her element, and therefore somewhat safe. For now.

Shaking his head, he turns on his heel to leave.

"I heard your wish by the way," Athena adds, halting Kellan mid-stride, "The one you made on your birthday?"

"What about it?"

"I scoffed at the idea originally," Poseidon scoffs as he chimes in once more, "But then Wren requested the same desire. I do not want your already inflated ego to misconstrued what I'm about to say for genuine acceptance or admiration, but I'm beginning to see that perhaps Athena had a point. Perhaps you are worthy of being Wren's equal after all."

Kellan parts his taut lips to say something snarky, but Athena catches his eyes and silently begs him to listen. It's the face same Iseult often gave Kellan as a child when he's temper flared up against his father. The familiarity of the expression is enough to diffuse him. Slightly.

"I already told you I cannot change this game of war, nor can I meddle with its outcome, but perhaps I can even the playing field and at least give you a fighting chance. Ares granted you a gift before, I cannot see why it would be against the natural order for me to do the same."

Kellan arches a golden eyebrow. His fury twisting into frustration and confusion.

The Maiden begins frantically moving her hands once more. As her crazed fingers dance with the threads until even the Mother begins to make movements. Something big is about to happen. And soon.

More gods in the form of wildlife begin to descend across the meadow. Whatever is about to happen is intriguing enough to whet the interest of the gods.

"Try not to appear so confused, boy. You're about to get everything you wished for," Poseidon says.

The god hoists his hefty Trident upwards with ease, as if it weighed no more than a blade of straw.

Athena, who has witness centuries of bloodshed and carnage, subtly drops her gaze. Her desire to not see what's about to happen sets Kellan's heart racing.

"If you wish to survive, I suggest you hold still," Poseidon warns.

And before Kellan can ask what the Hel is going on, the Trident is lunged straight through his flesh.

NINETEEN

Wren

 ven as the ichor faded from his veins, Pip had told me everything. He answered every question and spared no detail. His honestly was both a blessing and a curse.

Now, I know every aspect of what those 'Trojans' have planned. The True Prince. Yarrow. Eliminating all magic. Marrying Aveen to a man double her age.

Shuddering, I grip the side of the boat until my knuckles turn white. An urge to sing, to scream, to shout any sort of song to get us to the Lunar Lands quicker, looms in my core once more.

But I cannot. Mainly because there are mortals onboard who I do not wish to turn into lured zombies.

Centaurs are warriors, not sailors, so Arthur's mortal presence was very much required aboard otherwise we would have never left the dock.

And it turns out Nessa determination is rather unbreakable when she decides she wants to do something. Refusing to wait on Seven Spikes whilst I gathered a crew to leave, Nessa insisted she knew castle back passages and Aveen's schedule better than anyone. She made herself a key part of this operation. Pip now goes wherever Arthur and Nessa go, so there was no chance of him staying behind with the harpies.

But even if I were alone and free to use my magic to lure a powerful bow wave to propel me towards the isle, I doubt I'd be able to.

Between the injuries which feel like a lifetime ago and the worry which has plagued me every day since my body is beyond exhausted.

Releasing both a weary sigh and my grip of the boat, I lean forward and let my hand drape towards the water. The wind and currents might be on our side, but time is not. On and off over the past four days, I've tried drip-feeding my power into the waves. I kept the amount small, to not harm my travel companions or myself, but even this gentle trickle of magic is depleting my already low levels of ichor.

The constant *whoosh* of waves morphs into a

whisper crying *rush, rush* that apparently no one else hears.

"You really shouldn't be doing that," Nessa says softly, materialising out of thin air.

Glancing over my shoulder, I shoot her a hardened look and keep my fingers skimming the water, "Kellan always jokes how you should don a bell to stop you creeping up on people."

Just saying his name causes an ache between my lungs. I shake my head and plunge my hand further into the cold waves.

She offers a small, sympathetic smile, "How about I promise to wear any hideous jingle-jangle bracelet of your choice if you promise to stop hurting yourself in this way?"

As tempting as dragging Nessa around the agora to find the clunkiest, noisiest jewellery possible sounds, I turn my gaze back to the sea, "I can't. I have to do something to help, to get there faster. If I don't get there in time...."

My voice trails away with the sea breeze. I guess no one really knows for sure what will happen if I arrive after the Trojans. Premonitions are reserved for the Weavers and gods, but my imagination can paint a picture.

One that at best depicts Callum yet again being

tortured into giving these brutes whatever they want. And at worse...well, the self-preservation part of my mind won't let me envision that. When we arrived tomorrow morning, I'll have my answer.

"We have to stay together. So, unless you're strong enough to propel the entire trio, there is no point in you draining yourself for nothing," Nessa says, giving a sweeping gesture towards the boats on either side of us.

We set sail in a V-formation, with this vessel taking the charge and boats carrying six centaurs each flanking our rearing.

The colts are warriors, not sailors. The boats stay close, with Arthur doing his best to captain three boats from one helm. He shouts orders and direction as needed. This trip was meant to be a break for him, an apology and a thank you for everything he's done yet it somehow became yet another task.

"Do not question my strength," I mutter at her.

"I'm reminding you to take care of yourself. To eat. To drink. To sleep. All important things which you have done none of since we left Seven Spikes. I'm simply saying what the King would say if he were here."

Her words hang in the air.

I retreat my hand from the salt water and let it hang by my side, dripping onto the deck. I peer past

Nessa's shoulder to Aengus.

He is the only Centaur aboard this ship for the simple reason he refused to leave my side. I knew he would defend me against Nessa's tone. With a silent eyebrow raise, I call on him to speak.

"I find myself agreeing with Nessa, your Majesty," Aengus says, clearing his throat, "A few hours rest can only be beneficial to you and your abilities."

My jaw flops open like a hooked coy.

Huh. I never thought I'd see the day where Aengus Blackhock and Nessa Shay team up to defend my welfare.

In the background, Pip busies himself with winding up a length of rope which doesn't need tidying, whilst Arthur buries his gaze into the wooden wheel beneath his hands. Their silent agreement is deafening.

The hefty sigh I release leaves me feeling empty, "Fine. I'll nap. But just for one hour, and I demand to be immediately woken up if anything changes. Understood?"

Once I've received their assurance, I firmly nod before turning on my heel and pace towards the cabin, keeping my head held high.

It isn't until the cabin door is shut behind me, that I sag into the bed which still holds Kellan's scent and sob for most of the hour.

Nessa nor Aengus stuck to their word of waking me. My weeping leeched away whatever energy I had left, and unbeknownst to me, I'd succumb to sleep. For hours.

I awake alone, in the dark and cold cabin, with hunger making my stomach feel like it's freshly glued to my spine.

Swinging my stiff legs free from the sheets, I set them onto the bare timbers and stiffly hobble as I begin my hunt for food. The sleep might have been needed, but all my aching muscles have seized up with the lack of movement.

As I hobble onto the silent and still deck, the only movement and rustling comes from Aengus who unfolds his front legs as he goes to rise from his reclined position.

Waving away his gesture, I shake my head, "No, please. Just rest."

He relaxes by barely a fraction, shifting his weight and rubbing his bleary eyes with the back of his hand. "Thank you, your Majesty. Truth be told, there's a chance I would accidentally trodden on you if I tried to stand right now. My legs aren't used to the sea and have not been this wobbly since I Changed."

"How long has it been since you Changed? Like a hundred years?" I ask.

Centaurs are born in their human form and remain that way until the age of about ten. Like Lycanthropes or Shapeshifters, Centaurs turn under the glow of a full moon. Once they Change into their equine form, they remain that way for the rest of their life. To ensure the continuation of their herd and heritage, they have the ability under a full moon to return to the mortal state for that night only. I'd seen some of the colts Change to their male form to play football or take a pretty fae dancing, but come to think of it, I'd never seen Aengus on two legs.

Aengus release a low but deep laugh, throwing a quick glance to the barrel beside him where I spot Nessa fast asleep.

Lowering his tone, he answers, "Although I feel that old at times, no, your Majesty. This autumn will mark fifteen years since my Change."

I nod before jerking my chin towards Nessa. Wrapped up in her woollen blanket, with her thumb nestled between the pages of a book, she looks like she dozed off in front of a fire, not on the damp deck of a ship sailing towards a battle, "Why is she not in her cabin?"

Aengus's souring face tells me he asked her the same thing.

"I don't know Ms Shay well, but from the little I've learnt of her, she's the only person in the realm whose helpfulness is a burden. With the bunk in the cabin being too narrow for me, I came out here to rest awhile. She refused to leave me alone. She was worried you would skin me alive for not awaking you when you wanted. I don't understand why she thinks her presence will offer protection. She fell asleep before I did."

Biting back a grin, I make my way towards the food crate, whispering loudly, "Remember *she* is the one who attacked Fynbarr. With a mere scarf and a stone no less. And then single-handily moved the attacker from the woods to the barracks."

"If it weren't coming out of a syren's mouth I would not believe it," Aengus mutters, watching Nessa's rhythmical breathing.

Selecting an apple from the crate, I bounce it between my hands and look out towards the dark, endless stretch of sea before me.

I keep my eyes locked onto the sliver of the ocean where the Lunar Lands outline will loom in a few hours. But for now, there is nothing. No inclination of what may lie ahead. No telling what we will see as we arrive with the dawn light.

"What if we're too late?" I quietly ask myself, the sea, and Aengus. With Yarrow and only gods know who else already within the walls of the Lunar Lands, there's no telling how much damage has been done already.

"It's never too late to teach traitors a lesson," Aengus says sternly, not bothering to whisper, "And that's what they are, *traitors*, make no bones about it. Even before Kellan made you their Queen, you deserved the utmost respect from them, yet they riddled you with arrows. This band of fools have appointed themselves 'Trojans', but come tomorrow they will be known as 'Deceased.'"

"I'm incredibly grateful to have you on my side Aengus, I don't think I could do this without-"

My sentence is hindered by the primal scream erupting from my lips.

Pain explodes within my chest as I drop to my knees with a bone-crunching force.

Aengus scrambles to his hooves in an instant, bellowing for back-up. His wide eyes scan the horizon and skies for threats.

But there are no enemy vessels. No archers. Nothing.

The ships flanking either side somehow tuck in

even closer, until we're sailing abreast, yet their shelter offers me no protection from the pain.

Unable to hold myself upright, I collapse from my kneeling position onto my side.

Nessa half-leaps, half-crawls her way across the deck. Still swaddled in her blanket, she screams, "Sweet Zeus! What's wrong?"

Her shaking hands uncurl my contorting body, her terrified eyes glancing over every part of me looking for injury.

She wrestles the apple from my stiff grip, "You didn't even take a bite, so it can't be poison."

Nessa chucks away the uneaten fruit, which rolls across the deck. Aengus stomps it into a pulp with his rear hoof, just to be sure.

I wish it were poison coursing through my veins.

Hel, I even wish I were the crushed apple. Maybe a stampede of hooves could stomp out this wildfire ripping through me.

My lungs are solid timber, being cleaved in half by a rusted axe. Prised apart, fibre by fibre, only to be fed to the growing inferno within me.

Yelling, I rip at my chest, clawing at my tunic until the fabric gives way to my skin. My fingertips grow warm as my own blood and ichor saturate them.

Aengus lurches forward, grabbing my wrists with

one hand, "Quit it! What's wrong, your Majesty? Speak to us!"

I try to answer him, I do, but drawing in breath to speak only fans the flames within me.

Placing the back of her hand against my clammy forehead, Nessa yelps instantly and whips her hand back, "Gods above, she's burning up. Badly."

She demands a pail of water over her shoulder. Arthur answers her plea, skidding onto his knees, with a bucket of icy water and a strip of cloth.

After dunking the rag, he slaps it onto my forehead without sparing a second to wring out the excess droplets. Granted I could be feverish at this stage, but I swear I hear it *hiss* as it hits my skin.

"Is that...." Arthur's voice trails off.

"Steam." Aengus confirms.

Nessa flings the damp rag aside and instead dumps the pail onto the planks by the shoulders. The water runs down the timbers beneath me, drenching my back. Within seconds, I transform it into a cloud of mist.

"I've seen her in a bad way more often than I'd like, but never anything like this. Except maybe when Kellan performed the ritual of Meraki, but that was a broken binding vow!" Nessa cries.

Hearing Kellan's name sets off my sobbing once

more, though he's been the only thing on my mind since dropping to the deck.

No. It cannot be true. I refuse to believe it.

Even as my ichor bubbles within my veins, threatening to evaporate me until I'm nothing more than a husk, I cannot believe it.

Aengus inelegantly lowers himself onto bent front legs and leans close to me. Muttering an apology, he presses his big palm between my breasts where I scraped my skin apart with my nails. He jerks his chin towards a hanging lantern by the cabin door, and once again Arthur wordlessly follows orders.

Using the glow of candlelight, Aengus examines my blood which inks his hands as dark as the tattoos with mark his shoulders and torso.

Arthur gasps, "Why...Why is her blood black?"

"It's not her blood." Aengus corrects sombrely, swallowing hard, "It's her ichor- and it's charred. But only one thing could scorch magic like this. I think Nessa might have been onto something when she mentioned a broken-"

"No." I choke out through my bone-dry throat, my ears unable to hear the words *binding vow* when it's already echoing through my mind, "It has to be something else."

Aengus moves closer, lightly squeezing my shoulder

with his stained hand, "Well, do you have any other outstanding oaths at the moment?"

Nessa and Arthur look to each other, then me. Confusion and worry dances across their faces in the dim light.

I have no other oaths.

I am bound to no one else.

Just to him. Just Kellan.

Unable to form the words, I shake my head.

Aengus keeps his tone low as if it will stop the others hearing, "And when you enacted Kairos, when ye took that vow, did you speak the mortal words?"

I swear to honour and defend.

I vow to love you in this life until you take your last breath, and then I'll find you in the next life.

Until you take your last breath.

Perhaps the oath I had taken was more mortal than I ever realised.

The overwhelming urge to scream no, to deny it and fight anyone who suggested otherwise holds off just long enough for me to nod.

Aengus winces, and then carefully pulls me into his solid frame.

"I'm so sorry, Wren."

Wren, not *Your Majesty*. Gods, it must be true.

"What's going on?" Nessa asks Aengus as he

carefully holds me out at arm's length.

His eyes find mine, and any cobweb of denial that survived the inferno of my soul are blown away as Aengus gently says, "I believe King Kellan has passed into the after-life."

TWENTY

he journey I'd been trying to speed up, is now ending too soon. I'd spent so long staring overboard that when I eventually drag my bleary eyes up, dawn is breaking. Apparently, the sun will still rise today, though I don't know how. I don't understand how the world has the nerve to simply carry on as nothing happened.

The subtle lifting of my head catches Nessa's attention. Sitting side by side with our faces to the sea mist, we have not moved or spoken for over two hours.

Salt stains mark our cheeks, a mixture of sea and tears. She wordlessly offers me the water canister she clutches between her hands. And when I decline, she doesn't push it.

No one has asked me to eat, drink or rest since my

insides caught fire. They know I'm not here, not really.

Physically, maybe, but I think whatever is left of my shredded soul slipped into the sea whilst I was staring at it. It drifted to the bottom of the seabed just to sit in the quiet a little while, to not have to worry about the arduous act of breathing.

Once my ichor had frazzled itself to the point of exhaustion, it settled. The burning which ripped through my chest has been replaced with a sense of hollowness, as if I am a vacant shell.

Now I feel no pain. I feel nothing except unanchored.

Adrift.

Off course.

I've lived without Kellan before, for seventeen years prior to knowing him and the weeks spent apart thereafter. We have been separated by seas and islands, by duty and thrones, but even when days passed without a new letter arriving from him, I never truly felt alone. Knowing he was somewhere, doing something, or talking to someone was enough. But now...

Now I don't even know where his body is.

"I don't even know where to.... retrieve him," I whisper aloud, my voice hoarse and cracking, "I don't know if the gods punished him on Eastern Acropolis, or did he even make it that far? What it his body is in the seas?"

To this Nessa pales further. Her silent tears begin once more, though I'm not sure they ever stopped.

Aengus remains at the helm where he's been since Arthur slumped onto a barrel, but his deep voice drifts across the deck, "When this is over, you say the word and we'll find him, your Majesty. The syrens and merfolk can take the seas, and I'll scour every corner of the realms until our King is brought home."

Not trusting myself to speak, I nod courtly and bite the inside of my lip as if to physically hold myself together. The tang of copper coats my tongue as my lower lip bleeds.

The crew around me fall silent once more, and in quietness my mind speaks volumes. A small but growing part of me wishes I had never fled the Queendom to escape Kestrel. A sadistic sliver of my soul wishes I was still at my mother's mercy, and that Kellan had never caught me in his damn net. Granted if I still lived under the rule and fear of my mother, my existence would be sombre and desolate and horrid, but I would have never known any better.

But knowing love and happiness and hope only to lose it is the greatest torment of all.

Grief warps time more than the Water World, and

what could have been five minutes or two hours later, Aengus clears his throat once more, "Your Majesty."

Dragging my bloodshot eyes upwards, I spot the dark jagged rock of Meteoroid Spit ahead of us. The dense archipelago is the most northern part of the Lunar Lands, with its two sea pillars acting like natural gates into the bay. Except the rocky arch which normally welcomes us is barricaded.

Two warships stationed stern-to-stern block the sea gateway. Waves which funnel into the opening, force the sterns of the boats to repeatedly smack into each other, whereas their bows scrape against the sharp shale on either side.

Another hour or two of this, and these vessels will be heavily damaged and unlikely to be fit to use. But then again, I doubt their passenger's intent to retreat home anytime soon.

"Let me guess," I say on the exhale of a weary sigh, "More Soleil vessels?"

Arthur slumps off his barrel and crosses the deck to stand between Nessa and me. His sober curse is his only confirmation. He quickly returns to the helm, unfurling a map and flipping open a compass as he tries to find another route into the bay.

"You know, my patience for hearing the word '*Soleil*' is starting to wear really fucking thin," I admit, turning my back on the sea, facing the deck for the first time all morning.

Young Pip offers me a small smile before disappearing back to his cabin with half a loaf of bread in hand.

Gods above I forgot he was even onboard. I doubt my writhing and screaming, followed by this subsequent zombie state is aiding his fear of non-humans much.

"You're the Queen of *that* island, you can change its name if you wish," Nessa offers, as she pulls her hair over one shoulder and begins braiding it.

My own wind-swept wild mess of mane should be braided out of my face as well, but I promised myself Dove would be the last person to plait my hair. A stupid promise made by a stupid girl who thought she would only grieve one person in her life.

"I was a mayfly Queen. I had my day. And it's over now before it's even begun."

"Of course you're still our Queen?" Arthur protests, glancing up from the map, "I doubt Prince Callum will have objections and-

"Not a word of this to Callum. And no-one utters a word about Kellan either, I mean it." My voice hitching a little as I say his name, "Callum isn't to hear about his brother until I can guarantee the safety of his sister."

Silent nods are the only reply I receive.

Movement begins to stir between the ships. The centaurs on the accompanying boats start strapping up their leathers and weapons.

Tarlock, a dappled grey colt, releases a low whistle to snag Aengus' attention before he tosses a set of leathers over the narrow gap between our vessels.

"I brought a spare," Tarlock says, jerking his chin towards me, "It should fit you, your Majesty."

Aengus catches the protective vest with one hand and then hands it to me, "You will not need this, but..."

"But I'm cursed with shit-luck?" I finished for him, grabbing the well-worn, softened leathers.

He gives a stiff nod, trying his best not to wince as I withdraw my blade and begin hacking two slits for my wings.

With Nessa's help, I wiggle my way into the snug vest and fasten the arm straps. Though Tarlock and I are similar in height, our body shapes are completely different. His leathers fit a few inches loose around my stomach yet it clings to my chest. I thought the pressure would irritate me, or feel restrictive, but it's a blessing in disguise.

It's almost tight enough to hold me together and stop me unravelling. *Almost.*

Rolling up the map, Arthur clicks his tongue, "I found another route in, but we would have to deviate now. We can take a south-easterly approach, by-passing the blockade at Meteoroid Spit, and enter through the Star Spike passage instead. It's an easy-to-navigate route, but the detour would take hours. We probably arrive close to sunset."

"But we don't have hours," I growl, tilting my face towards the sky, squinting at the white sun, "You're really going to make this as difficult as possible, aren't you Poseidon? Alright fine, we'll climb."

"Climb?" Arthur asks, following my gaze towards the skies as if an invisible ladder where before us, "Climb where?"

"The lower rocks of the Meteorite Spit. We'll make our way up, and then use the rope bridges to get across to the mainland."

So many arguments rush to Arthur's lips that he physically chokes for a second. Knocking his chest to clear a cough, he splutters, "I...I *really* would not recommend that, your Majesty,"

"Well, no one with eyes would bloody '*recommend it*' but do we have another option? No. So why not use what we have? This armada is brimming with hooves and wings, we might as well use 'em. Pip is frightfully light so Tarlock can bear his weight. Diarmuid can carry you up, Arthur. And Nessa can go with Aengus."

I cross my arms the way I'd seen Kellan do it a hundred times. A clear signal that this is not up for discussion so do not even try.

Nessa offers her most unconvincing 'Of course' to date, and Arthur mutters "Steady as she goes" as he realigns the ship to direct us towards the chaos.

TWENTY-ONE

 edging the anchor into a fissure within the dark rock helps the boat stay flush against the cliff. The climb is as steep as it can be without being completely sheer.

Craning my neck to see the summit, I swallow hard, "Ugh. Maybe we should try to find another way. Arthur is right, this is a stupid idea."

"No one is disagreeing with you or Arthur, but as you said, we don't have a lot of other options, your Majesty," Aengus says firmly, offering his outstretched hand to Nessa.

A loud explosion sounds.

It echoes across the cliff wall, loosening some smaller rocks and clumps of moss.

"Was that a canon?" I ask, brushing fallen dirt off my arms.

Arthur swallows hard as he helps Pip mount up, "I believe so."

"No time to waste then," Aengus offers, shaking his hand towards Nessa once more. She tentatively takes his palm and is immediately swung onto his solid back. Stretching his arms back on either side, he grasps her calves and tugs her towards where his mortal side blends into the dark coat of his withers, "Closer. I don't need you falling off halfway and pulling me off the cliff with you."

"But there are no reins for me to grip?" Her empty hands splaying in a questioning fashion.

"Bridles are for horses, Ms Shay." He growls, reaching back for her arms this time. He wraps them around his torso, and with a tight squeeze clasps her hands together, "Now, lean forward and hold on."

Nessa yelps as he lurches into a canter. She presses her forehead against his back and squeezes her eyes shut as they zig-zag their way up through the craggy pillars and loose stones.

With a colossal stride, he bounds onto the grassy overhang above, kicking up a spray of dirt and alpine flora in his wake. As they land on the top of the cliff edge, clumps of earth come away as his hooves scramble for better footing.

"Did you track my path?" Aengus hollers to the

other centaurs, his breath labouring, "Canter as far as that thicket of wisteria, then leap fast. But be careful of the edging, it comes away under hoof."

Nessa, visibly flustered even from down here, leans forward to mutter something in his ear. He throws a look over his shoulder and the two have a silent stare off for a moment.

"Alright, fine, apparently it's not wisteria- it's rockcress. Ms Shay is worried you would somehow get confused and therefore lost on the side of a cliff," Aengus sighs, with Nessa nodding approvingly from his back, "Tarlock you're next, then Diarmuid followed by the rest of the herd. Your Majesty, I think you should see this."

I throw a silent glance to the rest of my crew. My eyes begging them to be careful. Tarlock gives me a nod and encourages Pip to hang on.

As they begin their ascent, so do I. Springing from bent knees I soar into the sky, hugging the rock front as I propel myself upward. Nothing but black rock and clumps of moss fills my vision until I burst above the coastline- and that's when I see it.

Hundreds of citizens fleeing towards us. The rope bridges bounce violently as a surge of people pile across them. The ropes groaning under the strain.

As they clear the main bridge, they begin piling

onto the open grounds of Meteorite Spit.

A bell chimes as Ludwig weaves his way through the crowd, "Keep going! Don't stop until we reach Star Spike!"

"Ludwig!" I cry over the throng of terrified people, "What the Hel is happening?"

Ducking and diving, he makes his way over to us, taking no time to glance at the steady stream of centaurs appearing over the cliff edge. Pip vaults off Tarlock the second they land on solid ground.

"Prince Callum ordered an evacuation. Only sailors and guards remain," he explains between heaving breaths, "The whole town is being captured. There's a Soleil man calling himself the True Prince and people called Trojans that-"

"Oh, I've heard of them, don't worry," I interject. I beckon Pip forward with a finger wag, "Go with Ludwig. He's not a creature of magic, or from Soleil so you've no need to worry about him. Stay with him until someone comes to get you later."

Ludwig nods eagerly, grabbing Pip's slender hand and tugging him along as he takes off running again.

Pip's wide, brown eyes latch onto Nessa and Arthur for reassurance as he's pulled away, but they're too busy gawking at the pandemonium before us.

The bay is crammed full of Soleil boats displaying

armed and ready canons. Even with their sails lowered, the old sigil they don is visible. The crest from before Kellan's rule. As if he never existed.

Swallowing the rising anger and bile in my throat, I scan the town below. By the dock, I spot Callum directing sailors in one direction and civilians in another.

I take flight once more, soaring over the heads of those fleeing.

"Clear the bridge," I shout, swooping low enough for them to hear my order, "Make way for my cavalry!"

Obedience or sheer fear locks the knees of those running for their lives just long enough for my crew to burst through. A thunderous rapture of hooves follows in my wake as we storm towards town.

Like salmon swimming upstream, we fight our way against the current of people. As I near the town, those fleeing below me dwindles to the last dozen or so.

"When you cross the bridges, burn them behind you," I shout to the stragglers, knowing it's the quickest way to keep them out of Trojan reach.

Hearing the charge of hooves heading his way, Callum snaps his neck up to find me landing beside him.

My boots have barely touched the cobbles before

he lifts me off my feet with his back-slapping embrace.

"Gods am I glad to see you," Callum says breathlessly, squeezing me tightly into what I think is our first ever hug, "When I woke up Ludwig was ringing the bell, boats were arriving, and I had no idea what the Hel was going on. By the time I got to the dock, they had already barricaded the bay. That's when I spotted one of your song-shells on the beach. I almost didn't open it because I thought it could be another mushy love note to Kellan. But it wasn't. Your warning gave me enough time to get people out. And you came, and you brought...friends."

He releases me for his grip, giving a nod of appreciation to those behind me. His golden brow arching slightly as he spots Nessa dismounting Aengus.

"I thought we could use the back-up," I offer without hearing the words I say. Not when my mind is so pre-occupied with studying Callum's face. I don't know if it's a blessing or a curse how closely the brothers resemble each other.

"Back-up is most certainty needed. But what I need most is Kellan so I can say a big fat "*I told you so*" about Yarrow," Callum says flatly, his eyes scanning those behind me, "Where is Kell?"

"Fate has taken him a different route." I say the response I've been rehearsing since dawn without pausing to draw breath.

"He'll arrive soon," Nessa lies effortlessly, stepping forward and adding, "Did you send Aveen across the bridge? Have my mother and sisters been evacuated too?"

"I was surprised your mother didn't stay and offer one of ye for this bastard to marry instead," Callum offers with a sarcastic smirk, "But yes, they all got across safety, as did your parents, Arthur. And as for Aveen, I kept her closer to home. She's absolutely terrified."

"Well, where is she?" I ask.

"No offence *Little Miss Truthful*, but I think you *not* knowing is the safest thing for her," Callum says, "But Nessa, could you go to her? Aveen is petrified about being kidnapped again and I doubt the eight guards around her are much comfort."

"Of course," Nessa nods, moving closer to Callum and offering her ear from his to whisper the Princess's location.

I open my mouth to protest how ridiculous this is, but Callum has a point. If only he knew the truths I'm fighting to keep buried within. I'm one forced question away from choking out that his brother is dead, so I'm hardly trustworthy with information about his sister.

"...And make sure you make your presence known

as you approach. The guards are heavily armed, trigger happy and on edge," Callum finishes in a normal tone.

Nessa takes a half step to jog away, but Aengus lightly grabs her wrist.

Removing a mini-canon ball on a chain and stick from his hip, he wraps her hands around it, "Take my flail. You just swing it. Think of this as a new and improved scarf and stone. Try not to hurt yourself."

"Thanks, I think." She cringes as she almost drops the heavy weapon straight away, but before Aengus can say anything else, she takes off.

A high-pitched whistle signals from the end of the dock. Fletcher. He gestures towards the castle gardens with a wide arm.

"Shit. They're gathering in the lawns as well," Callum mutters as his eyes land on what his husband motioned toward. Dozens of heads bobbling over the hedges.

"Keep your sailors defending the dock, and we can take the gardens without them," I say, feigning confidence in my voice.

A syren's life is one of honesty, yet Callum nor my crew need reminding of the stark truth awaiting us. We'll be facing guards who Kellan himself selected for their strength and savagery. We'll be heavily outnumbered and going toe-to-toe with people who want to eradicate magic creatures from this realm whilst simultaneously steal the mortal throne for themselves.

Callum throws one last look towards his husband before giving me a solemn nod, "Alright, but Yarrow is mine and mine alone."

He makes the claim with an eerie calmness. As we stalk towards the lawns, he reaches for where his hipflask would usually hang, but in its place now lies a sword belt.

"That's fine by me as long as I get Fynbarr," I say, rolling my shoulders and wings.

As our feet hit the centre gravel path, at least eighty heads turn in unison to see us.

I unsheathe my knife. Whether it be the Trojans or my own, I intend to fight to the death.

"Are you ready?" Tarlock asks.

"Nope," I admit, "But I'm going to rattle the stars and ripple the seas anyway."

Callum claps my shoulder, then lightly pushes me towards the mayhem, "Good."

TWENTY-TWO

-she's meant to be dead." A splotchy faced teen mutters to his comrade as we waltz onto the lawns.

Both boys are not much older than Ludwig or Pip, yet there was no one telling them to evacuate or arranging guards to protect them.

"Oh, we'll remedy her living status soon enough." The man responsible for placing these boys in danger steps forward. Yarrow runs a hand through his greying hair. An attempt to look calm and collected. But with gauntlet gloves on, it's hard for him to appear casual. Especially when beneath the shiny Master pin he still has the nerve to wear, he dons a thick layer of chainmail.

"An army of orphans?" I spit at him, "That's low even for you, Yarrow."

"At least my army will grow into men," Yarrow sneers, his gaze of disgust locked firmly on Tarlock, "*Actual* men, not magic mutant scum."

"I can smell your fear from here," Aengus says flatly, crossing his arms and swishing his tail.

Huh. Maybe Callum will have competition when it comes to ending Yarrow.

"Isn't it hypocritical for you to act concerned about their welfare when *you* are the very reason they are orphans to start with?" Yarrow asks with a toothsome grin.

For a split second, I'm grateful it's Callum by my side and not Kellan. Out of the *Lazy Twins*, Callum is marginally less impulsive. If his brother had just heard those words, Yarrow's head would be trundling across the lawn.

"I did what I did because of Alistair. Your previous ruler made a grave mistake, and his people paid the consequences," I say flatly, before glancing over at the teens, "You learnt last winter how King Kellan will stop at nothing to protect his family. A family which can include you if you do not rebel. So, choose carefully which side of this fight you wish to be on."

Yarrow prattles on, but I ignore him.

With as much sincerity as I can muster without emotion clogging my throat, I address all the armed youths surrounding us, "Harming people is not my greatest desire, despite what you may have been told about syrens. So please, *please*, stand down."

The weapons they point in our direction do not falter- but their gazes do. Hesitation and bewilderment creep across their young faces.

I swear their bows and blades are lowering when a gigantic *boom* jolts them into tightening their grip.

Dizziness washes over everyone in the lawns.

I spin swiftly towards the blast. My eyes scan the docks and bay a dozen times in a breath, but the blast wasn't a mere canon. The explosion came from the hills, from the top of all those bloody steps, from the-

"The Temple!" I cry aloud. Or at least I think I do, but with ringing ears it's hard to tell.

Sunlight shines through shards of stained-glass as they drift towards the ground. For a fleeting moment, the Virginal Temple of Athena is surrounded with flashes of colour.

But like butterflies, these bursts of fluttering colour don't last long. Soon plumes of smoke and licks of flames spew out of every shattered window.

I lurch forward, but Callum grips my shoulder in an instant.

"Let me go! I can lure water and try to put out the fire," I protest, as the smoke bellows towards us on the

spring breeze. A strong scent of iron drifts from the slope and fills my nostrils. Gunpowder.

The Temple never stood a chance.

"It's too late, Wren. She's already gone," Callum says flatly, his throat bobbing as he watches his church crumble. The church where his wedding took place. And his brother's coronation. His father's funeral. So many memories would now be tainted with smoke and ruin.

I'd managed to shoehorn all my grief into a dark corner of my soul for safekeeping. But watching the Temple incinerate before my eye's changes something within me. I may be guilty of not always cherishing mortal life, but these bastards don't even fear the gods. They don't appreciate architecture and art. Nor do they appreciate the idea of sanctity and shelter.

The heat and pressure from the groaning Temple replicates within me. My sorrow forges into something else. My slab of dark sadness begins to heat, cracking its way through whatever hold I had on it. Like coal forming into a diamond, what comes next is crystalline, hardened, and pure. Rage.

Like the Temple, I explode.

With a guttural roar, I sprint forward, throwing my arms wide until I catch air. With a single wing beat, I tower above the nearest Trojan. And with a single breath, I come down blade-first into his neck.

By the time his body slumps onto the dew-softened ground, chaos has blossomed within the garden.

As Callum launches himself at Yarrow, Arthur guards his back, sparring with anyone who tries to get close.

Unlike Arthur, the Centaurs do not wait for opponents to come near them...they gallop straight towards them instead. Whilst Tarlock's tactic is rearing up and slamming down on his rivals, Aengus and Diarmuid opt for rear kicking. With bone crunching force, men fly across the lawns at the receiving end of their powerful hooves.

Seeing the sheer destruction surrounding them, a dozen or so of the younger boys drop their weapons and sprint out of the gardens. It's a mercy, albeit a small one. Their disappearance doesn't seem to lower the number of traitors surrounding us, but I try not to think about how many we have left to fight. Nor do I spare a glance towards my crew. I only focus on one rival at a time. Once they're defeated, I find another. And then another.

Once we begin turning the tide, the Trojans start changing their tactics.

The archers who patiently flank the hedging, raise their longbows, and knock their flaming arrows.

With a synchronized release they sent blaring arrows raining through the skies. but none land in people.

Huh.

Knowing *all too well* the accuracy Soleil archers have, I do not accept their missing as a mere mistake. Not when nearly all the arrows have landed by the edge of the lawn, by the gravel. Another arrow *whooshes* overhead, landing right in the centre of the path, biting into the shallow stones- and then the gravel catches fire. A heavy metallic scent fills my nose once more.

Okay, not stones, more gunpowder. Camouflaged perfectly, the substance trails from the bottom of the lawn to the wooden doors of the castle and beyond.

I whip around, trying to alert Callum, but I only spot a figure barrelling straight for me.

Fynbarr.

His eyes drink me in as if I'm something to eat. His smirk letting me know this is a moment he has imagined before. A moment he has dreamt of. He already knows what my blood across his teeth would taste like.

He closes the gap between us with two bounding strides, before slamming me into the ground.

We roll twice down the gravel path until his weight

pins me flat against the pebbles. Stones press into my skull. I try to lurch up at the hip to headbutt him, but he suffocates the space before me.

"I don't see your demon-blooded King-slayer protecting you this time," Fynbarr shouts into my face, his cheeks reddening.

He grabs my right hand, bending it backwards until my wrist nearly cracks. I yelp and release my knife onto the gravel.

"It was so easy to fool him, to fool you, into thinking Yarrow was my deeply ashamed guardian who would teach me a lesson."

His hot breath caresses my cheeks. It's rich with the smell of sugar and rot. I crane my face away from him only to see the blaze creeping its way towards us. Like a serpent slithering through the heart of the garden, the blaze *hisses*, blasting smaller stones out of its way as it scorches the land.

"Oh, how Yarrow laughed as he put me in that fancy cell. He gave me a pat on the back and a packet of biscuits and said he'd see me tomorrow. He was *proud* of me."

Fynbarr smacks my face to get my attention. Heat rushes to my cheek, staining my skin lilac. My non-mortal complexion only angers him further.

"He would have been prouder if you didn't miss

the first time around," I spit with my burning cheek and smouldering eyes.

Heat licks at my feathers. I try to retract my splayed-out wings, but any attempt to tuck them fails. I cannot move, yet sensing my mere attempt, Fynbarr eyes up my twitching feathers. Stretching out his grubby hand, he pins my wing directly in the flame's path.

Amongst the clatter of swords and the twang of bows, I hear someone bellow my name, telling me to fight.

My lack of struggle must be obvious. But I'm tired, so bloody tired, and I'm running out of reasons to carry on anymore.

"You know, if you had killed me the first time around it would have saved me a lot of grief," I grate out through gritted teeth.

Sparks land on my plumage, singeing the membrane below. His hand must be blistering at this point, but he doesn't release his hold. He would rather burn with me than ease my suffering.

"Well in that case, maybe I won't kill you. Maybe I'll keep *you* in a cell. In a cage, like the crow you are. You could be my plaything, you useless-"

The words are knocked straight out of his mouth as a flail swings into the side of his head. The momentum of the solid ball blasts him to one side.

Towering over me in his place stands a panting Nessa.

"Get up!" She offers me her left outstretched hand. The blood-splattered flail hanging in her right.

Instead of accepting her help, I dive for my knife. I lunge onto Fynbarr's limp body, driving the blade deep into his soft flesh. I drag down until a torrent of blood emerges and then flip him onto his side. His warm blood quenches the advancing flames.

"I understand why Kellan loves you now," Callum bellows towards me, kicking his defeated foe under a hydrangea bush with the toe of his boot, "Would the guards not let you through, Shay?"

"All the guards are dead." Nessa hauls me off the ground, but her words floor me, "And I can't find Princess Aveen anywhere. She's gone."

"What do you mean *gone*?" Callum kicks the body by the bush out of temper and not necessity, "Where the Hel is my sister?"

Rounds of canon detonations fire in quick succession. Seven teeth-shaking and ear-ringing blasts bellow across the bay as the Soleil's open fire. But not on the buildings and town as one would suspect.

"Are they...." Nessa's voice trails off with confusion as clouds of dense smoke rise from the bay.

Fletcher releases another loud whistle, before

shouting, "They're blowing their own blockade asunder. We should chase them out whilst they're fleeing!"

Arthur eagerly agrees with his captain, telling Callum, "The *Iseult* is our best warship, we could easily take 'em, sir."

For some reason, the thought of Fletcher and Arthur boarding that boat turns my stomach, though I don't exactly know why.

I go to stop him, but Arthur is already sprinting towards his Master. He ducks and dives through the remaining guards, and leaps over the perfect circle of unconscious men encompassing Aengus and Tarlock.

"I don't think this is a retreat, Callum. I think it's a quick getaway."

The archers begin receding from the lawns, relentlessly emptying their quivers as they go. Having foiled their plot to blaze the castle, they now focus their arrows on us.

Callum growls, diving to the left to avoid a sharpened arrowhead by mere inches, "Why the Hel would they conduct a morning raid, burn half the Kingdom and then leave whilst they still have troops standing?"

A screech of pure terror comes from the docks.

"Because they've gotten what they wanted," I gasp,

fighting the urge to drop to my knees as I spot Aveen. Her petrified cry fluctuating in pitch as her small body bounces and slams into the Soleil's shoulder she's flung over. And glinting atop the bastard's head, a flimsy tiara- the True Prince.

Trojans flank them on all fronts, some even jogging backwards as they make their way towards an awaiting boat. At the rear of the group, hobbling along is Judge Bevin, cradling his quill and hefty tome.

With Callum's roar acting like a war bugle, we wordlessly bolt into motion.

I opt for the skies, but my ruined wing roars in protest. Along with the barely-closed hole Fynbarr bore through the centre of it, the edges of my feathers are now scorched. Thick clumps matt together and drag through the air instead of cutting it.

With a frustrated snarl, I drop to my boots and sprint after Callum and Nessa instead.

We barrel towards the docks. Callum uses both the blade and hilt of his sword to blast anyone in his path out of the way. He doesn't hesitate to check whether they're a Trojan or Lunar sailor. He doesn't care. Nessa and I sprint side-by-side behind him until she drops to the ground with a high-pitched cry.

I skid to a halt, grabbing her slender arm to haul her up, but she barks in pain.

"I'm fine, Wren," she shouts, panic rich in her voice, "Go to Aveen!"

But I cannot tear my eyes away from the silver throwing knife buried deep into her thigh. Her trembling hands desperately trying to hold her upper leg together as a torrent of blood pours out.

"Keep moving, your Majesty!" Aengus bellows from behind, bucking an opponent off, "I've got her, go!"

I turned my back on Dove before and never saw her again. I flew away from Kellan and never got to say goodbye.

Aengus is already galloping over, but it doesn't chase away the growing dread in my core as I step away from her. It might be selfish, but I cannot lose another person. I can't. I want to stay with her, but I can't. I want to promise her she'll be okay but judging by the pulsating flow of hot blood rushing from her, I can't do that either.

"Go," she reassures with paling cheeks and ashen lips.

"I'm really proud of you," I admit truthfully, needing to say something, needing her to know before I turn my back on her.

TWENTY-THREE

s a syren, I spent most of my life practising different tunes and notes. Various *ooh's* and *ahh's* which carry no meaning, just music. And granted a scream is just another sound. A note without meaning. But as I run away from Nessa's shriek and head towards Aveen's, I decide it's the worst sound in all the realms.

The Trojans who flanking The True Prince and Aveen do not board the boat. Instead, they wade waist-high into the water and give a vigorous shove until the vessel is soaring into the bay. As quick and nimble as an eel, the boat effortlessly weasels its way into the shadows and shelter of the Soleil warships.

"Hold your fire!" Fletcher roars from the helm of the *Iseult*, knowing his sister-in-law, *our* sister-in-law, is now nestled between the chaos.

The Lunar Land men obey the Master of the Sails, but the Soleil's do not. A lone warship groan's as it rotates within the bay, sluggishly shifting to aim its loaded canon towards Fletcher.

As I catch up to Callum by the dock, I rip off my leathers and toss them aside. I won't need their protection once I'm under the water. What I do need is my gills free from obstruction as I labour hard to reach Aveen.

"I'll get her," I shout, kicking off my boots, "You get Fletcher and the crew off their boat."

"In my brothers most problematic absence, *I* am the ruler of this Kingdom, Wren. Don't try and stop me from saving my sister."

If only he knew.

"Do as I say," I growl, and before I get the chance to say something I'll regret, I jump off the timber edge of the dock.

But I do not land in cool waters. Instead, damp silt squishes beneath my bare feet. Running a few more steps doesn't bring me to the waterline. No matter how fast I move, the water retreats away from me.

Even without touching the waves, I know something is off. Gurgling bubbles ripple where the blasted barricade sinks to the bottom of the bay and the fleeing ships displace waves, but the disturbance I sense is something else. Something bigger beneath it all. *Much* bigger.

"Go."

The word erupts from my lips in a feral tone I'd never heard before. And this time Callum doesn't argue. Not when he notices what I see. The choppy waves smacking off each other without natural pattern or flow in the heart of the bay.

A vortex of ebony scales and endless teeth begins to whirl furiously.

Well, that explains the dropping water level in the bay.

With the sea being so vast, us marine dwellers had had to come up with different means of communicating our messages through-out the millennia. Song shells are the quickest. Hippocampi are the most dependable. But *this* means of messaging is by far the most terrifying.

"Charybdis!"

As if my cry lures the beast, it erupts through the surface. Bursting through the heart of its whirlpool, it rises up. And up. And up-until its immense reptilian body blocks the silvery sun and plunges me into the deep shadow it casts. Water gushes down its sides like a living, breathing fountain. Seafoam rushes from its endless mouth, as it froths like a furious Cerberus.

Charybdis only answers to the Queen of the Sea.

But I did not summon this creature? Since Kestrel used it to torment me with the cries of Dove's death, I have left it alone. Perhaps it felt my utter despairs around the seas and skulked out of whatever dark, dank cave it resides in. Or maybe Poseidon himself is beginning to pity my abysmal existence and sent the beast.

Charybdis begins its descent, and before it fully slinks back into the sea, it delivers its message. But there is no large shell this time.

From behind the rows of teeth and whipping tongues, a torrent of water blasts, drenching the dwarfed boat below. And within the wispy white waters is a ghost.

Rising from the puddle, drenched, and seething, is Kellan.

Armed with his glistening knife- and heaving gills.

I run until the returning waters suffocate my legs, and then I dive headfirst with the upcoming tidal wave. Thankfully, the boat Aveen is hostage on is small enough to ride out the rough waves caused by the retreating reptilian beast. Whilst they float over the cresting waves with little resistance, the larger vessels begin to capsize and crash into each other in the crowded cove.

Even without my tail skirt on, I press my legs together and pump hard. I propel myself through the choppy waters and plummeting debris.

I ignore the groan of my muscles, and the bitter sting of seawater entering my wounds, or at least I try to.

Staying close to the surface, I glance towards the boat in between broad strokes to make sure he's still there.

Between one glance and the next, the crisp, white blouse of the True Prince runs crimson as Kellan separates his spine from his body.

Three more broad strokes, and another glance.

But this time Kellan is nowhere to be seen.

My chest tightens. Maybe it was just a ghost? A trick of light fuelled by my delusional mind and grief.

Powering through the waves, I don't glance up again until my palms slap against the barnacle covered keel. Grabbing a tattered rope hanging overboard, I haul myself in. Tumbling over the wooden edge, I crumple onto the deck.

Aveen yelps and cowering away before she realises it's me. She's the last one standing amongst a myriad of death. Judge Bevin, the True Prince, and Kellan all lay strewn across the worn planks.

"He won't wake up," she cries, shaking her brother's limp shoulder with as much force as her trembling hands can muster.

Blood oozes from his nose and ears. It's not the mauve shaded blend of mortal and Descendant that I've seen before. This is near indigo- the same hue as mine.

I don't know how he gained so much ichor within his veins. And I don't know how the Hel he has gills. *Gills!*

But I take one frazzled look at him and know he is transitioning too fast.

Hoisting his lifeless scarred arm around my neck, I drag him towards the side of the boat. The strain on my body as I lift him onto the edge is glorious. It proves to me he is real.

Callum had listened to my roar to go to Fletcher, but rather than dragging him off the deck, he now stands steadfast beside him at the helm. Through the slew of sinking ships, the *Iseult* weaves its way towards us.

"*Mikros*," I sooth gently the way Kellan has a million times, "I need you to keep waving to Callum and Fletch, okay? Count to a hundred and they'll be here."

I want to stay with her.

I'm growing weary of having to decide who to save

first and turning my back on people is becoming far too frequent. But Kellan is starving for air right now and I cannot wait.

Half-lifting, half-throwing, I jump overboard, hauling Kellan with me.

We crash into the water. His limp body begins to sink.

Once he's submerged a dozen feet, I dive down and wrap my arms tightly around his waist. Threading water, I hold him close in silence. Although my ears are grateful for the reprieve from screams and blasts, it's too quiet. He is too quiet.

Plunging him into water stops his transitioning immediately. His gills flap open once more as I expected, but they do not look like mine. They're not the subtle, sleet slits of a syren. His are raw, raised and reddened.

A shadow creeps across our faces as the *Iseult* reaches Aveen overhead. I gaze through the distorted ripples just long enough to see her small frame jumping to the larger vessel. Relief knocks at my core, but I cannot let it in, not until I know her brother is safe too.

Turning my attention back to Kellan, I find the trickle from his nose and ears has finally eased to a halt. With the remnants of ichor and blood washing away, he becomes more conscious. But as alertness kicks in, so do his mortal instincts.

Human survival skills compel him to swim towards the surface and sunlight, but I tighten my grip. In his he jaded state, he tries to fight me off, writhing with my hold but I hold firm.

Clutching onto his shredded tunic, his eyes lock onto my hand. He traces a path from my fingertips, along my arm until he finds my shoulder...and then my face.

Kellan stops struggling. He holds me out at arm's length. His russet eyes blink rapidly a few times as he adapts to seeing underwater.

With a taut jaw and a wobbly voice, he asks, "Is this another vision, *lígo pouláki?* Or the afterlife?"

Another vision?

"If I'm dead, why are you here?" he presses, his beautiful face contorting with anguish, "You shouldn't be here, Wren. You can't be dead-"

"Shh, I'm not dead, Kellan. And neither are you. I don't know how, but you're here." I choke, sobbing with a mixture of joyous laughter and sheer emotion.

As the honesty of my words sink into his bewildered mind, I've never been more grateful to be a syren.

"Wren?"

He speaks my name softly, so softly, as if he's

afraid I'll vanish before him. Unable to speak, I nod, allowing my tears to blend into the sea around us.

Wrapping his arm around my waist, he yanks me flush against him. I tilt my face upwards needing to see him, needing to *feel* him. I offer up my lips, and he readily welcomes them.

His mouth captivates mine with a passion which takes me back, but the shock doesn't last long. Gliding my hand into his hair, I pull him closer. I kiss him as if he's the air I need to survive.

The world arounds us drifts away. Too wrapped up in our embrace, we stop treading water and begin to slowly sink towards the bottom of the bay. But it doesn't matter. Nothing else matters.

As our feet settle upon the dense sediment at the bottom of the bay, I pull away from his kiss slightly and mutter, "I have no idea how you're here. I *felt* you take your last breath. It broke our bond and scorched my ichor."

"Scorched you?" His wide eyes scan me a dozen times, looking for signs of injury, "Well, I guess I did take my last breath before your *daddy dearest* decided to poke holes in me with his bloody Trident."

"*Poseidon?* Poseidon did this to you?"

With a sagging sigh, he releases a stream of bubbles, "The one and only. In his defence, he did recommend I let the gills fully heal before going in the water but after seeing what the Weavers predicted I couldn't sit around and wait."

My own wounds which now look like papercuts in comparison to the rips carved into his sides, itch and burn with the saltwater surrounding us.

"Is it excruciating?" I ask. I have a long, *long* list of questions, but that one seems like the most important for now.

"It's not that ba-"

An explosive cough bursts from his lips. Winded from the inside out, and heaving for breath, he doubles over. He winces as he stretches his sides.

"The added ichor would be courtesy of Athena," he chokes out, "Granted it's mostly for gill function, but she figured everyone would benefit from me being more truthful. She hoped it would curb my habit of *'act first, think second'* if everyone could ask what I'm planning."

"I find myself agreeing with her."

He rolls his eyes, "As much as I disagree, I cannot be too annoyed with her. It was Athena's idea to provide me with transportation. It took a lot of persuading and elbow-bending to get Poseidon to beckon that... thing."

We both eyeball the murky waters for Charybdis,

but there's no sign of it. Only plummeting planks from the shipwrecks above disturb the waters around us.

As much as I want to stay down here in the muffled silence with Kellan, I know royal duty calls from above, but for once it calls *both* of us.

"Are you ready?" I ask, jerking my chin towards the surface.

Not wanting to burn his insides with lies again so soon, he shakes his head, "No, I'm definitely not ready. But our people and our family need us, so I'll do what I have to."

He does a good job at seeming strong and stoic, but I still see a glint of fear flashing across those bronze eyes.

Taking his hand, we begin to slowly swim towards the surface. As we ascend, I prepare him for what to expect whilst transitioning, like the popping of your ears. The mounting pressure in your lungs. The way your heart lurches in your chest. The drumming in your head.

But alongside all my warnings and advice, I also offer a promise. That he will not be alone for a second of it.

We swim towards the furthest edge of the bay, away from the diminishing chaos and peering eyes.

Being vulnerable for seven minutes during a battle is far from ideal.

Leaving the water, we scramble over a bank of marram grass. Each blade cuts like a razor against our bare skin but we don't have the time to carefully pick a path.

Once out of sight, we drop onto the thin layer of wind-blown sand. Sodden and silent, we lay side-by-side as we catch our breath. Prepared for the worse, we both brandish our knives, but I remain clutching his left hand for support. The feeling of suffocation is never enjoyable, regardless of how fleeting it is.

From the flat of his back, he stares at the cloudless sky above whilst I stare at him. Having years more experience and knowing not to fight it, my gills seal first. A few moments later, he joins me. Lurching upright, he gulps a large, greedy breath and forces it deep into his lungs.

"Gods above." He rasps, spitting out a mouthful of brine, "That is not enjoyable."

Although his gills are like no other, they close as intended though his scars remain.

"It will be easier next time," I sooth, patting his back to help bring up the last dregs of saltwater.

Noticing the wisps of smoke rising from various

pockets of the isle, he grips his weapon tighter and shakes his head.

"The bastards even burnt down my bridges."

"Actually, that was me," I mutter, with a slight wince, "And aren't they *our* bridges? I thought I had a right to burn them if it protected *our* citizens. I thought it was rather ingenious."

An impish glint brightens his eyes, "My cunning, *lígo pouláki*."

Groaning, he rises stiffly to his feet and with his help, I haul myself onto my leaden legs.

He drapes his arm around my shoulders. I don't know if it's emotional support for me, or physical support for him, but I do not question his touch. His warmth reminding me he is here. He is real. And he survived.

TWENTY-FOUR

he bay before us is brimming with shipwrecks. Between the canons and Charybdis, most of the older Soleil ships are obliterated.

As we walk by the docks, we see the *Iseult* is berthed but barren. Sailors race towards us, bowing to Kellan with wide eyes as they stare at his maimed sides which are visible through his shredded shirt.

They inform us that the Prince, Princess and Captain headed into the castle, trying to calm Aveen who could not stop vomiting from stress and shock. Although the trio escaped relatively unscathed, the fear of being kidnapped again had sent Aveen into shock. The young Princess won't even swim in the bay for fear of fish nibbling her feet, so I can only imagine the trauma of seeing a monster most deemed a myth spewing out her brother would do to her.

"And the gardens?" I ask.

With a weary but encouraging nod, he says, "They're almost cleared."

Almost.

"Good." Kellan says sounding genuinely content there's enough lingering chaos left on the lawns for him. "Extinguish the fires smouldering throughout the town. Leave the remaining turncoats to us."

Us. Not just *him* as or *I* as usual. He might loathe placing me in danger, but from now on every battle we face would be met head-on, and side-by-side.

The men's chorus of '*Right away, your Majesty*', quickly turn into shouts for buckets and pails amongst themselves. As they get to work with haste, we march towards the gardens, only pausing momentarily along the way to pluck a grubby coat off the cobbles.

As he shakes it out and slips it on, I cannot help but smirk a little, "*Now* do you understand why I wear my capelet over my wings so much?"

Grunting in agreement, he bats away some of the mud and blood caking the sleeves.

"And I hate to burst your bubble, but I'm pretty sure everyone witnessed Charybdis spitting you out. Hide those gills all you want, but there's no way you can pretend to be mortal."

"I hope they did see it," he says flatly. "And I hope it scared the absolute shit out of them. They chose to side against the gods. Against Fate. Against you, me, and our crowns. They chose the wrong side of this fight. A grievous mistake, but one which they will not make again."

Complete faith and confidence chimes through him. He changed in more than one way on Eastern Acropolis. Kellan had always been a natural-born leader, that was never in doubt. But the crown he used to carry out of duty, he now wears with pride and a sense of entitlement.

Stalking through the lawns once more, I notice any trace of spring has been weeded out. The ground is churned up from the dozens of hooves. The hedging riddled with holes and burnt patches from the archers. The sweet musk of roses blends with the metallic whiff of gunpowder and blood. Bodies and petals are scattered everywhere.

"Stand down." I do not know if his order is directed towards the centaurs or the Trojans, but the colts obey instantly and lower their head towards us.

The last twenty or so Trojans ease their flailing, sword-wielding arms, but they do not bow.

No surprise there.

"Listen to your King and bow before him." I snap.

I'm probably the last person in the realm to care about the intricacies of royal etiquette, having waved away more bows and formalities than I've accepted, but I refuse to let them snide him like that. Not after everything he's done to be their King.

A Trojan standing at the back of the rounded-up group spits out, "We do not take orders from demon-blooded princelings. Nor the squawking crow he has chosen to bed."

A wild snarl burst through my lips. A lesser man might have flinched at the sound, but not Kellan. He doesn't move an inch from my side. He doesn't move at all. With taut tension and through grated teeth, he simply clicks his tongue.

"Unfortunately, I cannot kill him twice, love. Would my Queen like to end him, or shall I?"

My Queen.

"Hmm, I cannot decide. Maybe we should flip for it?" I offer Kellan with a playful wink. Like a hunter teasing its prey, I watch the Trojans' squirm.

Effortlessly reaching into his pocket, Kellan withdraws a lone gold coin and hands it to me with a wolfish grin.

"I like your thinking." He flips the coin off his thumb, sending it high into the sky, "Though should remember I don't lose. Face or fin?

Even though I'm the Queen of the Sea, I chose '*face*' as '*fin*' tends to be Kellan's prefer gamble. Perhaps that's why he was Fated to end up with a syren.

When the coin lands in his palm, he offers his outstretched hand to me without even bothering to look himself.

"Damnit." My whisper under my breath causes him to smirk. Pocketing the coin, he gestures to Diarmuid who wordlessly tosses him a sharp axe.

"Now, no-one calls their Queen a crow and survives, so this offer does not apply to you," Kellan starts, pointing the hatchet towards the paling man at the back, "But if anyone would like to surrender, I will offer you the opportunity. Though be warned, your future entirely depends on my brother's approval. I distrusted his opinion about a Soleil guard previously and look where it got me. If Prince Callum deems you unworthy of redemption or unwilling to rehabilitate, I will not stand in his way."

"Do not surrender," the man bellows, "And she is not our Queen. We serve the True Prince and no-one else."

Tarlock paws the ground. His hooves itching to kick something, but like the other colts, he holds his position. Barely.

"I think you'll find the True Prince is now

as *spineless* as his personality." Kellan says, swinging the hatchet in a figure-of-eight and rolling his shoulders. As he steps into the squad, the colts and I wordlessly follow. Within seconds the man who had so much to say falls silent, and after fifteen minutes only three stragglers remain.

Even before he had additional ichor flowing through his veins, Kellan tended to be a man of his word. Yet it still surprises me when he accepts surrender from the remaining guards. Knowing their own deaths were as inevitable as those of their leaders and their cause, as our blades swung towards them, they tossed their broadswords onto the grass. Seconds later, they threw themselves onto their knees. With an inward sigh, I realise this is almost over. *Almost.*

"Take them to the cells. As I said, Prince Callum will oversee your Fate." Kellan says, panting slightly. It's a wonder he's still standing.

As the trio of traitors are towed away, Kellan turns his attention to the castle. "As much as I want to see my family, I don't have the strength for a Callum-*esque* spiel."

"Well, be warned you're in for a Wren-*esque* lecture the moment we both have the strength," I threaten with a staggered exhale.

As adrenaline fades, exhaustion takes its place. I spare a glance towards the upper right section of the castle which houses his suite. The thought of crawling into bed and *finally* sleeping with him beside me is enough to make my mouth water.

"I'm sorry for putting you through Hel," Kellan says, stepping before me. Sweat and grime aside, he's a pretty mouth-watering view too. "I wanted to be worthy of you. To be reborn as your equal so our people would either love us equally or fear us together. I had no idea things would go so south whilst I sailed east, Wren."

"I know, I know" I soothe, gently taking his scarred forearm as we begin walking towards the castle doorway, "But you're not *exactly* my equal. You don't have wings."

A slow grin pulls at the corner of his lips, "Ares was actually willing to grant me wings. He deems himself high enough in Aphrodite's esteem to ask a favour of her. She gave Eros his wings, so Ares figured she could do the same for me, but Athena and Poseidon whole-heartily disagreed. Your creator refused to have me on the same pedestal as you, whereas the goddess deemed every woman should be able to get a break from men. She said you'd thank her someday for being able to get a sky break from me if we're to be bound for decades or centuries."

Centuries.

With Kellan now equipped for the Water World, it's a possibility should we want it. And even if we opted for a more normal life, if that's even possible for the two of us, reigning over the merfolk and syrens would require regular visits. Spending time beneath the waves would elongate our lives to one extent or another.

"Will you tell me about the gods? Tell me about *him*," I say, wincing a little. Saying *creator* makes me feel like a project, yet *father* feels too relaxed.

As we enter the cool, stone corridor of the castle antechamber, he nods, "My life in all its entirety is yours, Wren. Once this whole mess is somewhat over, I'll tell you everything you want to know."

Turning right, we march our way towards the working quarters of the castle. Kellan spares a glance for the lengthy passageway before us. "I'm surprised all this is still standing. In the visions, there was so much destruction I assumed my castle, my home, would just be another thing for me to lose."

I open my mouth to ask about the vision he saw but pause. Like he said, we have enough time for that in the future, and I doubt delving into more death and destruction is what he wants right now.

"They had plans to burn it down, but as you would say, *I took care of it.*"

He arches his brow, silently demands an explanation but I wave him away. The tales of what I did would take place at a different time too. A time when the memories were not as fresh as the blood splatters on my face and hands. A time when my skin isn't peppered with imminent bruises and a coating of saltwater and sand.

We've both seen enough pain and suffering for today, but we're not done. Not yet.

As we near the scullery which has been turned into a makeshift hospital, wounded sailors line the corridors. Their years of discipline shine through as they arrange themselves in order of injury severity. With each hurried step I take, their suffering becomes more prominent. And as Kellan and I round the corner into the scullery, we are fronted with the most injured patient yet.

Sprawling across the sturdy oak table in the centre of the cramped room is Nessa. To her left towers Aengus who's steely stare is firmly locked on the person to Nessa's right. A butcher, donning blood-stained white overalls and an apron. I pray the smears are from previous meal preparation, and that he just didn't have time to change. Judging by the bundles of herbs, onions, and pots strewn across the flagstones, I doubt they spared even a moment to prepare themselves or the area.

With a pair of poultry shears, the butcher cuts a crooked rectangle into Nessa's slacks. In the centre of the opening juts out the knife. The weapon buried up to the hilt within her flesh.

"What can we do to help?" Kellan asks, as we squeeze our way into the sliver of space surrounding the table.

Aengus's head snaps from the butcher to us. His usually unflappable face displays pure shock.

"Your Majesties," Aengus breathes, as he hastily offers a bow to both of us, but his wide gaze never leaves his King.

"We were running towards Aveen when she was struck. I...I had to leave her behind," I explain to Kellan, leaning forward to take Nessa's limp hand.

Her skin is slick with cold sweat. Her eyes shut but twitching behind the lids as if she were living her worst nightmare. And her leg.... well, her leg makes me feel nauseous, so I try my best not to look at it.

"I carried her off the lawn right away but finding someone to fix her has proven difficult." Aengus runs a hand through his dark and dishevelled hair, "I sent half a dozen colts to scale the Star Spike cliffs and retrieve some healers. In the meantime, I've charged this pig carver with keeping her alive."

Glowering at Aengus's remark, the butcher fashions a tourniquet around her thigh out of some unused pork twine. As he tightens the knot, Nessa lurches upright, reanimated by pain. Gripping my hand with bone-crunching force, a gnarl escapes her unnaturally pale lips.

"Easy lass," Aengus bellows, splaying his wide hand across her torso and pinning her to the table. "*Apparently* he's trying to help you."

Nessa spits a vile curse I didn't think her polite mind had to ability to form.

"The meat I work with is usually dead and therefore more cooperative." The butcher retorts, using the back of his blood-speckled hand to swipe sweat off his brow, "Your Majesty, truth be told I have no idea what I'm doing. But *that brute* threatened to hoof me off the nearest cliff if I didn't help."

Aengus scowls at the man but doesn't deny it. He simply keeps his gaze and hand fastened on Nessa who has gone completely limp.

With a wordlessly nod, Kellan dismisses the butcher into the corridor with a pot full of water, a dishcloth and more pork twine. The worker might not be a healer, but he could do his damn best until better showed up. We have all had to do tasks beyond our comfort zone today, he should be no different.

"Stay with us, Shay." Kellan urges quietly as he drapes a sodden cloth over her forehead. I'm not sure what he hopes the rag will achieve, but I understand the need to do something, *anything,* to not feel useless. Idle hands only fuel a racing mind.

Aengus cautiously elevates her injured leg into the air, resting her calf on his sturdy shoulder as he attempts to rush blood back to her core. Through a taut jaw, he mutters, "I should have locked you into your cabin on the boat. Or bucked you off on the far side of those burnt bridges. You're far too fragile to survive this realm."

I open my mouth to scold him on Nessa's behalf, when he threatens, "So *when* you wake up, I'm training you with the rest of my herd for at least a month. That ought to toughen you up a bit."

Nessa remains still and silent, but I swear a faint scowl crosses her face.

Like a storm rolling in, a rumbling thunder begins to echo through the castle. A dozen hooves canter their way down the flagstones. A chestnut colt skids into the scullery. The sheer speed of his veer around the corner almost unseats the healer on his back. Dismounting onto wobbly legs, the woman stumbles the few steps to Nessa's side.

"I know you'll do all you can," Kellan says firmly, giving the healer an encouraging pat on her shoulder.

Four more colts pile into the doorframe. The already crowded room grows smaller. The remaining healers slide off their mounts and launch into assessing the sailors awaiting care. They shout instructions to each other and bombard the butcher with questions.

Elbowing her way through the towering centaurs around her is a familiar face.

"Shelli?" I gasp, trying my best to make room for her by the table, "What are you doing here?"

"I thought my skillset could be useful." She unfurls her toolbelt which hangs around her hips to expose an array of sewing needles, yarn, and pins. "I figured a few people might need putting back together again."

Selecting her longest needle, she dampens twine against her lips and threads it effortlessly.

Another healer sticks his head around the door, clutching a glass bottle containing a milky mixture. "Your Majesty, I heard the Princess Aveen is in shock. I have a valerian and chamomile tincture for her, but the sailors have warned me not to step within a fifty-foot radius of her unless I wish to lose my head to the Prince."

Kellan blows air through his lips, before muttering,

"There's a strong chance my presence will only heighten his desire to stab something. But I'll accompany you."

As he moves towards the door, he throws me a glance over his shoulder.

Pray for me, his russet eyes wordlessly say.

In response, I lightly roll mine and offer a subtle smirk, *So, you're fine with facing the gods, but your brother is where your sense of fear finally kicks in?*

I love you, he says ferociously without ever parting his lips.

And I you, I declare with a small nod before Nessa almost detaches my hand from my body.

"Sweet Zeus," I yelp, twisting to find the healer sprinkling crushed calendula powder over her wound. Although the goldfish-hued powder is meant to numb the area completely, it stings and burns the flesh when first applied.

"Are you ready?" Shelli asks gently, but Nessa doesn't respond. Yet her pain arched back, and claw formed fingers speak for her. This needs to be over.

At the healer's command, Aengus lowers Nessa's leg and begrudgingly step aside.

I glance towards the door to find Kellan gone, and when my gaze returns to the table I almost gag at the sight before me. The healer painstakingly fishes the blade from her thigh. It's slow work to ensure she doesn't nick any arteries. Even with the healer's care, more blood trickles onto the table regardless, though I don't know how Nessa has any left to lose.

Tossing the Soleil blade onto the flagstones amongst the scattered herbs and pots, the healer wipes her hands on the front of her skirt. "Alright. Let's begin."

For the next hour, I remain holding Nessa's palm but keep my eyes as far away from Shelli's stitching work as possible. Aengus opts to keep his hands to himself, firmly folding them across his chest. But his eyes never leave Ms Shay.

TWENTY-FIVE

nce Nessa is somewhat patched up and marginally more responsive, the healer gives the nod of approval for her to be moved to a bed for rest.

With her sisters and mother still stranded on Star Spike, I refuse to let her be carried to an empty home. Aengus offers to stand guard over her, but with the Shay family home being a narrow two-story townhouse, I doubt it was built with centaur proportions in mind. Whatever about squeezing through the doorframe, he would never be able to carry her upstairs.

"Take her to my cottage at the top of the hill," I suggest over my shoulder, busy squeezing the clear gel from aloe vera plants which the healer handed me, "There's a large bed for her and plenty of space for you. There's a key under the mat. Make yourself at home."

The sailor before me awaiting treatment for the burns he received from a barely missed blazing arrow, awkwardly winces at my words.

"The Trojans found out you reside in the bungalow, Queen Wren, and eh...." The man pauses to clear his throat and pick a bit of ash from his sleeve, "Well, it's destroyed."

"How destroyed?" I ask, tossing the wrung-out aloe vera leaves onto the floor. An overwhelming urge to sit down floods through me.

"I'm afraid to say it's flattened, ma'am".

Even without seeing it for myself, I can imagine the damage. The bathtub overflowing with rubble. The oil painting of Lachlan and Iseult-shredded. The wide window where Kellan first kissed me-shattered.

I deflate with an utterly defeated sigh, before the sailor kindly adds, "There is always a spare room at the barracks if it's any good? Ground floor. Wide doors. It isn't glamourous but a bed is a bed, right?"

Appreciating the soldier-like response he instils into his own colts, Aengus nods firmly, "Aye, that will do. Thank you."

Carefully scooping her off the table, Aengus holds her flush against his chest whilst resting her bandaged leg in the crook of his elbow. The healer tucks another sachet of calendula powder into Aengus's pocket to reapply later in the night. He bows his head to me before plodding down the dim passageway, trying his best not to move his torso. And once the gentle clop of hooves no longer echoes through the tunnel, I return my attention to the men seeking aid.

Hours later, as the level of sailors and sunlight dwindles, I strike a match and begin lighting the lanterns lining the passageway. Rooting around in the scullery cupboards, I find a basket brimming with apples and pears. It isn't exactly dinner but at least it will line the men's stomachs. Swinging the wicker basket onto my hip, I begin handing out fruit to the last few patients and healers. Having arranged themselves in order of injury severity, the remaining wounded were in reasonably good spirits. The screams of earlier have faded into light laughter amongst the men, and gods above were my ears grateful for the change.

I'm relaxing ever so slightly when a tap on my shoulder jolts me.

"I only have pears left," I say, spinning around. But my weary feet don't react as fast as the rest of me, causing me to stumble. An arm lashes out to steady me with lightning speed.

"I think it's time for this *lígo pouláki* to nest,"

Kellan says, taking the basket from my stiff arms.

"Hey," I say breathlessly, scanning his face for any signs of a rising shiner. But his weary eyes are free from bruising.

Huh. I guess Callum's lecture didn't comprise of brother beating. "How long have I been down here?"

"About five hours. I tucked Aveen into bed and I'm coming to do the same for you. You didn't have to stay here until I returned, you know?"

"I wanted to help our people."

"We are all very lucky to have you." He says it with a tired smile, before quietly adding, "And I cannot wait to announce to everyone that you're their Queen."

We bid goodnight before finally traipsing our way down the passageway. Thankfully, Kellan doesn't even think of heading for the cottage. I guess neither of us have the energy to climb those damn steps, but I'm grateful I can stave off the news of its destruction until tomorrow. There has been enough damage done for one day.

Once we reach Kellan's suite, we slump onto the plush bed and groan in unison. We managed to kick off our boots, but the filthy, blood and sea-salt stiffened clothes remain. Kellan fights the woollen blanket free from beneath us, but I've succumbed to sleep by the time he drapes it over us.

For days and days, we sleep and sleep.

I might have avoided telling Kellan about the cottage being flattened, but when he caught wind about the Temple, he snapped into a state of alertness which I struggled to keep up with.

On the fourth morning since the attack, I find myself jogging to keep up with Kellan's bounding strides as he takes the steps three at a time.

His hast grinds to a halt the moment he lays eyes on the Temple. Granted those bloody steps normally take my breath away, but I find myself gasping at the sight of it.

With an audible swallow, he ascends the three marble steps and stands in the archway where the heavy oak doors hung for decades before.

"I am the King of ruin." He speaks with a quiet, hoarse voice, but his words echo across the remnants of the Virginal Temple of Athena.

Climbing the marble steps, I stand behind him in the archway to survey the damage. Thankfully, most of the structural stone survived, but the good news ends there. The oil paintings, the colourful windows and the roof have disappeared without a trace.

Dawn songbirds fly overhead. A lone blackbird descends through the remnants of charred rafters to land atop the creamy marble sculpture of Athena. Though the dais is covered in a dense layer of soot, the layers of ash fade as the flames failed to reach the top of the ten-foot statue. The bird sprays its wings upon the goddess's gently sloped shoulder, and the pair bask in the early morn light.

I want to ask Kellan if the statue has a likeness to the goddess, but he's so buried within his own thoughts I doubt he would hear me.

With his eyes never leaving the lines of undisturbed ash where the pews once were, he mutters, "This wreck and ruin is just the beginning of what I could have lost, Wren."

I open my mouth to bat away his worries, but I pause. Disregarding his fears because they didn't happen would be an insult. In his mind, he lived through the devastation that could have awaited him a hundred times over. As he travelled in the belly of a beast, the real monster would have been his own mind-replaying every possible outcome in a kaleidoscope of misery and sorrow.

"We will rebuild it." Stooping over, I lick my thumb and press it into the cinders at my feet, "Do you remember when you anointed me with ash?"

"The Phoenix Blessing?" he asks, with an arched brow, "That ritual is carried out so the sailors are connected to the boat for a safer journey. I doubt this pile of rubble is going anywhere soon."

Rolling my eyes, I smoothen out the frowning wrinkles of his forehead by smearing my thumb across his skin, "Well, may you always be connected to your land. To your buildings. Your people. Your gods. Try as they might, no one can take this from you, Kellan."

He lowers his forehead against mine, smudging the ash onto my skin too, "As you said, this can be rebuilt. It's just brick and mortar. At least those who cannot be rebuilt are still with me."

I tilt my chin up to find his warm lips and part them with my tongue. He wraps an arm around me, lifting me onto the balls of my feet.

We remain lost in each other for a few moments, until the blackbird takes flight. The sudden movement reminding us of the real world.

"We best not keep them waiting." Kellan says, tucking my hair behind my ear, "Royalty or not, someone wise once told me it's rude to keep others waiting for trivial reasons."

"Oh?" I chuckle, biting my lower lip slightly, "Well aren't you lucky to have someone so wise to keep you on the straight and narrow path."

"Incredibly lucky." He offers in a tone far more serious than mine. His lips lower against mine once more.

Oh well. What's the point in being King and Queen if we can't be a few minutes late?

TWENTY-SIX

we waltz into the West Wing, I find Fletcher and Callum already engrossed in paperwork. An array of scrolls and parchments lay spread across the long table.

"Aw, look at you trying to impress Fletch by *actually* reading something for a change," Kellan taunts his brother, pulling out a velvet backed chair for me to sit in.

As quick as a viper, Callum leans back in his chair and smirks, "Not everyone can rely on the '*Charybdis almost ate me*' sympathy sex like you."

Although I gasp, Kellan just chuckles as he takes his seat beside me.

"Are those the building plans for the Temple?" I ask Fletcher, my ear tips blushing with embarrassment.

Fletcher bites back a grin and swivels the

construction drawings around for Kellan and me to see. "You'll notice a lot of the original design is replicated, but there are a few modifications to allow for magic creatures."

"What's that?" I point my finger towards the back corner of the Temple where an azure square is drawn.

"That is one of the adjustments. A tunnel is to be constructed from the edge of the bay. It'll flow underground and emerge into this deep pool within the Temple walls, offering somewhere safe and secluded to transition away from prying eyes. Not just for you or Kellan, but any syrens visiting this isle."

"That's really thoughtful of you, Fletch." I offer, swallowing the lump of emotion thickening my throat.

"It was actually Cal's suggestion."

Kellan and I both look to the Prince immediately, but he simply shrugs. "You and your people have done a lot for this isle. Besides, I thought you might want to invite them to your wedding."

It's a struggle not to roll my eyes. "I think you care more about the party you're envisioning, more so than the actual ceremony."

Feigning hurt, he raises a hand to his chest, "I'm offended you think so little of me, Wren. Why the ceremony is a vital part. No sibling of mine is eloping like a teenager struck by Eros. You two are royalty and therefore will be wed like so. I'll even hand over Mom's ring to sweeten the deal."

"*You* have Mom's ring? Gods above, I spent weeks looking for it." Kellan says.

My heart swells. *Weeks.* Perhaps his vow to me was not as impromptu as I was led to believe.

Callum laughs. "Dad gave it to me when I was proposing to Fletch. I guess he was trying to be supportive but..."

"But it would have to lose the emerald gemstone and double in size for me to even consider wearing it." Fletch chimes in with a quick wink in my direction.

The first time I ever walked into the West Wing I had deemed it somewhat barren and overly exposed from all the windows. But as I grin toward the Lunar men around me, I'm grateful the room is large enough to contain our long overdue joy.

Through our laughter, a firm knock raps on the door. A moment later Aengus plods into the hall with a scowling Nessa atop his back.

"Apologies for the delay. Ms Shay and I had a difference of opinion about her ability to walk here."

Judging by how Nessa bats away his outstretched hand to help her dismount, I'm doubting this centaur commute was her idea.

"We were just about to get started," Kellan says,

gesturing towards the vacant seats across from us.

Aengus doesn't force his touch on Nessa as she stubbornly hobbles forward. A jingle sounds with each slow step she takes.

"I see someone finally put a bell on you, huh?" I grin, noting the flail still attached to her hip.

"How else would I protect myself for the ten minutes I'm left alone to bathe?" Nessa sighs under her breath, but with his heightened hearing Aengus effortlessly picks up on it.

Ignoring the chair Aengus pulls out for her, Nessa picks up the drinks tray waiting on the side table.

"What are you doing?" Kellan, Callum, and I all say at once as she hoists up the tray and limps forward.

Our collective cries cause her to jolt. Water sloshes out of the carafe and drips off the tray. "I...I'm here to serve you, aren't I?"

"Gods above, have I really been such a terrible employer? Did you honestly think I'd ask you to hobble down here just to serve me water, Nessa?" Kellan asks in a manner which doesn't need answering.

"You're far from a terrible employer, your Majesty. Working for your family is a privilege." Her tired eyes still shining as she offers one of her iconic smiles.

"I'm glad to hear it because that's precisely why we asked you here today," Kellan says.

Her smile slips as confusion creeps in, but she quietly takes her seat. Although Aengus pulls out another chair, it's obvious it's not for him. He simply couldn't fit. Instead, he taps the cushioned seat, giving Nessa a knowing stare. She subtly rolls her eyes as she fishes out an embroidered handkerchief from her pocket. Covering the seat with her cloth, she tenderly stretches her stiff leg out, resting her boot heel on the chair.

She raises her brow towards Aengus in a *'Happy now?'* fashion. He nods once and takes his place standing beside her.

Swallowing a smirk, I clear my throat and say, "Right then. Let us begin."

The meeting kicks off with the building plans. Along with the Temple being rebuilt, construction plans for a new naval fleet and bridges are discussed. Even though Nessa jokes how she enjoys the reprieve from her sisters, everyone agrees Crescent Cove is eerily quiet without the hustle and bustle of its citizens.

The burnt rope bridges of yesteryear are to be replaced with drawbridges. Although Kellan vows a mass evacuation will never need to occur again, it never hurt to be prepared.

There are also plans for the cottage to be rebuilt, but there will no longer be a key under the mat for me. The key to this new home will solely belong to Arthur. I may not have gotten him those gifts in the agora, but I somehow think he'll like this more. Fletcher agrees the young sailor has faced challenges tougher than any naval exam. Arthur is to be promoted to Lieutenant, moving out of the barracks and take up his role with training the recruits.

The vacant skipper roles and barrack bunk which Arthur leave behind will be offered to Pip. Once Callum caught wind of a fellow orphan tortured by Soleil's, the Prince had a fondness for the teen before they'd even met. It seems the youngster's dream of being a sailor would come true after all.

The buildings, bridges, and barracks aren't the only things changing. Instead of finding recruits to take the Master titles now vacant by Yarrow and Bevins deaths, Kellan opts to dissolve all Master titles instead. There will be no more advisors. No councillors. Kellan and I will only seek advice and judgment from those we trust most. Our family and friends.

Friends who I am eternally grateful to now have by my side. Turning my attention to Aengus, I finally explain why his presence is required today.

"Without the support of you and the hooved army, there is no way we would be sat here today." I allow the truth of my words to hang in the air. "The level of fortitude and discipline instilled into the colts speaks volumes of your leadership, Aengus. You move, they move. You give an order, they follow."

Subtly rolling his shoulders as if to shuck off my praise, he clears his throat to say, "It's my job, your Majesty."

"Well, how do you feel about taking on another job?" I ask.

"I'll do whatever is asked of me."

I make a mental note of his answer, knowing I might need to hang it over him once he hears what I want from him.

"We all know how resilient the Soleil troops are. We've fought against them a few times and narrowly won. The idea of incorporating them into our army and navy is still a good one, but we need to go about it a different way. If there is any good we can take away from a radical group emerging from Soleil isle, it's that it highlights all the issues they have with us. Yarrow, the True Prince, and the Trojans might be gone, but I doubt we eliminated every thread of hatred. There will be Soleil people who do not agree with Kellan being King. Or with a syren being their Queen. The idea of magic creatures now being an equal part of this Crowndom will infuriate some Sols. And that's where you come in Aengus."

I pause to search his face for a reaction, but I don't find one. Kellan gives my hand a light squeeze and takes over.

"Nominating a stranger, a Soleil, to oversee those who dislike me was a mistake. One which my brother warned me off, and one which he won't let me forget anytime soon. So instead, Wren and I nominate you to oversee the remaining Sol men. You will train them as hard as your colts. Sweat their hatred out of them. Normalise them to magic. Instil your loyalty for the crown into them. And if you deem them unable for rehabilitation then...."

"Then they will be *taken care of* in whatever way I see fit," Callum says flatly.

His hand tightens around his glass, but for once it's a glass of water. Come to think of it I hadn't seen him reach for rum in days. Not since he cleared away his hipflask to make room for his sword. Not since he almost lost everything.

Kellan and I nod stiffly as Callum's words. We knew this would be his response, but we would not fight it. We needed Callum on our side, and he needed a sense of control and retribution. He allowed the men one more chance. *One.* But he said if they so much as snickered at the opportunity, they wouldn't live long enough to be granted another. And any other Alistair relatives Fletcher tracks down through his research will not be offered the same opportunities. Callum plainly said a single acorn can lead to an orchard of rot. Kellan snorted to himself as if he knew his brother would say that.

"I will bring them to heel." Aengus says, "And if I cannot, I will bring them to my Prince."

Before I get too worried about the wicked grin Callum flashes towards Aengus, I turn my focus to Nessa.

"And how do you feel about a new job?"

"I too will do what is asked of me," she offers, though I sense the hesitance in her voice.

"The Trojans topped up their legions with orphans from the Omphalos Stone house. Pip is a relatively shy teen, but the few details I wrangled out of him all point towards the place being less of a home and more a holding pen. He lost much more than just an ear in that desolate place." A shudder rushes down my spine. "They need someone to teach them compassion and empathy. They won't be recruited by evil if they have a figure of love protecting them. And that person will be you, Nessa."

Nessa straightens herself in her seat, spluttering, "I...I am flattered you thought of me, but I don't have the experience needed. I would mess it up."

"You've practically raised your sisters. If Cal and I are busy, *you* are the person Aveen looks to torment with her songs and dancing." Kellan argues, "You most certainly would not mess it up."

"And no offence Nessa but fussing over people and managing everyone is kind of your forte. You're a natural mother-hen," I say with a shrug. Fletcher echoing a gentle *hear, hear* in agreement.

"Look, if you don't want the job then I will try to find someone else. I just thought you'd like the opportunity to get away from your mother for a few months and redecorating an entire castle, but-"

"Redecorating a castle?" Nessa blurts.

"Oh, did I forget to mention?" I tease, biting back a grin, "Omphalos Stone is being demolished. The children and teens will be moved into Alistair's vacant estate. I'll need someone to organise the bedrooms, arrange swings for the gardens and hire staff."

Pulling at her organization-loving heartstrings, I see her eyes light up. "And whoever runs the new home will need to stay close to the children in case they are needed during the night. I guess the old royal quarters would be converted for them. It would be a big change for someone who has always shared their bedroom with their younger sisters."

Not being subtle at all with the game I'm playing, everyone around the table grins.

Nessa shakes her head at me, freeing a golden lock, but sighs, "Alright. You won me over. But could I keep my current coin arrangement, your Majesty?"

Kellan had mentioned when he took over his fathers' bookkeeping tome, he noticed Nessa only gets paid half of what she's owed. She asked Lachlan that the rest goes to her mother to support her in place of her father. In the four years since beginning her employment, she had never taken the full coin amount for herself.

"If that's what you desire, then sure. But know the Shay household will always have the additional income from Ada."

"Ada?" Nessa chokes, "What poor fool hired my sister? She's hardly renowned for her work ethic."

"I guess I'm the poor fool then." Kellan leans back in his chair and crosses his arms, "I sent a messenger seagull to Star Spike yesterday and she accepted this morning. It's a good thing you accepted Wren's job offer because your current role has already been filled."

"Luckily, you're not leaving for Soleil until next week, so you'll have some time to train in your replacement," Callum taunts.

"Lucky me," Nessa mutters quietly, causing me to burst out laughing.

Reaching across the table to take her hand, I give her a sympathetic squeeze, "All of this will be a wonderful adventure. And just think of all the new stories you'll have to tell me."

"You'll write to me, won't you?" Nessa asks with her doe-eyes locking onto mine.

"Of course," I say, a habit she has given me which I know will linger even without her presence. "I'll need updates on how you're training with Aengus is going?"

"*Training?*" Nessa and Aengus squawk in unison.

"It was Aengus's idea. He thought he should *toughen you up a bit* if I remember correctly."

The subtlest shade of red tints Aengus' cheeks.

"What does she mean?" Nessa asks, twisting in her seat to glance up at him.

"I'll explain on the journey to Soleil. It seems we'll have enough time together Ms Shay."

Before the awkward silence between those two can leak into the rest of the hall, I scoot back my chair and rise to my feet.

Everyone follows suit, though it takes Nessa a moment longer.

"To new beginnings," I say, raising my glass. Granted it's not champagne, but as a daughter of the sea, water has always been my element.

Glasses rise around me, catching in the crisp, midday light. We clink our vessels together and the gentle sound resonates in my core.

With our toast and meeting concluded, Nessa begrudgingly accepts Aengus transport to her home to begin packing.

Kellan and I go to leave when Callum lightly calls, "Make sure to enjoy the rest of your evening. News of your engagement will be spread tomorrow, and chances are you'll get a headache from how loudly Ludwig is going to ring his bloody bell."

"Engagement? Wren is already my wife in every way." Kellan says, failing to hide his primal tone as he takes a step closer.

Callum rolls his eyes at his brothers' eagerness, "As I said, our citizens will want to celebrate. Let them have this sliver of joy after everything they've been through. Let Aveen have this."

"Alright, but you know neither of us can lie," Kellan sighs, draping his arm over me as we make our way towards the door. "I guess I'm lucky to have a lying, cheat as my brother."

"Oi, I might lie but I never cheat."

"Please, you're a notorious cheat. You'd always whine to Mom about how I only won the race because I *got an unfair head start*." Kellan mimics in a whining tone.

The *Lazy Twins* silent stare at each other for a moment. I'm unsure whether one of them is going to start laughing or throw a punch.

Kellan gives a wink before wordlessly spinning on the heel of his boot and sprinting away.

Callum darts after him, blowing a chair out of the way. As the pair race down the corridor, Callum shouts his complaints about Kellan's head start.

"I'm glad I'm not the only one who married into this madness," Fletcher muses, squeezing my shoulders as we pad after them, "Welcome to the family, Wren."

TWENTY–SEVEN

Five Weeks Later

ibiscus or lavender?" I ask over my shoulder as the pot begins to whistle on the stove.

"I'll have whatever you're having," Kellan says with a yawn, slumping himself onto the sofa and running his hands through his damp hair.

Hibiscus, I choose, worrying that lavender tea will make him even sleepier.

Although it's been weeks since he gained his gills, his body is still adapting to the strain of transitioning. I offered to go to the Water World alone today to give him a break, but he insisted on coming with me. Tired or not, I doubt he would miss an opportunity to coo over Robin whilst Rhea and I discuss syren and merfolk matters.

Rhea rarely lets anyone hold Robin for long, but

Kellan is an exception. Actually, most people treat Kellan as an exception now. He has become something of a living myth.

Handing him the steaming mug of tea, he straightens up a fraction to make room for me. He tosses aside the jacket he had resting over the arm of the sofa. As it lands in a heap on the floor, a single golden coin rolls free from the pocket.

"Life as a King must be treating you *too* well if you can throw your money around," I joke, reclining onto his chest.

Nuzzling a kiss into my hair, he laughs quietly, just a brief puff of air through his nose. His faraway gaze stays firmly on the coin as it rolls in ever constricting circles, eventually flopping onto one side. It lands *fin* side up- Kellan's go to gamble.

"I had that coin in my pocket whilst journeying to Eastern Acropolis. I placed a bet on myself to succeed, or...or I would lose and forfeit it as my Charon coin."

I take a sip of my tea to help swallow down the rising emotion and buy me a few seconds to gather my thoughts. "Was this before or after you met them?"

Them. The gods. Something I still have a hard time saying and a tougher time believing. But it's true. He has the only mortal known to man who conversed with the gods. Well, the only one to do so and live to tell the tale.

"Before," he answers without missing a beat, "If it had been after I wouldn't have been optimistic enough in my odds to place a bet."

I wince. "That bad, huh?"

He shifts his weight behind me. "I know I haven't been the most forthcoming about what I saw but living through that kaleidoscope of horror is enough for any lifetime, regardless of how long a life I'll live. And I just don't want to burden you with what could have been. It doesn't matter now anyway."

"Of course it matters, Kellan? Don't think I'm unaware of the way it haunts you at night. I hear you mumbling in your sleep. The reason I don't ask you about it is because I don't want you to relive those visions unless you want to, not because I'm disinterested."

I twist over my shoulder to look at him, but his eyes are burying into his mug. With a slight sniffle, he nods.

"I won't be able to lie. I can skip over some parts completely, but with this new ichor, sugar-coating details isn't really a possibility."

"I don't want you to glaze over details for my

benefit. Tell me everything. Every inch of darkness. Every fear. Everything."

He remains silent for a moment. I'm considering asking about the construction work on the Lunar Lands just to change the subject when he sighs and says, "There were these three women, well, it was one woman technically. The Weaver and eh…"

And just like that, he reveals what he saw within the Tapestry. The threads of Fate he demanded be woven a different way. He tells me about The True Prince hoping Aveen would perish during childbirth like her mother. How he thought Arthur and Fletcher would perish. How his brother would never forgive him and end up drinking himself into an early grave. How my citizens and I, along with any other trace of magic would be eliminated.

His deep voice turns hoarse. His words rumbling through my back until they seem to shake my heart. I want to turn around and face him, but he so rarely speaks this freely. I'm afraid the slightest motion might cause him to stop. So I remain against his chest, blinking back tears and listening.

After almost an hour, he falls silent. Finally pivoting within his hold, I set the cold cup I've been clutching to on the cobbled floor and face him, "I always knew you were fearless, but I have no idea how you braved the waters once more knowing what doom could lie ahead of you."

Kellan thumbs my lips, and gently tilts my chin towards him. "Because I would rip this world apart for you, Wren. To hold you one last time. And if I cannot hold you then just to see you. And if I cannot see you, then to scent you upon the wind as I took my last breath."

I kiss his hand which cradles my face as if he cannot believe I'm here. Closing any remaining space between us, I crawl onto his lap and allow my legs to fall on either side of his solid thighs. His fingers slide from my cheek to my nape as he draws me close. I find his velvety lips and part them instantly.

Brushing a loose strand of hair off my face, he says, "The visions I saw were possibilities. Outcomes I could try my best to avoid. But when your ichor scorched within you, you thought I was lost forever. Out of the two of us, I think you're braver for carrying on when you had no hope."

Resting my forehead against his, I say, "It took me many years to learn this, but I understand the importance of family now. I couldn't protect you, but I thought if I could save the extended parts of you, then you wouldn't be gone. Your sister. Your brother. Your community. I'm not sure if it makes sense but-"

"No, it does," Kellan argues, nodding firmly, "I understand. I eh...Could I tell you about one more vision I had? I wasn't going to tell you, but I guess it was the one which spurred me on the most when I needed it."

I force myself to nod and say 'Of course' in a Nessa like fashion, but inside my heart picks up to a canter.

Gods above after all the horrors and fears he told me; this one must be bad if he wants to shield me from it.

"Just before Poseidon shoved me off the threads, I caught a fleeting glimpse of a painting. An oil portrait of a boy no more than five. The artwork was as tall as me and hung between two colourful stained-glass windows. Perhaps in the West Wing or Temple. It was the glimmer of hope I needed. It was breath-taking and glorious. It was...Well, it was a portrait of our son."

"That's.... impossible." I say, unfurling myself from his lap. Scooping up my mug, I pace my way towards the sink.

Rising to his feet, he says, "I don't want you to feel pressured, Wren. Nothing has changed, and I remember the vow you purposely skipped during your coronation."

"No, I mean it's *literally* impossible," I say with

a shrug, rinsing out my cup, "Syrens only ever birth daughters. Any children we could have in the future, the *far* future, would be girls."

Noting my change in tone, and my lack of immediate rebuttal, Kellan grins a little as he leans against the wall beside me, "Well Lunar firstborns are always boys."

"There is no such thing as a male syren. They do not exist."

"*That* is what you have a problem with?" he asks, cocking his head to side, "You're the first Queen syren to have wings in decades, and I'm the only King to have gills. We hardly live by the norms of the realms ourselves now, do we?"

I roll my eyes but remain quiet. He has a point. Turning my back on the sink, I cross my arms, "And this boy you saw had gills? Wings?"

"I can't guarantee about the gills as he donned a ceremonial jacket. But he had wings," Kellan says, smiling to himself as he recalls the memory, "Plumage of cream and sepia hues to match his fair hair. His hair might be my doing but his dark eyes, they were all you, my love."

"It's not possible," I mumble with disbelief under my breath, but he hears me anyway.

Kissing my crown, he pushes off the wall and pads

towards the window, "I wonder how much of the rebuilt will be done when we arrive for this month's meeting."

I scoff slightly. Apparently, I wasn't the only one who used our royal duties as an avoidance subject for our private life when needed.

Shaking my head, I sigh, "I just can't believe it's possible. But...but I would like to meet him."

As Kellan spins on his heel and stalks towards me with determination, I quickly add, "You should be warned, vision or not, there is a very high chance I'll birth a typical syren daughter. One who looks just like boring ol' me."

"First of all, don't ever refer to my Queen as *boring* ever again. If anyone else had said that there's a chance I'd behead them. And secondly, any child, of any gender, any blend of mortal and magic, at any time in any future, would be perfect, Wren. Because it would be ours."

"Careful Kellan, you're making me eager to meet *her*," I tease.

"You should want to meet *him*," Kellan says a wolfish grin, "I find myself pondering over the painting at least twice a day. The portrait captured this cheeky grin so full of life it brings me joy just to think of it."

Huh, I wonder where he got that feature from, I muse

to myself staring at Kellan's beaming face.

"You do seem awfully sure." My heart swelling so much I fear it may burst.

As he nods, I take four steps and stop before him. Laying between our feet is his Charon coin. I pluck it off the floor and balance it on the edge of my thumb, "Shall we place a wager then?"

With a wolfish grin, he nods, "Be warned, *lígo pouláki*. I never lose."

As I flip the coin high into the air, Kellan lifts me up at the waist and tosses me over his shoulder. The gentle clink of the coin landing on the cobbles is drowned out by my laughter as he storms towards my bathroom.

"Good thing we both have gills. I plan on us being in here for quite a while." He winks, setting me down on the edge of my new, extra-wide bathtub. He turns on both faucets and kicks the door closed behind us.

Keep up to date with
Naomi Kelly publications,
giveaways, and upcoming
events by following:

naomikellywriting

Naomi Kelly Writing

Head over to
Goodreads to find
reviews and quotes
about the Syren Stories
and feel free to leave
your own thoughts too!

Printed in Great Britain
by Amazon